RUNNING

FROM THE

DEAD

RUNNING
FROM THE
DEAD

A CRIME
NOVEL **MIKE**
KNOWLES

Copyright © Mike Knowles, 2020

Published by ECW Press
665 Gerrard Street East
Toronto, Ontario, Canada M4M 1Y2
416-694-3348 / info@ecwpress.com

Cover design: Michel Vrana
Author photo: Danielle Persaud

This is a work of fiction. Names, characters, places, and incidents either are the product of the author's imagination or are used fictitiously, and any resemblance to actual persons, living or dead, business establishments, events, or locales is entirely coincidental.

LIBRARY AND ARCHIVES CANADA CATALOGUING IN PUBLICATION

Title: Running from the dead : a crime novel / Mike Knowles.

Names: Knowles, Mike, author.

Identifiers: Canadiana (print) 20200154427 Canadiana (ebook) 20200154435

ISBN 978-1-77041-519-5 (softcover)
ISBN 978-1-77305-501-5 (PDF)
ISBN 978-1-77305-500-8 (EPUB)

Classification: LCC PS8621.N67 R86 2020 DDC C813/.6—dc23

The publication of *Running from the Dead* has been generously supported by the Canada Council for the Arts which last year invested $153 million to bring the arts to Canadians throughout the country and is funded in part by the Government of Canada. *Nous remercions le Conseil des arts du Canada de son soutien. L'an dernier, le Conseil a investi 153 millions de dollars pour mettre de l'art dans la vie des Canadiennes et des Canadiens de tout le pays. Ce livre est financé en partie par le gouvernement du Canada.* We acknowledge the support of the Ontario Arts Council (OAC), an agency of the Government of Ontario, which last year funded 1,737 individual artists and 1,095 organizations in 223 communities across Ontario for a total of $52.1 million. We also acknowledge the contribution of the Government of Ontario through the Ontario Book Publishing Tax Credit, and through Ontario Creates for the marketing of this book.

ONTARIO CREATES

ONTARIO ARTS COUNCIL
CONSEIL DES ARTS DE L'ONTARIO
an Ontario government agency
un organisme du gouvernement de l'Ontario

Canada Council for the Arts

Conseil des Arts du Canada

Canadä

PRINTED AND BOUND IN CANADA

PRINTING: MARQUIS 5 4 3 2 1

MIX
Paper from responsible sources
FSC® C103567

For Andrea.
It could be for no one else.

JONES NOTICED THE BLOOD ON HIS SLEEVE WHEN HE REACHED FOR HIS wallet. For a second, he thought the barista had noticed it too, but the look she gave him was too brief for shock. She sidestepped the length of the counter and pierced a Danish with a cheap pair of tongs while Jones turned his body to conceal the evidence he had missed. The young woman left the bagged pastry in front of the well-dressed man who had been standing ahead of Jones in line and reused the same parting words Jones had heard her use with the previous two customers.

Jones had initially pegged the barista's age at twenty, but up close he was less sure. The toque and pigtails had influenced his initial hunch, but the tattoos climbing her right arm changed his mind. A winding branch populated with colourful birds started at the wrist and continued under the sleeve of her t-shirt. The quality of the work varied, and Jones could tell there was a degree of trial and error until one final artist completed the bulk of the work. There was something tough and not at all twenty about her.

"What can I get you?"

Jones had already looked at the menu board while he waited out of the range of the well-dressed man's cologne. His regular was listed and so was his backup; the presence of both meant the coffee shop was good. Jones had never set foot in Brew before. He had only found the place after a minor fender-bender caused a massive traffic jam on Queen Street East. The red tail-lights stared Jones in the eye and refused to blink first. When Jones did, his mind was waiting. The split-second of empty thought was all the opening his brain needed to start rolling. His thoughts picked up faster than the cars on the road around him and Jones knew where they were headed. He searched hard for a distraction, any distraction, that would put the brakes on his mind. Jones found what he was looking for buried back from the road on a quiet looking side street. A U-turn and few right turns got him a closer look at the busy café, and at the vacant parking space far from the crawling traffic on the main road.

"Cortado."

The barista nodded and turned her back to Jones. She stepped to the espresso machine and let her hands simultaneously reach for a container of beans and a cup. When she spoke, it was over her shoulder.

"You want it for here, or to go?"

He should have asked for it to go, but *to go* implied a destination and Jones was not ready to go anywhere.

The barista tamped the coffee and started the drip before she turned to ring Jones up. When his change was in his palm, he dropped the coins in the coffee mug that had been stationed next to the register and heard the money clink against the other tips. The sound produced a nod of appreciation from the barista and she said, "Thanks," just loud enough to be heard over the noise of the espresso machine.

It was just after six, and there was a steady choral hum in the busy coffee shop fueled by the conversations taking place at most of the tables. Jones stepped left and glanced around the room; people were either focused on their companions or their phones—no one was looking at him.

The slap of metal against granite pulled Jones' eyes toward the barista, who began adding steamed milk to his coffee. The waitress turned faster than anyone with a hot drink in their hands should have and set his order in front of him. Jones paused and stared at the coffee. The drink had all the qualities that he had expected; it was the cup that threw him. The barista had made the cortado in a cheap juice glass instead of a mug. Jones glanced toward the woman to see if she was going to offer an explanation, but she had already side-stepped toward the register and the next customer.

The glass was uncomfortably hot and it made the journey to the corner table feel longer than the few seconds it took to cross the floor. The table had just been vacated and Jones had noticed a few people debating a seat change as he approached it. Jones put the drink down and gave his fingers a small shake as he shrugged off his coat and took his seat against the exposed brick wall. The coffee shop had been filled with eclectic pieces of furniture and antique bric-a-brac to give it a sense of history. The décor felt forced; the wall was the real deal. The bricks lacked uniformity and the mortar in-between displayed long fractures. Jones was sure that he could have picked chunks of the aged concrete away with his fingernails if he tried.

The table afforded Jones with a view of the entire room and the door. There was only one table separating him from the entrance and it was occupied by a woman waiting for her companion to return to the jacket left draped over the backrest of her chair. The short window of solitude left her unable to resist the impulse to pick at the cement. Jones watched a shiny blue fingernail probe the cracks the way a bird uses its beak to probe the dirt for worms. She eased the sliver of mortar free and spent a few moments looking at it before she suddenly dropped it so that she could inspect her nails. She suddenly had no further interest in the wall or the piece of concrete next to her cup.

Jones braved a tentative sip of the coffee and found the heat of the misappropriated juice glass manageable, but the coffee still too hot to drink. He let his fingers loosely linger on the glass and felt the warmth diffuse into his palm. He liked the feeling almost as much as he liked the taste of coffee. He swung his focus from one physical sensation to the next, as though they were monkey bars that allowed him to stay above the feelings lurking beneath. He had no emotions for what he had done—this was not the first time he had killed a man, but it was the first time he had done it at home. There were different rules about murder on the other side of the world: there, it earned you a medal; here, it was more complicated. The dead were victims even when they weren't.

Jones felt his focus turning inward and he began searching for another diversion. Jones watched the woman at the next table take another sip from her glass. Her sips were frequent and she paired the wine with glances around the room. The last look caught the eye of the barista. There was a nod from behind the counter and Jones pegged the woman as a regular. A mane of dyed blonde hair resisted the impulse to move as the woman tilted her head to drain the last of the wine in her glass.

Jones glanced at the counter and saw the barista rise from a crouch with a bottle in her hand. She removed a stainless steel stopper a fraction of a second before a dull tone announced the bottle had made contact with the counter. The blonde rose from her seat to get the bottle, as though beckoned by the sound, and slipped past a man waiting in line. Judging from the amount of contact and the dirty look from the guy in line, the blonde had either misjudged the space or the width of her hips; either way, she didn't apologize.

"Thanks, hon."

"No problem, Diane."

Diane's status as a regular allowed her the perk of refilling her own drink, and when she turned to make her way back to the table, Jones saw that the wine was flirting with the lip of the glass. She paused before taking her seat to again look around the room, and Jones noticed that Diane was a pleasant looking woman made less attractive by her efforts to emphasize her sexuality. Her clothes were just a bit too tight and her make-up just a bit too loud. The overall effect held Jones' gaze longer than he had planned, and he realized too late that the cosmetic decisions had been a trap. Diane sensed his attention and she turned her head in his direction. Jones shifted his glancing eyes back to his drink and lifted the glass to his lips. He heard the tinkle of the wine glass touching the tabletop, but he didn't hear the chair move. He glanced toward the other table and found eyes looking back at his. Jones met

Diane's stare, and she responded with a tiny smile and a slow shift of her shoulders that lifted her chest and elongated her torso. Jones didn't respond to the subtle carnal introduction; instead, he took another sip of his cortado and then fished out his phone.

Jones heard Diane's chair scrape over the uneven pre-war floorboard before making a final bark as she jerked it toward the table. Even though the coast was clear, Jones didn't lift his head again; his eyes drifted from his phone to his sleeve and again the spot of blood he had missed. The blood that had been red inside the veins of Kevin McGregor was now black on his sleeve. Jones lifted his arm and rotated it back and forth. There were no other stains, but he could pick up the faint scent of gunpowder from his hand. He rolled up his sleeve and then sat back in the chair to give his shirt and pants another look. He didn't see any other signs of missed evidence, but the light at the table wasn't much better than the light in the basement.

Jones slid his phone back into his pocket and then lifted the glass. The thin material that had radiated with such ferocity a few minutes ago had given away most of its heat. The coffee inside was colder than he liked, but Jones drank it quickly. He let the glass linger at his lips until the last of the coffee lost its fight with gravity and then he stood up. He draped his jacket over his arm as his right hand lifted the chair and quietly brought it back to the edge of the table. Jones scanned the room for anyone who might be looking his way and found that only Diane was interested in what he was doing.

She was staring at him, and Jones didn't need to guess what she was looking at. Diane caught herself and lifted her eyes away from the jacket over the forearm that ended so abruptly. Jones had never been comfortable with an empty sleeve. He had always thought that the cuff made his arm look like an elephant's trunk, so Jones made it a habit to roll up his sleeve. His forearm was capped with a synthetic fabric sock that a physical therapist had once described as space age. Jones had wanted nothing to do with a prosthetic. An artificial limb had always been more artificial than limb for him, so he scrapped it in favour of the sock. He still got looks like the one Diane had given him, but it was better than looking at a hand that wasn't his.

Jones had expected Diane to be embarrassed for staring, but she surprised him. She looked at him and slowly raised an eyebrow as though she was waiting for the answer to a question she had just whispered in his ear. Jones held her eye for a moment and then reached for the juice glass and stepped away from the table. He walked along the counter and placed the glass next to a collection of other empty mugs and glasses before turning to walk through an archway in the brick wall that bisected the coffee house. The other side of the wall offered bigger tables, a few more comfortable chairs, and a sofa for customers interested in a bit of distance from the din of the coffee machines and stream of customers coming in off of the street.

There were several people alone at tables for four, each working on a silver laptop bearing the single white Apple. Each of the people working on a computer had attempted to assert their independence with decals and stickers. The attempts at individuality were so uniform that they made the laptops even more similar.

Jones found the bathroom door open and the light off. The flea market décor in the room was done no favours by the aggressive hundred-watt fluorescent bulb in the ceiling that exposed every flaw and imperfection left by age or carelessness. Jones hung his coat on a thin metal hook that had once been a yellow brass, but now was mostly black, and looked at himself in the mirror. He checked his clothes for blood but found only flecks of mortar and concrete on his shoulders and in his hair. Jones tousled his hair clean and slapped at his shirt until it stopped giving off plumes of dust. He used the washroom and took his time washing up. Jones pulled the sock off his wrist so that he could use his arm to rub at the soap. He worked the lather all over his hand and up his wrist. The fancy all-natural soap wouldn't erase the gunshot residue or eliminate the DNA evidence— Jones knew he would need a stiff brush and something that wasn't natural for that, but the soap would at least do something about the smell. The cordite had been a gift at first. The scent exploded into existence and completely overpowered the dense odour that had crept out from inside the wall and invaded Jones' nose. Even now, in a bathroom reeking of lilac, he could smell the cellar as though he was still standing there. Jones squeezed his eyes shut; the thought of the bodies was pulling on him, but he knew better than to give in. He would have to go back to the memories soon enough, but not yet.

When he had rinsed as best he could, he used his forearm to release a tiny glob of soap on the bloodstain on his sleeve. The white bubbles went pink as he scrubbed and he rinsed them away. Jones figured the absence of a hand dryer was because it would have clashed with the old fixtures. The same logic must have applied to a paper towel dispenser, but the line of function over form was drawn at paper towels. A pile was lazily stacked in the indentation meant for a bar of soap. The proximity to the faucet had left the flimsy brown sheet on top brittle in the places where someone else's water had dried. Jones pulled up four sheets and dried his hand and arm, but the thin material had no chance against his wet sleeve. He pushed the shirt past his forearm and tossed the ball of wadded paper at the garbage can. The uneven lump bounced off the summit of piled trash and rolled toward the corner of the room. Jones sighed as he pulled the sock out of his mouth and fit it back onto his arm. Lifting the jacket off the hook, he realized that he had been in such a rush to wash his hands, that he missed the graffiti.

Jones took a step closer to the door as he shrugged the coat over his shoulders. This was not the colourful kind of graffiti that could pass for art; this was the ball-point kind of graffiti that could sometimes pass for wit. According to the door, Becky gave the best head in the world. Someone had left Becky's number and someone else had crossed it out and written a new number under-neath. Someone else had taken the time to draw a crude drawing of Donald Trump on the door. The only thing that really resembled him was the hair, but it was enough. Trump's head was oversized and someone had drawn small swastikas instead of pupils, and underneath the caricature someone had written *Make America grate again*. Jones bent down to examine the words written around the doorknob. It was clear that someone had taken their time with that one because each of the letters was a close match for Times New Roman font. Jones followed the words, *I know you are, but what am I?*

Jones bent down the rest of the way to get the wad of paper towel off the floor. As he stood up, he noticed some writing on the door that hadn't stood out before. The script wasn't ostentatious or illustrated like some of the other graffiti. The black letters were small and written with a calligrapher's skill. The message had been placed next to the hinges, and Jones would have missed them had he not been inches away. He took a small step back and tilted his head so that his shadow was no longer obscuring the tiny words. Someone had taken their time writing the message. They had rested a shoulder on the wall, committing to getting it right.

Jones put his body against the wall and slowly bent his knees until he was eye-level with the words. He had descended about a foot and a half, which put the girl at around five feet. Jones felt like the height confirmed the gender. Jones knew that his personal experience didn't make the idea of a man with beautiful penmanship impossible, but he had never come across a guy with beautiful handwriting.

Jones read the message another time before giving the bathroom another look. There was no reason a person would choose to hang around in the corner of a public washroom—except to kill time. Jones inched a bit closer to the writing. It was faded and a few of the letters had drifted to the right, likely after knuckles brushed against them. There was no period at the end of the sentence; he could forgive the sin—it was a door after all. Instead of punctuation, there was a small round smudge. Jones licked his thumb and gently put it on the edge of the dark cloud at the end of the sentence. Part of the mark came off without a fight. Lifting his thumb toward the light revealed a grey smear. Jones tried the same thing with a wet index finger on Trump's hair. When he lifted his finger, there wasn't a hair out of place.

Jones pulled his phone from his pocket and took shots of the message. He checked his work and repeated the task with the flash on. Satisfied, he took shots of every other thing that had been written or sketched onto the door before stepping back to get a final shot of the entire unintentional canvas.

Jones opened the bathroom door and almost collided with the woman waiting on the other side.

Jones nodded and moved past the woman as she made an obvious show of taking a deep breath in anticipation of the smell she thought was waiting for her inside.

Jones walked back to the counter and took up a spot behind a guy in coveralls who had just ordered.

While the barista was making change, she flashed a look at Jones and said, "We don't do free refills."

"I want to talk."

The barista poured the coffee and passed the cup to the guy in coveralls. To him, she said, "Thanks," and to Jones, she said, "We don't do that either."

"We're doing that now," Jones said.

The barista crossed her arms and looked Jones up and then down. She furrowed her eyebrows and two deep lines emerged in between. "No, that's what you're doing."

Her lipstick coloured her pursed lips a deep shade of red that seconds ago had been attractive, but now seemed more like the stained mouth of something carnivorous.

"It's about the bathroom."

The furrow released and she rolled her eyes. "Oh, gross. Did you clog it?"

The woman waiting behind Jones cleared her throat. Jones stepped left and let her order. After money changed hands, and the steamer stopped hissing, Jones said, "I didn't clog the toilet."

The barista put the coffee down and pointed at the tip jar after the customer walked away. "You see her drop anything in there?"

"No," Jones said.

"That's on you."

Jones put a loonie in the cup. The tip seemed to satisfy the barista. "We out of toilet paper?"

"It's about the graffiti."

"Oh." She rolled her eyes and started to wipe the counter. "I don't know Becky."

"It's not that."

The barista took another order from a guy in a suit who wanted a gluten-free cookie and a latte. She rang him up and then spoke to Jones while she worked. "Look, we take care of the graffiti ourselves, but you can leave a business card if you want. I'll pass it on to the owner when she comes in."

She put the latte down and lifted a glass top off a cake stand that doubled as a cookie display. The glass was heavy and exposed ropey veins running up the barista's tattooed arm as she held it. She thanked the guy for his tip and sighed when she looked at Jones again. "You're still here."

"I don't want to remove the graffiti. I want to talk about it."

"Christ, man. I don't have time for whatever this is. I'm paid to sell coffee, not talk about the bathroom."

Jones stepped over to the register.

"What now?"

"Another cortado."

She sighed again, louder this time, and took his money. "You said *we* take care of the graffiti. Did you mean you when you said *we*, or is it someone else?"

"What do you care? You said you didn't remove graffiti."

Jones fished a twenty out of his pocket. He let the barista see the money before he fed it into the tip jar. "I think we got off on the wrong foot. I just have a few questions. I have no problem paying you for your time."

The barista looked at the tip jar. "My time is worth more than that."

Jones lifted an eyebrow. "How much do you make an hour?"

"What's that got to do with what I'm worth?"

Jones doubled the tip. The barista nodded and turned her back on Jones to make the second cortado. She set the drink down on the counter. It was in a juice glass again. "You've got until you finish your drink, or five minutes—whichever comes first."

"Alright."

The barista took the twenties and put them in the back pocket of her jeans. "We paint over the graffiti ourselves."

"How often?"

She shrugged. "Whenever it gets bad and there's a lull. There's a can of paint under the sink. Painting over it is easier than scrubbing it off."

"When was the last time you painted it?"

The barista jutted her chin at the glass. "You're still on the clock whether you drink it or not."

"It's too hot in that glass."

"Wuss."

"Why not a mug?"

"Most of them are dirty so I have to be selective about giving them out. I thought a big guy like you could handle a warm cup."

"When did you last paint the door?"

The barista thought about it for a second. "Four days ago."

"You know that for sure?"

She nodded. "I painted it myself. I remember because I got paint on my jeans." She took a step back. "See?"

Jones saw a whiskered patch of white just below the pocket from an unintentional brush stroke.

"You're still wearing them?"

She rolled her eyes. "They're still jeans. Why do you even care about this anyway?"

Jones pulled out his phone and showed her the picture.

The barista flicked a glance at the phone and then looked again when she saw that Jones hadn't paid her forty bucks so that he could flash her a picture of his dick.

She leaned into the phone and stared at the words for a long time.

"That wasn't on the door when I painted it."

Jones took back the phone and looked at the picture. "And you never noticed it when you were cleaning the washroom?"

She shook her head. "We done?"

"Almost. You remember a girl that came in recently—under twenty, around five feet tall, probably wearing a lot of make-up?"

The barista thought about the question long enough to give the impression that she was putting effort into it. "No. Why?"

"Because she's the one who left the message."

The barista smiled. "Bullshit. What is this, some kind of scam to hit on me? You come around with money and some bullshit story about graffiti so you can get me into the back of your Mystery Machine?"

Jones raised his palm to slow her down. "This is exactly what it looks like. I don't have a Mystery Machine, just a mystery."

"What do you care, dude? You took a piss and read a note on a door. What's it to you?"

Jones knew that there was no way he could explain the answer to her. "Under twenty, around five feet tall, a lot of make-up. Ring any bells?"

"Do you know how many people come in here every day?"

"I only care about the last four. Do you have a security system?"

She snorted. "Of course."

"Cameras?"

The barista shook her head. "Just an alarm. It's the kind that calls one of those companies that can talk to you directly if it goes off. I hit the wrong code one time and they started talking to me. It scared the shit out of me."

Jones went into his pocket and put some more money into the tip jar. "Another twenty for you to ask your co-workers about the girl."

The barista leaned forward and took the money out of the jar. "This is forty."

"The other twenty is for you."

She raised an eyebrow and rested a hand on her hip. "Why?"

"To keep you from painting the door for a little while."

She put both bills in her back pocket. "I think you're crazy."

"Doesn't make the money any less green. Do we have a deal?"

She nodded.

"What's your name?"

"Sheena." She said it with an edge; like she was daring him to say something about it.

"Like the Ramones song."

Sheena crossed her arms. "Uh hunh."

"You here tomorrow, Sheena?"

"Yup. Maybe some other weirdo will come in and start dropping cash to talk about the gum under the tables."

Jones tested the glass and found it bearable. "I'll check in tomorrow to see if you found anything out."

"Sure thing, dude."

"You want to know my name?" a woman's voice said.

Jones looked to his right and saw Diane looking at him. Sheena smiled and busied herself down the counter.

"It won't cost you a twenty to find out," Diane said. She swayed slightly and overcompensated when she realized it. Her heel made a loud tap on the floor and Diane laughed it off.

"Do you come here a lot?"

Diane smiled and put a hand on Jones' shoulder. She glanced down for just a second, but Jones caught it. "I'm here all the time."

"So you know the regulars?"

Diane laughed and Jones smelled the wine on her breath. "I know the irregulars too."

"I'm looking for a girl. She'd be under twenty, around five feet tall, and wearing a lot of make-up."

Diane flashed a look over Jones' shoulder, probably at Sheena, who was still out of earshot. She turned up the volume. "You're looking for a girl?"

Jones held up his hand. "I'm not *looking* for a girl, Diane. I think this girl might be in trouble."

Diane looked Jones over. "You a cop or something?"

"I'm a something."

From her tone, Jones could tell that the possibility of a yes had excited her. "What does that mean?"

"I'm a private investigator."

Diane laughed. "Shut up. That's not a real thing."

"It is," Jones said. "So tell me, Diane, do you remember a girl under twenty with a lot of eye make-up in here in the last four days?"

Diane thought about it for a second and then she laughed. "Hey, how'd you know my name was Diane? You really must be a private investigator." She put her hand on his arm again. "A good one."

"The girl," Jones said.

Diane leaned closer and laughed. "Oh, right. Duh. I'm such a scatterbrain. It's the wine." She leaned in a little closer. "I get into so much trouble when I have too much." With her hand still on Jones, she said, "Let me think." Her thumb moved back and forth over the fabric of his jacket. When she spoke, her voice was quiet—an invitation to come closer and share a secret. "I think I might remember someone like that. Why don't you buy me a drink and we can talk about it?"

"You think you saw her?"

Diane smiled. "Maybe."

"She would have been left-handed."

Diane looked. Jones caught her.

"Sorry."

Jones shook his head. "Nothing to be sorry about. I'm

not left-handed. Listen, why don't you let me buy you that drink."

Diane smiled wide. "If you insist."

"I do."

The promise of a drink loosened the grip on Jones' arm. He watched Diane walk back to her table with a lot of hip thrown into her gait.

"I gotta ask. How the hell do you know she's left-handed?"

Jones looked over his shoulder and saw that Sheena had made her way back. "The smudges," he said. "Her knuckles made them when her hand moved to the right."

"Bullshit."

Jones turned and rested his elbows on the counter. "The place she picked to write was another dead give-away. No righty would have picked that spot. It would have been too hard to write there. That's why most of the other tags are in the middle of the door."

"What are you, some kind of handwriting expert."

Jones smiled and lifted his arm. "Used to be left-handed."

Sheena looked at the empty jacket sleeve unimpressed. Jones put it down and instantly liked her more than he had a second before. She rested her back against the prep counter opposite Jones and crossed her arms. "Are you really a private investigator? Like in the movies?"

Jones shook his head. "If this were the movies, I'd have already solved the case."

"How do you know she wore too much make-up?"

Jones checked on Diane; she was using her phone to check her make-up. "Graffiti is a dying art. At least, the restroom variety is. Not many people carry pens around anymore. Students do, but this girl isn't a student."

"Why not?"

"She didn't use a pen or a pencil for her message; those don't wipe off that easy. She used eyeliner, I think. Something cheap."

Sheena wrinkled her nose as though the bullshit she was sure she was hearing smelled as bad as the real thing. "Watch the register." She walked out from behind the counter and turned the corner toward the bathroom. Less than half a minute later, she was back. A customer had approached the register and Jones had told her the barista had gone to use the restroom. The answer was accepted with an exasperated sigh and a dramatic gesture of checking her watch. The fact that Sheena appeared seconds later and attended to the customer before saying a word to Jones did nothing to generate a tip.

When the customer had walked away with her coffee, Sheena said, "You were right. It *was* cheap eyeliner."

"Makes you wonder how she afforded to drink here," Jones said.

"The coffee isn't that pricey."

Jones consulted the menu board. "It isn't that cheap, either. Maybe she wasn't the one paying."

He put a ten on the counter next to his empty juice glass, and Sheena waved him off. "It's okay. The second one is on me."

"You said it yourself, no free refills."

"That was when I thought you were a kook."

"Did you change your mind?"

"I'm open to the possibility of you not being a kook."

"Can I get a large coffee?"

Sheena took the ten off the counter and paused at the register. "You planning to not sleep for a while?"

The words hit Jones hard when he realized he wasn't, but he didn't acknowledge their truth to Sheena. "Not for me." He jutted his chin toward Diane. "For her."

Sheena looked at Diane. "She doesn't like coffee."

"I can tell what she likes; this is what she needs. Think you could bring it over to her?"

"She's going to like that less than the coffee. I think she wants you to stick around."

Jones shook his head. "I have to keep moving."

2

JONES GOT BEHIND THE WHEEL OF HIS JEEP AND DROVE NORTH IN THE DIREC-
tion of Martin House. Monday wasn't his day to visit
his father; Jones checked in on his dad on Tuesdays and
Thursdays, but that didn't stop him from driving toward
the residential care facility.

Behind the wheel, Jones thought about sharks for
the first time in a long time. When he was a kid, he saw
a nature documentary on television; the program was
about sharks and Jones could remember the narrator in
his distinct English accent explaining how sharks needed

to remain in a constant state of motion in order to breathe. It didn't matter how much water was around— if the shark stopped swimming, it would suffocate in the middle of the ocean. Jones didn't care about sharks. He was thinking about them for the same reason he was driving across the city on a Monday—it kept him from stopping. If he stopped, if he lost momentum, it would mean confronting the inevitable, and the inevitable was coming. Jones had a week before the inevitable became unavoidable. Seven days—his own Shark Week—unless he stopped moving.

The exterior of Martin House in Toronto's stock-yard district had all the charm of the shoe factory that it once was. No one had given a thought about the design, and Jones was sure that lack of planning was behind the series of failed start-ups that had first tried to convert the building into something new. The string of failures drove investor interest down and the property value followed. After a year on the market, a long-term care facility set up shop. Jones had not chosen Martin House for his father; his brother had picked it while Jones was in Iraq. Sometimes, sitting beside the fragile shell that housed what was left of his father, Jones wondered if he would have made the same choice. Thomas had told him once that wondering about the choice was a luxury he was not afforded. The facility was clean and the staff was competent. Those were the things that Thomas would have looked for. Jones could picture him at his kitchen table making a list of the things his father would require. But Thomas' selection process would have gone farther than just a list. Thomas was never more practical than when he was dealing with their father. He would have had a percentage in mind: a number of checks on his list that would have made for an acceptable choice. He wouldn't have thought twice about losing a view of the water, but for Jones that would have been a deal breaker. Their father had spent his whole life near the water; it was as much a part of him as the air he breathed. The stroke had taken the water from him and left him at Martin House; breathing was all he had left now.

Jones knew his thoughts were out of line. Thomas always had a complicated relationship with their dad. He seemed to sense early what Thomas didn't discover until he was in his teens. By the time Thomas was ready to come out, his father had already put enough distance between them to make the same room feel like different continents. Looking back, Jones had known about his brother before he knew there was a word for it; he just didn't have any of the feelings his father had. Thomas was close to Jones in every way he wasn't with their father. Thomas had had as much of a hand in raising Jones as any parent, and Jones loved him fiercely.

Jones found his father where he had left him. The only change was the angle of the bed. A nurse had moved it so that his father could get a better view of the television. The gesture was sweet, but the nurse had neglected to adjust the older man's head. His gaze was six inches to the right of the basketball game on the screen. The inches might as well have been a mile for Jones' father.

"Hey, Pop," Jones said en route to the bed by way of the TV. The screen was adjustable and Jones was able to move it directly into his father's line of sight with no trouble. He made a mental note to have another conversation with management and to grease a few of the rusty palms of the staff who looked out for his father.

"Raptors aren't the same without Kawhi," Jones said.

Jones sat next to the bed and rubbed his father's shoulder. Through the shirt, he felt the hard angles of bone under cold skin.

"I didn't see you come in."

Jones looked over his shoulder and saw Laverne in the doorway. The floral scrubs she always wore were about half as cheerful as her personality. Not for the first time, Jones wondered how a smile like hers managed to stay in bloom on the night-shift sixty hours a week.

"That's because I'm sneaky."

Laverne laughed. "This is my first chance to see your dad today." She held up a pair of nail clippers. "I was going to put on some music for him and cut his nails. I noticed they were getting long."

Jones paid Laverne on the side to look out for his father, and she did Jones the favour of taking care of his dad without making it seem like she was doing it just for the money. Laverne fought him at first; she knew it was against the rules to take money on the side, but she had family back home in the Philippines who depended on her and she wasn't making enough on the night shift to turn down free money. Had he known about it, Thomas would have been offended and would have considered the bribe a criticism of his systematic selection process—a silent message that in Jones' eyes, he had not chosen correctly. But Jones had no problem with Martin House, and he had no evidence that the staff were doing their father any harm. He paid the money because he felt guilty. The stroke had occurred while he was away and his brother was left to care for the man who had barely cared for him. Jones had let everyone down, and so he worked overtime to make sure nothing else ever fell on his brother's shoulders.

"Do you think I could take him for a walk?"

Laverne checked her watch. "I don't know. It's already after eight." She looked at Jones and then checked her watch again as though the face had changed in the brief seconds between glances. "You need to be quick, and you need to stay on this floor. Do you remember the ruckus you caused last time, when you took him outside and tried to get back in after visiting hours were over?"

"I don't remember any ruckus."

Laverne put a hand on her hip and looked at him over the glasses that had slipped down the bridge of her nose. "No? Maybe, that's because all of the ruckus happened after you went home. I was the one who had to explain to my manager why I hadn't told anyone that your father was not in his bed after visiting hours."

"I'm sorry, Laverne. I had no idea."

Laverne exhaled loud enough for Jones to hear on the other side of the room. "Just stay on the floor and have him back here in half an hour."

"I can do that."

Laverne wasn't satisfied. "Not thirty-one minutes, not thirty minutes and thirty seconds. Thirty minutes exactly. Got it?"

Jones held up his hand. "Got it, boss."

Laverne smiled. Her teeth were a little crooked, but incredibly bright. Jones liked her smile and felt a bit of pride that he had caused it to appear.

"Do you need help with the transfer?"

Jones stood and retrieved the collapsible wheelchair that had been stowed behind the head of the bed. "I can manage."

"Half an hour," she said before she moved on to the next room.

Jones opened the chair and took a few seconds to arch his back. He had felt his muscles starting to get tight while sitting in Brew. Some part of what had happened in the basement had left its mark on him—it clung to him in the dark and refused to let go when he climbed the stairs and stepped back into the light. Jones paused at the side of the bed and wondered exactly how much of what had happened didn't stay behind. He caught himself before his mind began to feast on the thing he was trying to ignore. He needed to keep moving.

Jones slipped his right hand under his father's back and positioned his left arm under his thighs. Every time he moved his father, Laverne asked if he needed help. It didn't matter that Jones was more than twice her size—she saw her two hands as an advantage over his one. While that might be true if they were eating a steak, one less hand meant nothing when it came to lifting his father. The bulk of the man who had spent a lifetime building houses had evaporated in a matter of months, leaving behind a marionette without strings behind. He eased his father's body off the bed and transferred him to the wheelchair. The only complaint was a sudden rush of air in Jones' ear when his father slumped into the seat.

Jones apologized as he bent to lift his father's feet onto the two metal rests. His father's chin had drifted forward onto his chest and Jones adjusted his body using a pillow from the bed so that it wouldn't happen again. He looked into his father's eyes and saw the old man blink.

"It was a bad day today, Pop."

Jones watched his father's eyelids slowly fall and reopen. The action wasn't a response, Jones had no illusions that his father was trying to dialogue with ocular Morse code, but pretending he was made it easier. Sometimes, he forgot he was pretending and the monologue felt like a real conversation, even if it was replicating something that had never really happened when it was possible. If he was honest with himself, Jones would have to admit that he and his father had communicated better after one of them couldn't. His father had always been a presence in Jones' life, and he knew that his father loved him, but it wasn't because it was said often, or at all. Words were mostly spent on trivial conversations about sports or the weather—never on things that mattered. Thomas was nothing like his father. His brother was an intimate conversation waiting to happen. He was passionate about almost everything. A condition that made small talk impossible. It didn't matter that Jones was quiet, Thomas would pepper him with questions the way a fighter used jabs. Eventually, he would find an opening to get inside, and a conversation would erupt.

Jones wheeled his father out of the room and rolled through the hall on a familiar route to the large bay window. There wasn't anyone seated near the windows so close to the end of visiting hours. Jones stopped his father next to a chair facing the windows and sat beside him. In the daytime, the window offered a view of the small patch of grass fronting the road. At night, the fluorescent bulbs turned the smudged glass into a mirror. Jones couldn't see the grass he knew was out there; his view was either of his father or himself—he looked at his father. Keeping his voice low enough for only his father to hear, he said, "You remember the case I told you about? The woman who hired me to find her son?"

Jones caught a blink.

"I found him."

Jones waited for another blink. Waiting for the response was habit, but this time he waited because he didn't like what was coming next. When he saw the eyelids close, he took a breath and said, "I haven't told her—not yet."

Jones let it hang there until the next blink. "It was bad."

Jones saw another blink.

"Adam had been gone so long. I knew better than to think I would find him alive, but part of me," he shook his head, "part of me hoped I could bring him home." Jones looked at himself in the window and shook his head. "No, that's not true. Part of me really thought I could find him."

In the mirror, Jones thought he saw a blink.

"I know I have to, but it's not that simple. Things with Ruth are complicated right now. She's not even in the country. A few months ago, she moved to Trinidad so that she could take care of her mother. The cancer in her lungs had found its way into her blood. She died last week." Jones looked away from his reflection. "The funeral is tomorrow. Ruth should have the time to mourn her mother. She deserves that."

Jones looked at the reflection of his father and read the slack expression as disbelief. He didn't argue; instead, he told him the rest. "When I found him, he wasn't alone." Jones watched his father's blank face waiting for him to say it all. "I made him tell me everything. It was a mistake. Finding out what had happened—what he did to Adam. After that, I couldn't just walk away."

Jones sighed.

"I managed to get out of that basement, but it's only temporary."

Jones shook his head when the next blink came.

"This can play out only one way. As soon as Ruth finds out, she'll go straight to Adam. When she walks in to claim the body, it won't take the police more than a few hours to get my name."

His father blinked.

"No, Ruth won't give me up. But she won't need to. I've been searching for Adam for six years, Pop. It's no secret. Hell, I've talked to the detectives who worked the case. The police will be at my door before she even leaves the station."

His father blinked and Jones ignored him. He didn't want to hear it, so he changed the subject. "Something else came up today. Something I need time to check on."

Jones looked back at his father and waited for it to come. The old man kept him waiting. He cursed under his breath. "I know how it sounds, but that doesn't mean I didn't find something. There is a kid—"

Jones saw his father blink.

"Another kid—a girl. Look, this might be nothing. It's probably nothing. But I need to know if I can help."

Jones didn't want to see his father blink again. He turned his head and caught sight of himself in the window.

The man in the chair looked like a bad drawing of Jones. One day had done that. One bad day.

"I have seven days until our meeting at the end of the month. That's less than a week. Even with her mother sick, Ruth hasn't missed a single appointment. She won't miss this one, and neither will I. I made her a promise, and I will keep it."

Jones didn't look to see if his father's eyes had an opinion; he had made his decision. "That gives her seven more days with that little bit of hope she says she doesn't have, but I know is there." Jones rubbed the knotted muscles at the back of his neck. "And it gives me seven days to do something right."

He leaned into the arm of the chair and slid his phone out of his pocket. A couple of swipes brought up the picture he had taken of the door. He let his father look at it. "What do you make of this?"

Jones waited a beat and then took the phone back. He looked at the phone and read the words out loud. "He is going to kill me, and I think I want him to."

He looked at his father. "Doesn't read like kid stuff, does it? Reads like something serious."

Jones saw his father's head start to nod and he reached over to place a hand gently on his cheek. He sighed. "It's thin. I know it's thin, but it's something. I need something right now. You get that, right?"

His father farted.

3

THE MURDER MADE THE FRONT PAGE OF THE *GLOBE AND MAIL*, THE *National Post*, and the *Toronto Star*. A murder in Toronto wasn't front page news; it was the remains found with the body that got all the attention. The police were not identifying the victim or giving any details about the remains, but the paper had a source that told them the second body found at the scene belonged to a child. Jones read the articles over, looking for any language that might imply something other than the obvious, but there was nothing—nothing about clues or witnesses, not even the name of the detective running the investigation. Jones should have felt relieved, but the paper did mention one thing that made relief impossible. The paper said police arrived on the scene just after six. If the reporting was accurate that meant there had been only minutes between the time Jones left and when the police arrived. A bad sign.

Jones closed the computer and made some breakfast. He ate the oatmeal and fruit at the counter and didn't notice how any of it tasted. Jones' mind was on the newspaper. If the paper had the time right, the first cops arrived on scene almost ten minutes after he left. That meant someone had heard the shots and called them in. He had been careful when he left; he used the back door and didn't do anything to draw attention to himself while he walked up the street to his Jeep, but it was a safe bet that whoever had called the police had seen him—worse, they had seen the Jeep.

Jones put the bowl in the sink and turned the faucet on to fill the bowl to the rim. When he shut off the sink, he noticed the spoon still on the counter. He picked it up and looked at his reversed reflection in the convex surface of the utensil. He had missed it; another careless mistake.

Jones put two elbows on the counter and rubbed his head. He had lost control in the basement. Every ounce of training that had gone into making him a soldier, a man who could keep his cool when the world was on fire, had not come with him down those stairs. He had been careless and it had cost him. He hadn't gotten the full accounting yet, but he was sure the bill would be in years. It wasn't that Jones was afraid to settle up—he just wasn't ready. He had left evidence behind; hell, he had been canvassing the neighbours the day before, but nothing the cops discovered would have led them directly to him. It was Adam who would point the cops to Jones, and Adam who would hang him. The task of determining the identity of a murder victim killed a decade ago would move at a scientist's pace and take weeks to produce any kind of lead the cops could use, but the detectives looking at McGregor's murder wouldn't have to wait that long. In six days, Jones would sit down with Ruth and tell her everything. After that, the cops would have an ID on the boy in the basement and a trail that led straight to Jones.

Jones stood and stretched his back until he felt the knots tighten. He dug his thumb into his lower back and worked at the worst of the kinks as he crossed the kitchen. When he became convinced the pain was going to be hitching a ride for the day, he gave up on his back and picked up his phone. He pulled up the pictures he had taken the day before and read the message again. He had six days until he had to meet with Ruth. Six days until everything fell apart. Six days to find *the girl*.

4

JONES WAS STANDING IN THE PARKING LOT WATCHING HIS JEEP GETTING
detailed when his phone buzzed. He pulled his phone
out, glanced at the screen, and saw that it was his assis-
tant, Melissa. Jones had a habit of throwing himself into
his cases; something that pissed off anyone who was
looking to get a hold of him. He eventually grew tired of
the constant complaints and hired a secretarial service to
take his messages and set up appointments.

"Yeah."

"Did you forget you had an appointment this morning?" Melissa didn't wait for Jones to come up with an answer. "I left you a message yesterday. You were supposed to call me back."

Jones remembered the text that had come in just before everything went to shit. "I got busy."

"Well, you have a nine a.m. appointment at your office with a potential client."

Jones almost reflexively told her to cancel the appointment, but then he thought about what Melissa would have to say about that. She knew his schedule inside and out and she would know any excuse he gave her was bullshit—his day was wide open. Jones had planned to keep chasing the girl, but it still was too early for that, and he couldn't face the prospect of going home to an empty house to kill time. He needed to keep moving and work was as good a destination as any.

Jones glanced at his watch and saw the minute hand flirting with the six. He judged the status of the Jeep and did a bit of mental math before he said, "I'll be there."

"Don't be late for this one."

Jones drove to his office in a vehicle that had been scrubbed clean of anything incriminating. He had no illusions about what was waiting for him at the end of the week, but he wasn't going to make it easy. The office was off Bloor West in Koreatown. The neighbourhood had none of the cachet of Chinatown and better food.

Jones owned the building, but kept only the upper floor for himself. He rented the first floor to a market that paid enough rent to cover most of his bills. The shop was busy and the sounds and smells of the produce found their way through the gaps in the aged floorboards and up to his office. Jones parked behind the market and let himself in a rear door. He went through the back room of the market past heaps of vegetables and boxes of Korean products that couldn't be found in a grocery store outside of Seoul. Mr. Mun, the owner of Moon Market, looked up from the box of mung beans he was inspecting and nodded at Jones.

"Hey, Ralph."

"Hello, Mr. Jones." The unlit cigarette in Ralph's mouth bounced when he spoke.

"Smells good."

"They do not." He pointed to the cigarette. "This is for when I get tired of the smell of beans."

"It's your place. Why sell them if you hate the smell?"

"They taste better than they smell." He slapped his belly. "The woman teaching yoga up the street recommends them to her clients. I can't keep them in stock."

"So I can expect more of this smell?"

Ralph nodded his shaven head and extracted a black bean. "You can also expect more rent money."

"I have someone coming by the office."

Ralph found another black bean. "She is already here."

"How do you know she's my client?"

The grocer laughed. "You can tell."

Jones clapped Ralph on the back and walked out through the market to the street. On his way past the register, he nodded to Ralph's daughter Linda. As usual, she was listening to K-pop music on one earbud. When she noticed Jones, she smiled wide. "This one didn't look happy."

Jones stopped next to the register. "You let her up?"

Linda nodded and held out her hand. Jones gave her a five for working the door.

"I should have done you a favour and kept the door locked."

Jones laughed. "She really that bad?"

"You could tell by the look on her face and the way she crossed her arms when she found the door locked— she thinks she's too good for a place like this."

"Maybe she just doesn't like the smell of mung beans."

Linda rolled her eyes. "Oh my God, I hate those things. My dad keeps trying to get me to eat them. He says they're full of fibre." She nodded to a woman with a basket full of produce and said something friendly in Korean. The customer started putting the items next to the register. "I'd rather be constipated."

Jones laughed and thanked her on his way out. The door fronted the sidewalk and opened to a stairwell. On the landing at the top of the stairs was Jones' nine o'clock appointment.

"You're late," she said.

Jones started up the stairs without bothering to check the time on his phone; he was sure that she was right. He stopped shy of the landing because his client refused to relinquish the high ground. She was older than him by ten years—more if the work that had been done on her face was really good. She was wearing thigh-high boots over a pair of jeans that were mostly concealed by an oversized blanket scarf. Her hair was too blonde to be natural, but the state of her hair didn't give that away. Her colourist must have cost a fortune.

"You're late," she said again.

"You already said that."

"When someone is late, it is customary to apologize."

"The same could be said for someone who is rude."

Jones lifted the keys out of his pocket and showed them to his nine a.m. She looked at the keys and then stared at him a bit longer before taking a step back.

Jones stepped up and turned toward the door. The surface was steel and the words Jones Investigations had been stencilled in white at eye level. In between the two words was a wide dent that Jones had used a man's head to create. He had never gotten around to getting the door fixed.

Jones turned the key and left the door open behind him. The woman didn't step inside the office until he had turned all the lights on. She crossed the threshold and gave the office a long look while Jones disabled the alarm system.

"This is . . . nice."

Jones let his gaze drift across the space as his finger glided to the enter key. When Jones had bought the building, he renovated the office space upstairs. The upper floor was part of the original structure while the lower floor had expanded in spurts throughout the decades. Jones had preserved the limited parking that remained behind the building, and as much of the original material as he could upstairs. The dark grey walls of his office were contrasted by the white trim. The contractor had wanted to tear out the thin uneven floorboards and start over, but Jones wouldn't let her. She reluctantly stripped them and stained them dark enough to hide all their sins. The furniture was old, but all of it was quality. Jones took special pride in his desk. He had found it on the curb and nursed it back to health with his own hand.

"Thanks," Jones said, nodding.

He circled the desk and shrugged out of his jacket. He tossed the coat on top of his file cabinet and pulled the chair back from the desk. He glanced at the woman and saw her eyes on his arm. You could tell a lot about a person by the way they looked at something that was different. The missing hand made her uncomfortable and she quickly averted her eyes so she wouldn't be caught staring. Jones let the chair catch his weight; the impact of his body against the leather seat generated a metallic screech that made the woman wince. He gestured to the chairs in front of his desk and waited for his prospective client to sit down. She looked around the room one more time before coming closer. She ignored the invitation to sit and stepped to the window that overlooked the street.

"I didn't even know there was a Koreatown."

"I would imagine that they haven't heard of you either."

"You're making fun of me," she said. "I don't like that. Especially, when I'm paying you money."

Jones grinned. "You haven't paid me anything at all. I haven't even agreed to take your case."

Her eyebrow dove like a predatory bird, creating a faint crease in her smooth skin. "But isn't that how this works? I pay you and you solve my case."

Jones grinned again. "That's how it works if I take the case."

"Why wouldn't you take my case?"

"I don't know what you want yet," Jones said.

"My father is missing, and I need you to find him."

5

"MY NAME IS IRENE HOGARTH." SHE PAUSED AND WATCHED JONES TO SEE IF HE was impressed. The name was familiar, but not impressive.

"Sam Jones," he said, but she already knew his name. "How long has your father been missing?"

"Three days." Irene paused again and seemed disappointed by the lack of effect the answer had on Jones. "He's eighty years old."

Jones nodded.

"Shouldn't you be writing this down?" she said, as she took the seat across from him.

Jones leaned back in his chair and rested his chin on his fist. "So far I have two numbers to remember. I think I can manage. Have you contacted the police?"

Irene nodded. "Two days ago. They told me I could come down and file a report. I did that and when I finished, do you know what they said?"

Jones shook his head.

"They said they would *look into it*. That's what they told me. I said that wasn't good enough, and do you know what the police officer said to me? He said I should *give it a few days*. He said that these types of situations often *resolve* themselves in a couple of days." She blew out a short breath. "My tax dollars at work."

Irene got up from her chair and walked back to the window.

Jones swivelled the chair and tracked her movement. "The police—"

She crossed her arms and examined the street below. "The police are useless."

"The police are busy," Jones countered. "They see a lot of missing person reports and they know that many people return home just fine."

Irene fixed a stare at Jones. "Well, it's been three days and my father has not returned just fine."

"Is it possible he just took a trip that he forgot to tell you about?"

"My father did not go on vacation. He is missing. Something happened to him."

"What makes you so sure that something *happened* to him?"

Irene pivoted and stepped to the desk. She gripped the corners of the desk and leaned in close enough for Jones to pick up her perfume. "Because he is eighty years old and has been gone for three days."

"Is he in ill health?"

Irene let go of the desk. "You sound just like the police. No, he doesn't have Alzheimer's or dementia, but that doesn't mean that nothing happened."

"You are right," Jones conceded. "But, it doesn't mean that something did. Plenty of octogenarians go on trips. Just look at a cruise ship brochure."

"Octogenarian?"

"A person between eighty and eighty-nine."

"I know what it means," Irene said.

"So you also know it isn't a terminal condition."

Irene sat down and crossed her legs before she answered. "What I know is that he is missing."

Jones nodded. "Fair enough. Tell me about him."

"What do you want to know?"

"Everything," Jones said.

Irene sighed and reached for her purse. "Can I smoke in here?"

"Nope."

Irene sighed again and dropped the bag. "God, I could use a cigarette."

Jones waited.

"Fine," she said. "My father's name is William Greene. He is—"

"Eighty," Jones said.

Irene's perfectly defined eyebrow arched in displeasure. "Yes. My father lives in a retirement community called Pacific Heights."

"I know it," Jones said. It had been far too pricey for his father.

"The staff provides meals and cleaning services, but my father is not under any type of supervised care. He can come and go as he pleases. That's my fault. He wouldn't agree to supervision, and I caved. I should have insisted."

"Not really your call," Jones said.

"It should be when I'm the one paying the bills."

Jones grunted.

"You disapprove?"

"Doesn't matter," he said.

"No," Irene said. "It doesn't."

"Does he have any other children?"

Irene shook her head. "I am the only family he has."

"So, no other family. How about friends?"

Irene thought about it. "He plays cards with a few of the other residents in his building."

"Hobbies?"

Irene bit her lower lip. "Just playing cards."

Jones nodded and brought the chair out of its lean. "I'll need to see his place."

"Does that mean you'll take the case?"

"I have some time to look into it."

Irene bent and began going through her purse. She raised her voice. "Just tell me what you want to know and I'll answer it." She straightened up and placed four photos on Jones' desk. "I have pictures you can use—for flyers."

Jones slid the pictures across the desk. The first photo was a shot of William's upper body. Jones picked the picture up and leaned back in the chair while he examined it.

"I think one of the others would be better."

Jones lifted the remaining photos off the desk and examined each of them; William was close to the same age in all of them. The man in the pictures looked like Irene and didn't. The physical features were similar—the sharp nose was dead-on—but there was a glint in the man's eyes that Irene didn't have; it was a look of youth that her doctors couldn't replicate. Jones took out his phone and took a photo of one of the pictures. He looked the image over to make sure that it had turned out and then put his phone away. He reached across the table and placed the pictures in front of Irene. She didn't move to take them back.

"I think you should hold on to those. I can get them back later. You'll need them for the posters."

"I think we should start with the apartment," Jones said.

"I told you, he's missing. He isn't at his apartment. You need to start putting up posters and canvassing the neighbourhood."

"That's how you find a lost dog, not a person. I need to see his place first."

"Why?"

Jones sighed and pushed the photos closer to Irene. "I get the impression that there is a lot you don't know about your father."

Irene opened her mouth to say something; it didn't look like it was going to be something friendly.

"I'm not judging," Jones said, "but if you want me to find your father, I need to know more about him than his name and his address."

Irene stared into Jones' eyes. There was a hard centre inside her that had been forged by crashing through whatever was in her way. Jones could tell that her first instinct was to push back and walk out, but she hesitated.

"Do you promise that you will find him?"

"No."

The word smashed into that hard centre like a sledgehammer, and Jones saw Irene's lip quiver. "I thought that is what you do."

"I look for people, and I find many of them, but not everyone. I will do everything I can to find your father, and I won't ever lie to you. That's what your money gets you here."

"I haven't paid you anything yet."

"Step one," Jones said.

"How much do you charge?"

Jones told her.

Irene picked up her purse and removed her cheque-book without looking inside. "For that much money, I should have my father back this afternoon." There was a hint of a smile on her face, and Jones could tell that the hard centre hadn't been cracked—it hadn't even been chipped. He liked that.

6

JONES PARKED THE JEEP AND CHECKED HIS PHONE TO SEE IF ANY OF THE
newspapers had updated the story on the bodies found
in the basement while Irene took two shots at adjusting
her Land Rover so that it was between the lines of the
parking spot. Jones got out after Irene killed the engine
and he stood waiting while she used the rear-view to
check her make-up. The cars in the lot of Pacific Heights
Retirement Community were a mixture of old and new.
Jones saw a few Town Cars and Cadillacs that remembered the '90s and figured that they belonged to the

residents. When Irene finally got out of her car, he said, "One of those belong to your father?"

Irene snorted. "My father doesn't have a car."

"Why?"

Irene had already started walking toward the door. She paused and gave Jones a look that told him she wasn't happy about having to stand around in the parking lot. "What?"

"Why doesn't he have a car?"

"It's not necessary here. Everything he could ever need is within walking distance." She made a show of adjusting her blanket scarf before setting her eyes on the Jeep. Jones watched as her lips puckered. "How do you know Daniel Adams?"

"Is that who gave you my name?"

"He attended a benefit I organized for the Hogarth Foundation."

Irene puckered her lips again when her words failed to produce a reaction.

"I established the Hogarth Foundation in memory of my husband, Aaron. Aaron loved sports. I thought it fitting that the Hogarth Foundation worked to provide others with the opportunity to be able to play them."

"No one should have to sit on the bench," Jones said.

Irene smiled. "That is our motto."

"Dan would like that," Jones said. "He tried to buy the Leafs not too long ago."

"You haven't explained exactly how you know Daniel Adams."

"No, I didn't," Jones said.

Irene frowned. "Well, he spoke very highly of you. But, I have to admit, you aren't what I expected."

Jones glanced at the Jeep. "Really, I'm surprised. Dan loves the Jeep."

Irene, realizing Jones wasn't going to engage her attempt to gossip, sighed and turned her back. "It's freezing out here. I'm going inside."

She didn't wait for Jones to catch up, and she didn't hold the door. Her lead gave Jones a unique vantage point. He watched from a distance as the staff of Pacific Heights reacted to Irene Hogarth's presence. Irene's heels pounded a steady aggressive beat that was too fast to be melodious. The sound drew eyes her way and Jones watched as the staff began pivoting their bodies to reduce the chance of any possible interaction. Irene ignored the employees as she deftly extracted a pen from her purse without breaking stride. She signed in without saying hello to the woman working at the desk next to the sign-in book.

She finished writing her name and looked over her shoulder to see that Jones had just caught up. "You have to sign in to be admitted." She didn't offer her pen.

Jones signed in and noticed the woman behind the desk looking at him out of the corner of her eye. Jones glanced right, saw that Irene had already moved toward the elevators, and stepped left.

"Can I ask you a question?"

The receptionist was younger than Jones and seemed apprehensive about the results of her eye contact with him.

"Don't worry," he said. "I'm scared of her too."

The receptionist smiled.

"Does everyone have to sign in?"

She nodded her head and pushed a braid that fell out of place behind her ear. "Every visitor must sign in, and they're supposed to sign themselves out." The receptionist glanced at Irene. "Not everyone does that."

"How about the residents? Do they have to sign out when they leave?"

The receptionist shook her head and Jones glanced to his right and saw Irene staring at him from inside one of the elevators. When she saw that he noticed her, she let go of the hold button, took a step back from the panel, and began looking inside her purse.

"I should run away, shouldn't I?"

The receptionist glanced at Irene and laughed before she nodded.

Jones managed to get a hand between the doors before they closed. "We are going to the fifteenth floor," Irene said. She was rubbing a generous amount of hand sanitizer into her palms and showed no indication that she was going to hit the button.

The button for the fifteenth floor had a greasy film that muted the light it gave off after Jones touched it. He wiped his finger on his pant leg and took a step back to stand beside Irene.

"What is she smiling at?" Irene asked, peering out the elevator doors.

Jones saw the receptionist look away when she noticed Irene looking at her. "A handsome detective," Jones said.

"You are on the clock, Mr. Jones. I am not paying you to flirt."

Jones saluted and said, "Yes, ma'am."

"And I'm not paying you for your sarcasm either."

"I throw it in for free. Most people find it charming."

"I'm not most people," Irene said.

"On that we can agree."

Irene adjusted her scarf and examined her hair in the cloudy reflection cast by the stainless-steel button panel. She pushed her hair from her face and checked it one more time before looking at Jones. "This elevator is far too slow."

Jones had the impression that she wasn't trying to start a conversation. The relationship had changed when the cheque left her fingers. Jones was on the payroll now—an employee.

When the doors opened, Irene went right and Jones followed. She used a set of keys to open apartment 1502. Calling the space an apartment was being generous. There was a living room large enough to accommodate an oversized leather recliner and a television mounted above a slim cabinet deep enough to hold a Blu-ray player. On the right was an open door leading to a bathroom that just managed to fit a sink, toilet, and tub shower. Jones wondered if it were possible to use any one item without touching another. He backed out of the room and moved along the wall to the next door. The bedroom was blessed with enough space to fit a double mattress and a bedside table; fitting a person too was the difficult part. Jones had to constantly adjust his body to navigate his way to the closet. He knew sliding open the door would depress him, but he did it anyway; he was right.

"Did you think you might find him in there?"

Irene had stayed in the living room. It was probably for the best; the bedroom wasn't meant for two. Jones ignored the question and scanned the length of the closet. "Five empty hangars."

"What?"

Jones leaned back and craned his neck so that he could look at Irene. "There are five empty hangars."

Jones stepped around the bed and out of the room. "Go and see for yourself."

While Irene checked the closet, Jones went back into the bathroom to confirm a hunch. He almost collided with Irene when he walked back into the living room.

She put a hand on her hip and gave Jones an exasperated look that felt like it relied on muscle memory more than real emotion. "I don't see what the number of hangars has to do with—"

"Sure you do," Jones said. "His toothbrush is gone too."

"Toothbrush?"

"Check it out."

Jones started opening drawers in the living room while Irene looked at the empty spot in the ceramic toothbrush holder on the sink.

"I can't find it," she said on her way out of the bathroom. She stopped in the doorway. "What are you doing?"

"I'm looking for clues."

"What kind of clues?"

"Bills are always a good start."

"You won't find any bills," Irene said. "I pay all of them."

Jones saw a small table on the other side of the recliner. He sat down in the chair and opened the top drawer. He lifted out the first sheet of paper and skipped to the best part. "Do you pay his credit card bill?"

"He doesn't have a credit card. He only has a debit card that I put fifty dollars on each week."

Jones took a picture of the bill with his phone and held the paper out for Irene. She snatched it from his hand and tried to read the bill but had to adjust the paper so that it was closer to her face. When that didn't work, Irene slowly moved the paper away from her in a furious search for some kind of personal sweet spot.

Jones made it easy for her. He got up from the chair and said, "He has a credit card and he has definitely been spending more than fifty dollars a week."

Irene threw her purse into the vacant seat and rummaged for her glasses while Jones went back into the bedroom.

Irene spoke louder than she needed to. "He's had this card for two months."

He figured she finally found her glasses. "Un hunh."

"His last charge was a dinner for three hundred dollars!"

"Must have been good."

Irene swore while Jones moved to the bed.

"He bought a suit for seven hundred dollars!"

Jones saw a red stain on one of the pillows. "Probably wanted to look good for his girlfriend."

"He's eighty years old. He doesn't have a girlfriend."

"You sure about that? Five minutes ago, you didn't know he had a credit card."

Jones heard Irene's heels march across the laminate flooring. "What do you know?"

Jones held up the pillow. "Nothing for sure. I'm just guessing this shade of lipstick wouldn't match his new suit."

7

"A GIRLFRIEND!" IRENE'S HAND TENSED AND CREASED THE BILL SHE WAS holding.

Jones had run out of things to check, and Irene took his presence as a sign to unload the anger she had been carrying.

"He's—"

"Eighty," Jones said.

"Don't be an asshole. What would a eighty-year-old man do with a girlfriend?"

Jones smiled. "The lipstick on the pillow says he figured it out."

Irene held out an index finger. "No. No. I do not want to hear it."

"On the bright side, we know he's not walking the streets like a lost dog."

Irene looked at the bedroom door. "I wish he were a dog. You can neuter a dog."

Jones laughed, but Irene didn't join in. "Judging by the missing clothes and toothbrush, the credit card, and the lipstick, I'd say your father is not so much lost, as he is out of town."

Irene turned her back on the bedroom door. "It would appear that way."

"Do you still want me to find him?"

Irene picked up the bill, put it back in the drawer, and slid it shut. "Perhaps we should take the advice of the police and give it a few days."

Jones took the cheque out of his pocket and held it out. Irene took the slip of paper and slid it into the depths of her purse. "You can send me a bill for your time, Mr. Jones."

Jones said, "Sure," even though he had no intention of sending her anything. Irene moved toward the door and Jones was happy to follow. He had been inside the cramped apartment for ten minutes and he was already itching to get out of it. He hoped William Greene made the most of his few days.

They rode the elevator together, and Irene felt no need to try to fill the quiet with small talk. Jones was happy for the silence. Irene took a step forward when she heard the muted elevator chime. When the door opened, she stepped out and, without looking at Jones, said, "Thank you for your help today, Mr. Jones."

Jones watched Irene Hogarth walk away. She didn't look back to see if he was following, so she didn't notice him walk in the other direction.

There was a common room on the first floor, and Jones found four men playing a card game at a battered felt-topped table. The soft green surface had worn slick and shiny in places where elbows had rested for countless hours. The men were playing euchre and the grunts and monosyllables told Jones it was a regular thing. He watched as a suit was chosen. The choice of spades earned a harrumph from the player to the right of the man who had chosen it and a grin from the bald man opposite him.

The first card hit the table and the sound it made was like a starter's pistol. Plans of attack that had been silently drafted in the moments between the call of spades and the drop of the first card played out in a steady rhythm that seemed to surprise no one at the table.

The bald man looked up as the cards were being collected. "Can I help you?"

Jones said, "I'm looking for William Greene."

That made the card players laugh. "No one calls him that except his daughter."

"She brought me here."

All of the smiles vanished and so did the friendliness in the bald man's voice. "You're with her?"

Jones shook his head. "She's gone. I stayed behind to look around."

"Thank God," the previous dealer said. He turned his head and looked at Jones through thick glasses. "That woman is real piece of work."

The bald man was dealt the first card of a new hand by an elderly black man to his right.

"She came in here the other day looking for Willy," the man with the glasses went on after he peeked at his card. "She was raising all kinds of hell downstairs about it. You know she threatened to sue the building for letting him walk off?"

The threat elicited snorts from the other players.

"Letting him walk off," he said. "Like we're prisoners who might escape."

"I'm new to this place," Jones said. "What's it like here?"

"We're playing cards at eleven o'clock in the morning," the bald man said. "What are you doing?"

"Working," Jones said.

"We win."

"What are you eating for dinner tonight?" the new dealer asked.

"I haven't figured it out yet."

"Me neither," said the dealer, "but it will be on the table at five o'clock, and whatever it is will be good. There will be ice cream for dessert too." He laughed and Jones saw a row of perfectly white teeth. "We win."

The man with the thick glasses turned his head away from his cards. "How many women do you live with?"

"None," Jones said.

"Last count, we live with seventy-eight. We most definitely win."

Jones looked at the fourth man. He was the oldest of the group and even from across the table Jones could see tufts of hair growing out of his ears. Jones waited for the last man's contribution. He spoke without looking up from his cards. "Do you ever get interrupted by people trying to sell you stuff?" Living in Europe had left a stain on the man's voice that would never totally fade away. Jones guessed Germany.

"Sure," Jones said.

"I guess we tie on that one."

The whole table started to laugh again.

"Can I sit?"

The man with the glasses said, "Sure, but you can't play and you can't offer advice."

"Deal," Jones said. He slid a chair away from the wall as trump was called and seated himself just behind the players.

"I hear Willy played poker here." Jones wondered if

the men would object to him talking during the game, but no one seemed to mind. Their actions were so practised that they seemed to be automatic.

The bearded man's smile showed his perfect teeth again. "He did, but this is euchre, son."

"Did Willy play euchre?"

"Just poker," the man said.

"Did any of you play poker with him?"

"We all have at one time or another, but not anymore."

"Why?"

The expensive smile flashed again. "Willy cheats. No one knows exactly how he does it, but he does."

"How can you be sure?"

"No one wins that often." The game ended, and the German began sweeping the cards toward him. The cards were shuffled quickly and tossed back toward the other players.

The bald man lifted the corner of his first card and evaluated what he saw. "Willy has taken our money more times than any of us want to admit," he said.

"Not mine," the German said.

Jones saw a smile creep on the bald man's face. "That's because you don't have any."

The jab earned another chorus of laughter from everyone at the table.

"Not to get too personal, but I get the impression that Willy doesn't have a lot of money."

The bald man was suddenly more interested in the conversation. "What makes you say that?"

Jones shrugged. "His daughter has him on an allowance."

"She's not hurting for money. That's for sure," the man with the thick eye glasses said.

The German leaned back in his chair and held his cards close to his chest. "She is rich," he said, "and yet, she treats her father like a criminal who just walked out of prison. Why do you think that is?"

"I don't know," Jones said.

The old man slapped a card down on the table and answered his own question. "Because he is a criminal who just walked out of prison."

8

JONES COULDN'T HIDE THE SURPRISE IN HIS VOICE. "WILLY JUST GOT OUT
of prison?"

"He didn't just get out," the bald man said. "He got
out about eight months ago."

"Willy served twenty years for armed robbery," the
German said.

"He told you that?"

"Nope," the bald man said over his cards. "I Googled
him after we figured out he had done time."

"Did he brag about it?"

"Nah, he just couldn't hide it. Willy didn't know anything about what was going on in the world. I mean *anything*. At first, we thought he was like a lot of folks in here, but he was sharp."

"Sharp enough to cheat us at poker," the old man said. He put a lot of emphasis on the word *us*, to let Jones know it was an accomplishment.

"Twenty years is a long time," Jones said.

The old man smiled. "Well, Willy robbed a lot of banks."

"His daughter said he disappeared two days ago." Something about what Jones said brought about another round of laughter, but the sound was different. The laughs were deeper and accompanied by the shared glances of men who were all in on a joke.

"Something you guys want to share?"

The German nodded. "He didn't disappear alone."

"He went with a woman."

The bearded man smiled. "You're not as dumb as you look. But he didn't go with *a* woman he went with *the* woman."

"Wore red lipstick?"

"How'd you know that?"

"Saw it on his pillow," Jones said.

The man with glasses let out a heavy sigh. "Charlene."

"Is Charlene Willy's girlfriend?"

The bald man barked a laugh. "Charlene is always somebody's girlfriend. Before Willy, she was with Phil."

He nodded to the bearded man, who had done most of the talking.

Phil smiled wide. "That's right."

"And before Phil, she was with Harry."

Harry adjusted his glasses. "Not right before." He smiled and elbowed Phil. "But I was first."

Jones looked at the bald man. "How about you?"

He shook his head. "I've never had enough money for a woman who wears lipstick that red."

Jones understood. When men closed their eyes at night and journeyed to the places their feet couldn't go, there was often a Charlene there. And when good men lost fortunes, or families, the way others lose car keys, there was usually a Charlene there too. Jones wouldn't have been able to make a living if there weren't Charlenes in the world.

"So when the money runs out—"

Phil smiled and shook his head. "That's when the fun is over. After that, she usually looks around for someone else. Maybe next time it will be Kurt's turn."

The old man picked up the cards and started to deal. "Fuck that." His accent made the profanity almost elegant. "I didn't spend my whole life in a steel mill to give my money to Charlene."

Phil laughed. "You didn't spend your life in a steel mill, Kurt. You owned the place."

"I was there every day."

Phil laughed again. "In your office."

The easy back and forth was felt comfortable and practised.

"I sweat through my clothes in that office every day for thirty-five years. Not one drop of it was for Charlene."

Phil tilted his head toward Jones, covered his mouth with the back of his hand, and whispered loud enough for everyone to hear. "He's full of shit. He's just too old to get it up."

"Maybe," Kurt said. "But officially I said no because of the principle, not the physical."

Jones laughed with everyone at the table. It felt good to laugh; like he hadn't done it in years. The feeling of happiness felt wrong all at once and Jones remembered the people who had nothing to laugh about and how he would be joining them soon enough.

9

JONES WAS BACK IN HIS JEEP BY ONE. THERE WERE NO MESSAGES FROM Melissa about appointments he had forgotten and nothing on his calendar except a meeting in six days. In six days, he would break Ruth's heart. He wanted to rationalize it. What was six more days on top of six years? It was nothing, but Jones knew it would be everything to Ruth. A feeling of shame crept up like a tentacle and tried to grab hold of something inside of Jones. He forced himself to push the feeling away.

The girl—that was the name Jones had given whoever had left the messages in the café bathroom—was out there, and there was a chance Jones could save her. He just had to keep moving for as long as he could and hope he had enough time. Jones scrolled through his phone, selected The Rolling Stones, and turned the volume up loud enough to drown out his thoughts. When he heard the opening chords to "Moonlight Mile," he turned the wheel and drove toward Brew.

Sheena was behind the counter again and the line was four deep. Jones made it five and looked around to make sure Diane wasn't at a table nursing another bottomless glass of wine. When it was his turn to order, Jones turned to the only other person in line and said, "You go ahead. I'm having trouble deciding."

Sheena rolled her eyes.

When it was his turn, Sheena said, "You manage to choose something?"

"Can I get a cortado?"

"Shocker." Sheena opened a jar and scooped out some coffee beans. "You know I don't even know your name."

"Jones."

Sheena put a hand on her hip. "That's not a name."

"Says the girl named Sheena."

"Is that your first name?"

"Nope."

"What is your first name?"

"Not the one they call me."

Sheena rolled her eyes and turned her back on him. Jones waited for Sheena to finish grinding the coffee beans before he said, "Did you get a chance to ask around about the door?"

She nodded. Without looking turning her head, she said, "No one knows anything."

"Did you paint over it yet?"

Jones saw her laugh. "It's yours until the rent money runs out."

"How long does twenty dollars get me?"

Sheena shrugged. "A week, or until my boss tells me to paint over it—whichever comes first." She set the cortado down on the counter and took Jones' money. "After my shift yesterday, I went and looked at the door. It's weird. I almost never even notice what is on it until I'm painting over it. Even then, I usually just pay attention to the pictures or the really good swear words. That message was there for who knows how long and no one paid attention to it except you." For a second, Jones thought Sheena sounded different. Her voice didn't seem to have any of the piss and vinegar that had been there the day before, but then she said, "You some kind of do-gooder, or just a lonely guy looking for someone to talk to?"

Maybe just the vinegar.

"Neither. I think I only saw it because I was looking for something to see," he said.

"What does that mean?"

Jones shook his head. "Nothing." He reached for the coffee before Sheena tried a follow-up and found the glass easier to pick up. "It's not as hot," he said.

She pissed in the vinegar and said, "You whined like a bitch about it yesterday, so I eased up on the milk a bit."

"Thanks."

Sheena put two hands on the counter and Jones saw the veins in her arms come alive. "Let me see that picture again."

Jones pulled out his phone and pulled up the image. He put the phone on the counter and Sheena picked it up. "Last night, I was lying in bed, thinking about that door." She used two fingers to zoom in for a few seconds. Then she zoomed out and began scrolling through the other shots. "I couldn't stop wondering about what other things I missed. How many other messages did I just paint over?"

Jones thought about that. How many other tags were buried in shallow graves under layers of paint? The bones were still there waiting to be uncovered; the problem was, this was no ordinary archeological dig. Scraping away the layers would require something other than shovels and brushes—it would need to be something chemical. There was also the issue of the site; it was a door and Jones didn't own it.

He looked around. "The art on the walls is for sale?"

Sheena glanced at the various paintings. "A local artist had an event here and the owner made a deal with him. We agreed to sell them if he agreed to leave them up on the walls. It was a good deal. They almost never sell and I like the way they look."

"What else is for sale here?"

The change in Sheena's posture told Jones that the question offended her.

"Don't be gross," Jones said. "I want to buy the door."

"There is no way my boss is going to let you walk away with our door. We run a place that serves coffee and bran muffins—people need to be able to use the bathroom."

"I'd pay for a replacement."

Sheena snorted. "He won't go for it. The door is vintage."

"Maybe I should talk to your boss."

"No offence, but you're kind of a kook." She held out two palms. "I think you're on the level, but my boss isn't going to see it that way. He will definitely think you're a kook."

Jones saw a customer coming in and moved down the counter. He drank some of the coffee while Sheena made a London fog. By the time Sheena finished ringing up the woman and putting the cash in the till, Jones had a plan.

"What are you doing tonight?"

10

AT ELEVEN, SHEENA LOCKED THE DOOR AND TURNED OFF THE LIGHTS.

Jones put the money on the counter. "Is there an alarm you're supposed to set?"

Sheena pulled a beer from the fridge and used the edge of the granite countertop to pop off the cap. The movement was done without any attempt to show off, making it even cooler than it looked. She picked up the folded stack of twenties and pocketed it without counting it. "I forget to set it at least three times a week and no one has ever said a word about it." She took a drink from the bottle and pointed the neck at Jones. "Did you get everything you need?"

Jones opened the backpack and tilted it toward Sheena so she could see inside. She paused to drink before looking. "You sure it will work?"

"Not as sure as the guy at the hardware store, but I'm confident."

"This shit won't screw up the new coat of paint you promised to put on when you're done, will it?"

"Shouldn't be a problem."

Sheena took another drink. "I didn't hear it in your voice."

"What?"

"Confidence. I can't get fired over this."

"You won't," Jones said.

"Won't what? I want to hear it and this time I want to believe you."

"You won't get fired over this."

Sheena drained what was left of the beer and put the bottle down hard on the counter. "Fuck it. Let's get this show on the road."

Jones diluted the mineral spirits in a tray and used a cloth to soak up the solution. Jones rubbed the cloth over the first quadrant of the door in slow rhythmic circles.

"You need a hand?"

Jones looked over his shoulder and saw Sheena biting her cheek.

"Proud of yourself?"

She laughed. The sound was loud and rough and had no trace of self-consciousness. Jones liked it. "A little."

"I'm fine," he said.

"How'd you lose it anyway?"

"High-fived too hard."

"Seriously."

"Army."

"They cut it off?"

Jones looked at Sheena again and saw her staring at him. Usually when he said *army*, people stopped asking questions. "They just trimmed off what was left," he said.

Sheena let a few seconds go by before she said, "Why didn't you get a prosthetic?"

Jones didn't look this time; he was too focused on the door. "Wasn't for me."

"I think I would want one if I was in your shoes," Sheena said.

Cloudy tears travelled in cracks and gouges and sought community in the grooves of the woodwork. Jones used a dry cloth to wipe them away before starting again with the mineral spirits. He treated each quadrant of the door one at a time and examined the face of the door before he started again. On the third application, he began to see evidence of graffiti that had been painted over. Jones carefully rubbed at each dark smudge and slowly brought it closer to the surface. As far as he could tell, no one else had ever tried something like this, so he did his best to work slowly and carefully to avoid erasing what was hiding within the layers of paint.

Sheena noticed his tentative wipes and came closer. "What is it?"

Jones gave the door a final scrub and then stood back to reveal a donkey with an erection.

"What does that even mean?" Sheena said.

Jones thought about it and the best answer he could come up with was a shrug.

"And why the fuck is that guy so good at drawing donkeys?"

IT TOOK TWO HOURS FOR JONES TO WORK HIS WAY DOWN TO THE ORIGINAL wood. Along the way, he uncovered pornography, crude jokes, lonely truths, and amateur philosophy. What he didn't find was another message from the girl.

Sheena had nodded off on the toilet. Jones looked at the woman who had been named after the punk rocker; sleep had quieted the fire inside her and relaxed her features. The person who had seemed so ready to argue the day before was dormant inside the small woman snoring on a public washroom fixture.

Jones repositioned the drop cloth and moved the tray of diluted mineral spirits out of the way. He carefully stepped over Sheena's feet and opened the cabinet under the sink where she had told him the paint was stored.

The sink was not antique; someone had picked it up at a box-store and paired it with a reclaimed seventies vanity that had been sloppily painted a robin's egg blue. Jones opened the cabinet doors and felt the hinge come loose from the door on the right. The door swung out and dipped eagerly forward like a loose tooth. In an effort to preserve the door, Jones kneeled and propped the door up with the toe of his boot while he reached inside to force the old screws back into their stripped holes. To be safe, he kept pressure on the open door with his toe and began to look through the vanity for the paint Sheena told him was inside. Jones found the paint on the left side behind three rolls of stacked toilet paper. On top of the stout can of paint was a stiff brush caked with hardened white paint. Jones knocked over the toilet paper lifting the can of paint out of the vanity and revealed another message inside the cupboard.

For a good time, call ~~416-647-0100~~
613-555-5897

The message was written in red pen, and not by the girl. The handwriting was nowhere near as beautiful. But the thick lines crossing out the phone number and the digits supplied underneath, however, were written with the same dark eyeliner and artist's skill as the message on the door.

"Hello," Jones said. The single word was quiet, but the acoustics of the room gave it a punch.

Sheena stirred. "God, you should have brought a fan. I've got such a fucking headache from those fumes. Doesn't your head hurt?"

Jones had been nursing a pain inside his skull that had started to send its roots down into his shoulders, but he forgot about it when he saw the second message a few seconds before.

Sheena looked at the exposed wood. "I'm guessing the door was a bust."

"It was," Jones said. "Not this though."

Sheena stared at Jones with her mouth open for a second before she surged forward off the toilet seat. The force of the sudden movement shoved the seat sideways with the loud crack of a plastic screw breaking. She planted one foot on the ground and was halfway to Jones when her brain seemed to register the feeling in her legs. "Fuck, pins and needles." Sheena changed course and walked a few circles around the room before she shoved Jones out of the way so that she could see what was inside the vanity.

"Holy shit! Do you think she wrote it?"

Jones regained his balance and pulled out his phone. He took a shot of the second message. "It was her," he said.

Sheena nodded. "She crossed the number out and wrote that new number in." Her head snapped toward

Jones a second behind the thought that had just exploded in her brain. "You don't think she's the good time, do you?"

The revulsion on her face was unmistakeable. Sheena had formed her own version of the girl in her mind, and that image had been a human, not a commodity. The sudden evolution of her girl from a kid crying out for help to someone advertising the sale of her body, was painful to try to imagine.

Jones had no answer for her, and he knew better than to speculate. He knew giving the girl dimensions was a mistake. Whatever container you designed in your mind would always be too small for the real thing, and it would end up hurting, like wrong-sized shoes.

"Do you recognize the phone number?"

The question was not the answer that she had been expecting, and it took Sheena a second to realize that she was not offended, but instead grateful for the chance to think about something else.

She looked at the digits. "No. Why? Do you?"

"No. I don't recognize the area code either. It's not local."

"Where's six-one-three?"

Jones shook his head. "Not sure."

Sheena stood up and pulled her phone from her back pocket. She began typing with nimble thumbs while she rotated her hips. "My back is *killing* me." She turned sharply and kicked the fixture. "It was this goddamn toilet. Do you know what that means?" Sheena didn't look up from the phone to see if Jones was listening; it didn't matter. "It means I'm getting old."

"I didn't know that was how it was determined."

"Well, now you do. You know what else you know?" She looked at Jones this time to make sure that she had his attention. She turned her phone and pointed it at Jones so that he could see the reverse lookup result. "You know that this number is for a place in Cartwright, Ontario."

"I GUESS THAT RULES OUT HOOKING," SHEENA SAID. SHE MADE A COUPLE quick swipes with her finger and tilted the phone so that Jones could see the screen. Google Maps put Cartwright out past Kingston.

Jones nodded. "It's definitely not in the neighbourhood."

"No shit, and no one is going to drive that far to get laid."

Jones shrugged and Sheena caught it. "Easy, big guy."

Jones took a few more shots of the door and then looked through the rest of the cabinet for any other messages that might have been left in make-up before opening the can of paint.

Jones managed to work the brush into something pliable that tested the paint; it was old, and a little thick, but it did the job. He had almost finished the first coat when Sheena said, "What do you think it means?"

Jones had been thinking about it. "Not sure. She left it there."

Sheena's voice got louder. "Are you trying to be a dick? I'm just asking what you think."

Jones didn't take the bait. He dipped the brush and worked the paint into the inlay. He gestured to the vanity with his forearm. "I mean *there*. The first message we found was plainly visible on the door. The second message was plainly visible, but only if you knew where to look."

"So visible, and not visible."

"Sort of like her, I imagine," Jones said.

"That was kind of profound. But why leave a note at all? Why not just tell someone?"

Jones dipped the brush and started back on the door. "Who would *you* tell?"

Sheena crossed her arms and thought about it. "Is this where you tell me that it's rough out there for girls because some of us don't have anyone looking out for them? You can skip the mansplaining. I'm up to speed.

I just don't understand why she left a note inside a cupboard. It's as good as talking to yourself."

The paint had a habit of collecting in the inlay, and Jones took a second to slowly drag the brush over the grooves before he said, "Yes."

Jones let Sheena work it out while he started to apply a second coat. "So she has no one because she's alone, or possibly because she's in danger. But she has something to say—something she wants to tell someone, so she leaves a message in eyeliner on the back of a door and inside a cupboard."

Jones dipped the brush into the can and carefully painted around the doorknob.

"That might be the saddest thing I have ever heard."

Jones wasn't sure if it was the saddest thing he had ever heard, but it was on the list.

"Maybe." The word was loud and full of promise. "Maybe this isn't that at all. Maybe it's all a prank by a kid with too much time and too much make-up on her hands."

Jones stopped painting and looked over his shoulder at Sheena.

"This doesn't feel like that."

"No, it doesn't," he said.

Jones got almost all the second coat onto the door before Sheena spoke again.

"Why do you think she put the second message under the sink? Why not put it on the door?"

Jones crouched down so that he could paint the lower part of the door and he heard his knees complain. Jones slowly let a breath out of his nose before he said, "I think the door was the first message. I think she was killing time in here and the door caught her eye. I don't think writing a message was anything she had planned. Graffiti isn't her thing; if it was, she wouldn't have used eyeliner. I think she read everything on the door. The confessions, the accusations, and the jokes and thought her message belonged there."

"What was her message?"

Jones looked at her.

"Confession, accusation, or joke?"

"All of them."

Sheena narrowed her eyes. "He's going to kill me, and I think I want him to.' That's what she wrote. There's nothing funny there."

"Not anymore. I think she changed her mind after she wrote the original message."

"What original message? You said the door was the first one."

Jones took out his phone and brought the picture up. He passed the phone to Sheena and said, "Zoom in on the words."

Sheena put her index finger and thumb on the screen and moved them apart. She looked at the screen for a couple of seconds and then at Jones. "What am I supposed to see here?"

"The end of the sentence."

"What, that blob?"

"She didn't use a period."

Sheena rolled her eyes. "It's graffiti, not poetry."

"That's what I thought at first," Jones said.

"But not anymore?"

Jones shook his head. "She was considerate enough to write a comma, but not a period? That doesn't make sense. I think she had a period at the end of the sentence."

Sheena looked closer at the screen.

"Another *O*—too," Jones said.

Sheena inched closer and spoke the words. "He's going to kill me, and I think I want him too."

"I think she made a joke at first, and then she thought about it. I think she saw something in that joke, something even darker, and she erased the last *O* and the period along with it."

Sheena zoomed in closer. It was pointless; Jones had already pushed the zoom function to its limits and come up with nothing.

She gave him the phone back and picked up the pan of mineral spirits. She walked to the toilet and tilted the pan. "Let's say you're right—"

"You're not supposed to flush that," Jones said.

Sheena stared at Jones while she poured. "We're not supposed to do a lot of things we're doing tonight." She went on. "Let's say you're right. Let's say there was a second *O* and she erased it. Why did she put another message on the second door? Why hide that one?"

"I think she came across the message in the cupboard the same way I did—by accident."

Sheena tossed the empty pan into the corner. "We're always out of toilet paper. She could have opened the door looking for some TP." Sheena leaned against the wall and crossed her arms. "So she opens the door, sees the tag on the door, and decides to do a bit of light editing."

"I think she found the message in the cupboard. It was a surprise waiting just for her. It made her think about something that wasn't dark. Something good."

"Something in Cartwright."

"Something not here," Jones said.

"Are you going to call that number?"

Jones nodded.

"When?"

"Tomorrow, after I get to Cartwright."

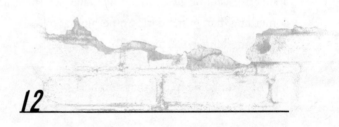

12

JONES GOT IN THE DOOR A FEW MINUTES BEFORE FOUR IN THE MORNING AND walked straight to his bed. His head ached from paint fumes and his back was sore from painting inside the cramped bathroom. He fell onto the mattress, closed his eyes, and let his body shut down.

Jones heard his alarm at eight and started the scavenger hunt for his phone with his eyes still shut. His hands groped across the usual surfaces and came up with nothing. He finally gave in and sat up so that his eyes could check his hands' work. It took about twenty seconds for him to see that they had told the truth and another thirty seconds to realize that his cell was in his pocket. Jones silenced the phone and plugged it in to charge before he walked to the bathroom.

After he was clean, Jones worked on getting fed. He had slept for only four hours, so he tried to balance the scale with food. He poached two eggs and ate them with an English muffin. He tossed the plate in the dishwasher and did a quick scan of the contents of the fridge for any fruits and vegetables on death row. The commercial-grade blender made short work of the old produce, and Jones poured the contents of the blender into a tall cup he could drink while he drove. He checked the cupboards and found a couple protein bars that had expired a few months before. He put the bars in a backpack along with an empty thermos and checked the street one more time before he walked out the door to his Jeep.

The 401 out of Toronto was slow, but that was just the city's default setting. The highway was a major artery and Jones had always felt the term was apt because it was always clogged. As the city became harder to see in the rear-view, the traffic thinned and Jones moved the Jeep into the centre lane and kept it ten over the speed limit.

After a couple of hours, Jones pulled off the highway to get gas at a rest station. Nothing much had changed since the last time Jones had been out that way. A little over five years ago, a case had brought him out to see an inmate at the Kingston Penitentiary. Jones' client was trying to prove that his brother had been wrongly convicted. Jones had interviewed the prisoner five times. The first time was to get the facts and the next four were to confirm what he had figured out on the first visit—the man was guilty. The con's brother, a former player for the Toronto Blue Jays, didn't take the news well. He fired Jones, and Jones hadn't driven up that way since.

When the tank was full, he parked near the entrance to a rest-stop that had used a Starbucks to fuse two fast-food chains together. He ordered a high-end coffee that got only the price right and walked back to the Jeep to make the call. He didn't check his phone for the number; it had been on his mind since he discovered it hiding under the sink.

Jones took a sip of coffee and listened to the phone ring. When he heard the machine pick up, he ended the call. He got back behind the wheel and reverse searched the phone number the same way Sheena had done the night before. The number gave him a name and Jones immediately went to Facebook to try to give it a face. Almost everyone had an online fingerprint, and most left their prints all over Facebook. It turned out, Norah Sinclair was not most people. There was no evidence that she had ever touched anything on Facebook. Jones took another drink and then started down another avenue. He narrowed the search to the name and the town and came up with a link to a church newsletter. Jones tapped the link and when the file was ready, he typed Norah's name into the search bar. The search immediately highlighted two words in incredibly tiny font in the header. Norah Sinclair was a church secretary.

Jones finished the coffee and then dialled the phone number for St. James United Church; the call was answered before he had the empty cup in the cupholder. "Thank you for calling St. James United Church. How may I help you?"

"Good morning, ma'am. My name is Sam Jones and I am a private investigator."

"Get out of town."

"I know. I don't seem so private after I finish telling you my name."

Norah paused a beat and then laughed. The laugh was loud and unrestrained. Jones got the sense that Norah probably knew that, and laughed anyway because she didn't care about what people thought. He liked the laugh, and felt a twinge of guilt about what he had to say next.

"I didn't know that was a real job. I thought private investigators were just something in movies."

"It's a real job, and I'm sorry to say it is nothing like the movies. There aren't any gunfights or car chases. I spend most of my time writing reports for lawyers."

"Oh," Norah said. "That can't be much fun."

She actually sounded as though she meant it. Jones felt another twinge, but he didn't let his voice show it. "Days like today help. I am working for one of those lawyers I mentioned on an estate case."

"Estate. Do you mean a will? Oh, no. Did someone in the community die? You should really talk to Father Tim. He handles all of our donations."

"This isn't about the church," Jones said. "I have been tasked with finding several estranged relatives named in the document."

"And my name was in the will?"

"That is what I am trying to determine. I just need to confirm some details with you. Could you please tell me your name?"

"Norah Sinclair."

Jones paused as if to consult a list, and then cheerfully said, "Perfect. Tell me, Norah, is your mother's first name—" Jones lifted the empty cup close to the phone and ran his thumb across the surface to simulate flipping pages.

Norah was kind enough to answer right away. "My mother's name is Barbara. Is that the name you were looking for?"

"Just give me a second," he said. Jones swiped the cup twice more before he said, "Bingo."

"What does this mean?" Norah said. "Who would have left me money?" She was too excited to wait for an answer, and immediately asked another question. Her follow-up was spoken in low tones with the receiver cupped close to her mouth. "How much money are we talking about?"

"I can't say," Jones said.

"Oh." Jones could hear the disappointment in her voice.

"I can't speak to how much money you are going to receive, but I can say that my client, Mr. Pembleton, is a lawyer of some importance. He doesn't take on small cases, Ms. Sinclair."

"Oh my goodness."

Jones could hear the excitement in her voice. She was already spending the money in her mind. She had likely taken a brief second to think about all of the bills she would pay before she dusted off all the dreams she had stored in the far corners of her mind. Jones heard a small chuckle and figured Norah was already past the bills.

"If I could just confirm your address." Jones paused, scratched the cup, and then gave her the address he had found online.

"That's it."

"And what would be the best time for Mr. Pembleton to reach you there?"

"I work until five every day. I have the weekends off, but I imagine your boss does too. So he can call after five, or between twelve and one. That's when I take my lunch. I usually go out, but I always have my cell on me."

She gave Jones the number and he jotted it down on the side of the coffee cup. He told her that Mr. Pembleton would be in touch the following day and said goodbye.

The feeling he had about lying to Norah matched the taste the coffee had left in his mouth. Lying was never a preferred first step; it made for a cheap foundation that was difficult to build anything upon. But with so little to go on, the lie was a necessity. He had one shot at getting a lead off a single phone number—he couldn't risk losing it. A cheap foundation was better than standing in the mud.

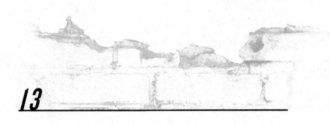

13

CARTWRIGHT WAS A BEAUTIFUL TOWN WITH A MAIN STREET LINED WITH boutiques and restaurants. Jones spotted a burger place and pulled into a vacant parking space out front. He couldn't see an empty table through the window and took it as a good sign. He walked inside and took up a spot at the end of a line four deep. The restaurant was filled with the scent of charcoal and a thin haze of smoke was visible in the light streaming through the window. Jones was grateful for the line; it gave him time to work his way through the menu. By the time he got to the counter, he had decided on a burger topped with avocado and a fried egg. The guy behind the counter took the order and then called Jones back to the register after he had taken a look at the avocados and decided they weren't ripe enough. Jones didn't bother looking at the menu board again.

"What do you get?"

The guy behind the counter had a lot of weight on a frame built on a deep respect for sitting down.

"Kahuna burger."

Jones scanned the menu board until he found the burger. "Really?"

He smiled. "Trust me."

The burger and fries arrived just as two men in mechanic's coveralls started wadding up their wrappers and bussing their own table. One of the men raised his chin toward Jones to let him know the table was all his. Jones nodded his thanks, slid into the booth, and immediately began to unwrap the burger. He lifted the sandwich and examined the layers. The kahuna burger had a thick patty that resembled nothing on the McDonald's menu. On top of the patty were two fat pieces of bacon, coleslaw, and a hefty pineapple ring. The concept was strange, but the smell made total sense. Jones bit into the burger and spent a second considering it, before he attacked what was left.

When he was finished, Jones got back in line. The guy behind the counter smiled when Jones reached the register.

"Told you it was good."

"You didn't lie," Jones said.

"You want another?"

Jones shook his head. "There's no way I have room for another. I'm just going to pick up something for a friend."

"Your friend want fries, or onion rings?"

"Not sure. I'll take an order of each."

The guy behind the counter smiled. "I wish we were friends."

Jones drove to St. James United Church and pulled into a spot next to one of the two cars parked there. Jones didn't know anything about the United Church, but the building told him that it had been around for a long time. He checked his watch and saw that he had five minutes until noon. He let the Arcade Fire song on the stereo finish and then walked to the church office door. At exactly twelve o'clock, he pushed the buzzer. No one answered. He waited half-a-minute and then tried again. His second effort got him the first response. Jones gave it another thirty seconds before he tried a third time.

"Can I help you?" The voice that came out of the intercom matched the one that he had heard on the phone. The words used by the tinny voice were window dressing. Norah didn't sound like she wanted to help anyone. She had been on her break and Jones had forced his way into her time.

"Norah Sinclair?"

There was a pause. "Yes?"

"We need to talk."

"I'm about to leave for lunch," she said. "I will be back at my desk in an hour. Well, fifty-eight minutes."

Jones leaned closer to the buzzer. "This isn't church business, ma'am. I need to speak with you about a private matter."

Norah thought about this for as long as it took her to imagine the worst. When she spoke, she sounded a little scared. "What is this about?"

"Someone is in trouble and I think you can help."

When Norah opened the door, Jones was surprised. He had imagined her older, shorter, and more matronly— he was one for three. Norah Sinclair was in her fifties, with a marathon runner's physique. She had her coat over her forearm, and Jones could see a rounded bicep that had escaped her sleeve. She had not tried to fight the grey in her hair and it had taken over. The sides were military short and the top long, like wild silver grass. Glasses covered a lot of real estate on her face, but she pulled off the look. She also somehow managed to pull off the Notorious B.I.G. t-shirt she was wearing.

Norah saw him looking at her shirt. She pulled it away from her body and tilted her head to get a better look at the man wearing a graffiti crown. "People always talk about Tupac being better. I never saw it. In my opinion, Biggie was always the king." She let go of her shirt and Jones saw that the fear that had been in her voice had crept onto her face. "Who are you?"

Jones put down the bag of food and reached into his pocket. He extended his hand and offered her his card. She took it. "My name is Sam Jones and I am a private investigator."

She suddenly looked more confused than afraid. "We just spoke."

"We did. I'm sorry, but I lied to you earlier. This isn't about an inheritance."

The confusion gave way to anger and Norah flared her nostrils the way a dragon might have before it set a knight on fire. She looked at the card again for a second and then clicked her tongue. "Talk fast, you're fucking up my lunch."

The profanity caught Jones off guard.

"This isn't fast."

"Sorry," he said. "The swearing threw me for a second."

"I'm a bad fucking Christian. Sue me. Oh wait, you can't because you don't really work for a lawyer."

Jones reached into his pants pocket and pulled out his phone. He used his thumb to unlock the phone and he held it out to Norah.

She took the phone from him and held it tight enough for the veins on her forearms to bulge. "You know, for that stunt you pulled, I should just smash the phone and close the door in your face."

Jones was worried she might do it. "Look at the picture first."

She ignored the phone and stared into Jones' eyes. "I'm serious. I should."

He believed her. "Please," he said.

She heard something in the word that was greater than the sum of its parts and she looked at her hand.

"What is it?"

"That's what I need your help with."

She sighed and lifted the phone up so that she could see the screen. Her eyes narrowed when she recognized the digits. "It's my phone number."

"I know."

"Who wrote this?"

"It was under the sink in a café bathroom in Toronto."

Norah looked up from the phone. Her eyebrows arched and created deep lines in her forehead. "You drove out here from Toronto because you saw in a bathroom? Look, pal, I don't know what this is, but there is no good time here. I don't give a fuck what you think you read."

"Swipe to the previous picture."

"If this is a picture of your junk, I'm calling the cops. My brother-in-law is a cop; he will fuck you up."

"Just look at the other picture."

Norah used her index finger to swipe the screen. Jones noticed her nails weren't painted. She bit them too much to put nail polish on them. She saw the picture, and Jones watched her closely as she read it. It almost felt like an invasion of privacy. There was a sudden wave of surprise that crested as a larger wave of sadness washed over it. In that moment, Jones saw Norah. She had been carrying something for so long that she had forgotten how heavy it was; the picture reminded her.

"Who wrote this?" Her voice was barely more than a whisper.

"That's what I came here to find out."

Norah forced herself to look away from the picture. "What is this to you?"

Jones shrugged. "She needs help."

Norah heard something she didn't like. She crossed her arms and the whisper in her voice became a growl. "You like to help young girls. Is that it? Why, so you can get them to thank you?"

"No," Jones said.

Norah put her hands on her hips, forming pointed triangles at her sides. At that moment, Jones thought she looked like a predatory bird. "What is this to you?"

"They don't always come back," Jones said. The words came out faster than he had expected. "But if you look, sometimes they do."

Tears fell in heavy drops onto Norah's cheeks. "Is that what you think? That I didn't give a damn? She ran on me. I was here. I was here for her. I was here the whole time and she ran. I thought if I waited, she would come back to me. So I waited, but she never came back."

"Who is she?" Jones heard a desperation in his voice that he hadn't expected.

"Her name is Lauren. She lived with me for three years."

"She's not your daughter?"

"Not by blood, but she's mine. Lauren came to me when she was thirteen. The church works closely with The Children's Aid Society, and the child protection workers know I foster kids. They give me a call whenever they have trouble placing a kid."

"That is kind of you."

Norah shrugged. "I needed help once and I got it. I try to be that for other people."

Jones held out his hand for the phone. Norah gave it back. "What makes you think it was Lauren who wrote this?"

Norah smiled. "The writing. I'd know it anywhere. It took her forever to put anything on paper. That kid would turn every grocery list into a calligraphy exhibition." She pointed at the phone. "That's her."

14

NORAH SCOFFED AT THE ONION RINGS AND FRIES JONES HAD BROUGHT WITH him; she did not scoff at Jones' offer to buy her lunch. She chose a tea shop that was across the street from the burger place and nowhere near as busy. Norah ordered an "chick"en-salad sandwich and a Darjeeling tea. She noticed Jones staring at the word on the menu board and said, "It's a vegan sandwich."

"Made by a chick," the woman behind the register said. She was wearing an apron covered in flour and when she pushed her hair behind her ear she left a streak of white in her bright red hair. She caught Jones' glance and laughed. "I used to try and be careful, but it never made a difference. No matter what, I always seem to go home with flour in my hair."

"Occupational hazard," Jones said.

"Nope. The occupational hazard is eating too many cookies."

"Did you just bake cookies, Cheryl?"

Cheryl nodded. "Madeleines."

"I will take one when they come out of the oven," Norah said.

"Sure." Cheryl looked at Jones. "You too?"

Jones shook his head. "Just a cup of coffee."

Cheryl let Jones know how she felt about his pass on the cookie with a sigh. "What kind?"

Jones glanced at the jars on display. "The Ethiopian."

She liked his choice and seemed to forgive him for turning down the cookie. Cheryl prepared the food and placed everything on a large wooden tray that Norah expertly transported to a corner table with a view of the street. She put the tray down and threw herself into the seat while Jones took his cup to the corner of the room to add cream and sugar. When he got back to the table, Norah was forcefully shrugging her way out of her coat, the way Houdini got out of a straitjacket. The sandwich came with a sliced apple and Norah ate a piece while Jones took off his coat. She saw his arm and took a moment to look at it before focusing on the food again.

Norah arranged the teapot and the bone china cup before she said, "They brought Lauren to me after she had run from another foster. This isn't exactly a big town, and Lauren already had a reputation at thirteen. She had run before, but this time was different—this time, she wouldn't go home. Something had happened." Norah slowly finished chewing and swallowed the apple in her mouth. "Something that had happened too many times before." The unpleasant memory took a minute to pass; then, Norah smiled wide as a new memory took its place. "So here is this Children's Aid worker I know at my door, with this wet cat. That's what she looked like—a wet cat. God, she was a nasty piece of work back then. She had an eye on the door every second of the day. Those first couple of weeks, I'd drop her at school and spend the night looking for her. Sometimes, I'd find her. Other times, my little wet cat would find her way home on her own. She'd just walk in the door and head straight for the stairs." Norah ate another slice of apple that had already started to brown. Jones used the moment of silence to try the coffee; it was excellent. "She learned early to skip over the first step because it squeaked the loudest, but she was never really good at being quiet. I'd hear her foot on that second step from the kitchen and I'd say, 'Here kitty kitty.' As soon as she knew she was caught, she'd come into the kitchen and I'd get her dinner out of the fridge. She'd pick at the plate and I'd ask her where she'd been, and do you know what?"

Jones put down his cup. "What?"

"She'd tell me. She'd tell me everything. At first, she was just trying to shock me. She wanted to make me sorry for asking." Norah laughed at the memory and tried a bite of the sandwich. She spoke over Jones' head with her mouth full. "So good, Cheryl."

Cheryl called out from the kitchen. "Wait 'till you try the cookie."

"Lauren didn't know me. I don't shock easy. She only surprised me once." Norah put down the sandwich. "I thought for sure she would come back."

After a minute or two of silence, Norah sniffed and picked the sandwich back up. "She eventually stopped trying to punish me. She stopped telling me things and we started to talk about things. It wasn't long after that that she started going to school. Like every day. Then she started singing. God, that kid could sing." Norah took a bite and when she put the sandwich down, Jones mimed wiping his nose. Norah swiped at her face with her thumb and licked off the vegan mayonnaise that had been on the tip of her nose.

"She won competitions. She was that good. I helped her get gigs, actual gigs, at some of the bars that played live music on the patio in the summer. She was just so fucking good." Norah pointed at Jones with a slice of apple before she shoved it into her mouth. "I wish she hadn't been." She saw the look of confusion on Jones' face. "She wanted to be a star. She thought she was good enough. A lot of people told her she could make it and she believed them."

She took another bite of the sandwich, this one smaller, and managed to get veganaise only on the corner of her mouth. Her tongue found it before Jones had to point it out. "I told her to wait until she finished high school. I wanted her to finish." She gestured toward herself with the sandwich. "I didn't finish high school and look how I ended up."

"You seem to be doing alright."

"I'm still here," she said, "but I could be somewhere better."

Jones looked around the restaurant. "Seems like a nice place."

"You've seen the burger place, the church, and here," Norah said.

"And all of them were nice."

"They better be, because there isn't much else." Norah picked up a chickpea that had fallen out of the sandwich and popped it in her mouth. "I understand how Lauren felt. I really do. I get wanting to get out of this place, but you can't just walk away. You have to be prepared to leave, and the first thing you need is an education."

"She disagreed?"

Norah spoke as she chewed. "Oh, she most definitely disagreed. It was the one thing we fought about. A few times, she got so mad about hearing me say the same thing again and again that she ran. The first time, she was gone for days. I was a fucking wreck." Norah paused to pose. "Nothing like the totally together vision you see before you." She laughed at herself and ate the last slice of apple. "People knew that Lauren was gone because they had seen me all over town looking for her. It's hard to stay hidden in a small town. Word travels fast. I imagine everyone already knows about the one-armed man who ate lunch twice today. So, I'd get these calls from people telling me that they'd seen Lauren here or there, and I'd get in the car and drive out to wherever she was last seen, and every time I got there she would be gone."

Jones watched Norah take a more measured bite of her sandwich so that she could keep talking. She was fighting a smile that was working its way onto her face.

"You know what I did?"

Jones shook his head.

"I put up posters." Norah leaned across the table and spread her hands in the space between creating an invisible poster in between them. "Lost kitten. Answers to Lauren." Norah laughed hard enough to send some of the food in her mouth onto the table. She used a napkin to wipe it and balled it up afterward without a hint of embarrassment; she was too interested in finishing the story. "I plastered the posters all over town. Everywhere. She saw one and came home to yell at me. We had one hell of a fight, but when it was over she stayed put."

Jones smiled. He liked Norah. She was not what he expected, and he guessed that he was not the first person to feel that way. Norah lost her smile a second after she finished telling her story. Jones watched her lip as she slowly ran her tongue over her teeth. She had laughed and enjoyed her meal and now part of her was regretting it.

"The next time she ran, she ran farther. See, the first time was an impulse. She was mad at me for telling her what she couldn't do, so she ran to prove she could. The second time wasn't a reaction—it was a plan. She had saved money and made arrangements. I never saw it coming. She was just here one day and gone the next. I knew something was different that time because no one was calling me to tell me that they had seen her around town. I called the police that time, but all they did was file a report and tell me to be patient." She shook her head. "Fucking cops tell me to be patient when my kid is missing."

Norah stopped talking for a while and Jones made no effort to change that. Part of detective work is knowing that when people are telling you a story, you ought to get out of the way and let them tell it their way.

A tear fell down Norah's cheek and she said, "She came back a month later. Wherever she had been, something happened to her there. She wouldn't talk about it. I didn't push her to. I thought she would tell me when she was ready, but she never did."

Norah took a small bite of the cookie, immediately regretted it, and put it down before she started to chew it.

"It was my fault. I knew something had happened and I handled it wrong. I was afraid to push her because I thought she would run again. I was selfish. I had her back and I was so happy—I didn't want to lose that."

Norah cried into her hands.

"I was so happy she was home, but she wasn't happy."

"Ever?" The question was a buoy to keep Norah from sinking into her grief. She took it.

She considered the question and remembered something that wasn't dark. "She was happy at first, but something was different—there was an anger there that I hadn't seen before. Something she couldn't get past."

"How long did she stay?"

"Longer than before, but I knew she would go again. I noticed her saving every penny she could, and she stopped telling me things. We still talked, but I could tell she was keeping things from me. And then one day," Norah held her hand in front of her and mimed an explosion. "Poof, she was gone. I remember checking her room and finding it bare. If it had value and would fit in a backpack, she took it with her. It was like she had never even been there at all. That time, I knew she wouldn't be coming back." She gestured at Jones' phone with her chin. "And I was right."

15

JONES HAD LISTENED TO NORAH'S STORY; ON THE WALK BACK TO THE
church, she answered his questions.

"When is her birthday?"

"October eleventh. She's seventeen."

"Does she have any family?"

"Lauren was born on a reserve not far from here. She
was made a ward of the Crown when she was four and
they took her away from her family. It was the wrong
thing to do. She told me that before she came to live with
me she had tried to go home. She thought that part of her

was missing and that she would find it where she came from. She said she went back and felt there was community there. She said you could feel it the second you put your feet on the pavement." Norah kicked a rock and watched it tilt off course. "She said she never felt so alone as she did right then. There was no home for her there. It was taken from her. She didn't stay a single day. She said it was too hard being so close to something she felt like she couldn't be a part of."

"Did she have friends?"

"Sure. I can get you some numbers and email addresses."

"I need a picture. The most recent one you have."

"I'll send one as soon as I get home."

"She a lefty?"

Norah stopped walking and squinted at Jones. "How did you know that?"

Jones smiled. "I wouldn't be much of a *private* detective if I told."

Norah thought about it for a second. "The writing was smudged."

Jones nodded. "Bingo."

Norah smiled, but hers was sad. "Her hands were always covered in ink."

When they got back to the church, Norah said, "You still haven't told me why you're doing this. You don't know a thing about Lauren. Why do you care?"

Jones looked at the tree growing in front of the church. The tree looked like it was as old as the building. It had endured years in the same spot; maybe that was the trick—taking root. Jones looked at his feet and thought about how far he was from where he started and wondered what it meant for him.

"It's a long story."

"I got time."

Jones shook his head. "Your lunch break is almost over."

Norah laughed. "I'm working the phones at a church on a Wednesday afternoon. All I got is fucking time."

"Does the priest know you swear this much?"

Norah smiled. "He knows. He also knows that no one else is interested in answering his phone for what he pays, so he puts up with it. He used to complain, but after the swear jar he put next to my desk paid for a new coffee maker, he shut up."

"Six years ago—"

"This is a long story."

"I warned you."

"You did." Norah leaned against the tree and wrapped her arms around herself to keep warm. "Well?"

"Six years ago, a woman came to me. I didn't know it at the time, but she had been famous once. She had a lot of money, but that wasn't why people knew her. She had been all over the papers about ten years before, when her son went missing. The story was everywhere. At first, the whole country was focused on the search for the eight-year-old boy, but as it dragged on, the country's collective attention turned to her and began to question how her son could have gone missing from her own home in the middle of the day without her knowledge."

Norah bit the inside of her cheek as she listened. Her mouth formed a small O when the story registered with something she remembered. "I think I know who you are talking about."

"Maybe. The case was all over the media and got a lot of attention. The cops had dug into everything and the press picked the bones of whatever turned up. The story was front page material for months, A-section for a year, and then it pretty much disappeared from the papers. My client had the kind of influence that came with wealth and she spent that currency looking for her son. She hounded the police, persuaded the press to keep the story alive, but without leads, and without scandal, there was no traction. She kept trying, but eventually she only had enough influence left to get lip service and empty promises. Skip forward a few years, and she calls me."

"Why?"

"Why me?"

"You said she was super rich, so why did she pick you? Do you work for rich people?"

Jones shrugged. "That was never the plan, but it's how things worked out."

"Another story?"

Jones nodded.

"Well?"

"It's not important," Jones said. "Anyway this woman comes across my name at a party and she has me brought to her home so that she can tell me a story about a little boy who was there one moment and gone the next. She asked me to find her son and offered to pay me very well to do it. I said no."

"What?"

"We were talking about a high-profile case that had been in the news for a year. There was nothing I could do for her that the police hadn't already done. They have more resources and are, despite what people might think, very good at their job."

"What did she say?"

Jones smiled. "She called me an idiot. She said, 'If they're so good, where is my son?'"

Norah smiled. "I like her."

"I did too. She offered me more money."

"And you took the case."

Jones shook his head. "I told her no again."

"Why?"

"It was a cold case that had been worked by good investigators. I wasn't going to take her money for something I couldn't do."

"Did she offer you more money?"

Jones shook his head. "She said, 'He is out there and

no one is looking.'" He paused for a moment and thought about the words; then, he held up his arm. "I had been out there once, and the only reason I came back was because there were people who didn't give up on looking for me."

"So you started looking."

"I started working the case. We talked about the difficulties of a cold case like this, and I explained that it would not be the only investigation I was working. She understood and we agreed to meet once a month to talk about what I had found out. We have met seventy-three times."

"You've been looking for six years?"

"And one month," Jones said.

"Poor thing."

"She's the strongest broken thing I have ever come across."

"Not her. You." Norah came out of her lean and stepped into Jones' personal space. She put a hand on his elbow. "You have been chasing that boy for six years. Six years looking for someone you can't find. I think you understand."

"Understand what?"

"Hope." There was no light in Norah's eyes when she said the word. "Hope is the worst kind of torture. Hope goes on forever. Hope won't let you die."

"There's something worse," Jones said and Norah let go of his elbow. "Knowing is worse than hope."

_16_

"YOU FOUND HIM?" NORAH TOOK A STEP BACK. "WAS HE . . . ?"

"No."

Norah began to cry.

"The lost live in your head," Jones said. "Hope feeds them and keeps them alive. Like any living thing, they grow bigger and bigger as time goes on. It gets harder and harder to carry the lost. You think you can't do it any-more, but somehow you just keep carrying the weight day after day. Putting it down should be a relief, but it's not. Somehow, it's worse."

Norah wiped away her tears with the back of her hand. "You're not here for her. You're here for you."

"Yes," Jones said.

"You're here for hope."

Jones nodded.

Norah took two fists of his coat. "I don't care if you're not here for her. Do you hear me? I don't care because you think you can bring her back. She's still out there and you think you can bring her back. Please—please bring her back to me."

"I'll try."

"Do better than that. Promise me."

Jones gently took hold of Norah's hands and pulled her fists away from his chest. "This world hates promises. All I can do it try."

Norah left Jones under the tree. He watched her close the door and then he walked back to the Jeep, thinking about what he had accomplished. He had a name and by tonight, after Norah got off work, he would have a picture. He got behind the wheel and took a second to cue up a playlist of rock music that had come out of Nashville that he planned to play loud enough to hurt his ears and kill his thoughts. Kings of Leon hit the speakers just as Jones noticed that he had a voicemail. He touched the phone and the music went quiet to make room for the message.

Call me, Jones. It's important.

Melissa's voice instinctively sent Jones' thumb to his contacts icon, but he paused before tapping the screen.

She was probably calling to set up an appointment with a client; Jones didn't want to lie to Melissa and he didn't want to tell her the truth, so he decided on telling her nothing. He swiped up on the phone and put his thumb down on the play button. The music erupted from the speakers and made it impossible to do anything other than drive.

It was close to dinnertime when Jones got back to Toronto and parked up the block from Brew. Sheena and two other employees were behind the counter, working their asses off. The coffee place made all kinds of sandwiches, and, for some reason, waffles, and people were eagerly after both during the dinner rush. Jones waited for his turn and ordered a coffee and grilled cheese. He was hungry and figured the grilled cheese was the simplest thing he could order from the already swamped baristas.

After Sheena took the order, she said, "No time to talk."

Jones said, "Sure," and waited for his food. He took his order to a vacant stool along the window facing the street. He had expected bread and cheese; he got both, but they brought friends. The bread was as much seed as bread, and the cheese was not at all orange, or alone. Sheena had used Brie and had slipped apple slices under the bread before pressing it in a panini machine. Jones drank some of his coffee while he considered the sandwich. He decided he was too hungry to wait in line for something else, so he ventured a bite. Jones took a few seconds to decide he liked the different textures and flavours. He ate the sandwich fast, but took his time with the coffee while he waited out the dinner rush.

After about an hour of watching cars drive by, Jones looked at the reflection in the mirror and saw that the line was a quarter of its former size and there were now only two people working; Sheena was one of them. Jones got off the stool and deposited his plate and mug on the counter on his way to the washroom.

The bathroom was occupied and Jones could hear someone inside. The guy who opened the door smiled regretfully to Jones, but that was nowhere near enough of an apology for what he had left behind. The smell was earthy and rank and contained no traces of the air freshener left next to the sink. Jones closed the door and fogged the room with Lysol. The spray didn't kill the smell, but it put up a fight. Jones put the can down and examined the door. His paint job had already been defaced with a swastika drawn in shaky ballpoint pen. Jones ignored the tag and pulled the Sharpie out of his pocket. The drive had given him time to think, and Norah had given him something he was happy to think about. He had a plan by the time he reached Kingston and supplies after he got into Toronto.

Jones moved to the left of the door and bent down to write his message over the spot Lauren had chosen for hers. In clear letters, Jones wrote: *Lost kitten. Answers to Lauren.* Under the message, he wrote his phone number and the words: *Ask for Norah.*

Jones took a step back and evaluated his work. His

handwriting was nowhere near as fancy as Lauren's, but it was easy to read and the right audience would understand the message. In the back seat of the Jeep were one hundred flyers with the same message and a tape gun he had bought at an office supply store. Jones figured he would start taping up posters in a widening circle around Brew. He would also stop into every bathroom he could find and leave a message behind for her. If Lauren was local, she'd see the flyers and make the call.

Jones finished up in the bathroom and found a line three deep waiting outside the door. He dodged the glares of what looked to have the makings of a lynch mob and found his stool still unoccupied. Sheena had taken the next seat and saved it for him.

"How'd you like the grilled cheese?"

"That was not grilled cheese," Jones said.

"You didn't like it?"

"It was good."

Sheena smiled. "I hate it. I like mine with regular bread and orange cheese." Jones noticed the familiar colour peeking out from under the bread on the plate in front of her.

She caught him looking. "Want half?"

Jones accepted the triangle. After he took a bite, he said, "I went there."

"You drove to Cartwright?"

Jones answered with his head while he took another bite of the grilled cheese.

Sheena watched him chew for a second before she punched him in the arm. "So?" The punch was solid and she fed it with her hips. She had trained somewhere. The pain in his shoulder did not diminish the glorious taste of the sandwich.

"This is good," he said.

"I used double cheese. Quit stalling and tell me what happened."

Jones told her everything.

"She has a name," Sheena said after Jones had finished. She was looking out the window, but she was seeing something else. "She's out there and she has a name." She looked at Jones. "What are we going to do? I mean there has to be, what—a few thousand Laurens in this city. It's not like we can just walk around asking every short sixteen-year-old girl if her name is Lauren and if she ran away from Cartwright two years ago?"

Jones liked that she said *we*. "You're not far off."

He told her about the posters in the Jeep and the note he left in the bathroom.

Sheena did not seem impressed. "You're going to put up flyers. That's your plan?"

"You got a better one?"

"No, but I'm not a professional private detective. Flyers is the kind of thing a kid would do. I mean it's not like she's a dog."

Jones laughed.

"What?"

"I said the same thing to someone yesterday."

"So you agree with me."

"The only move in this game is forward."

Sheena, suddenly no longer interested in her sandwich, pushed her plate away. "Still seems stupid."

17

JONES STARTED OUTSIDE BREW AND WORKED HIS WAY AWAY FROM THE coffee shop along the busiest streets. He put the flyers on poles, bulletin boards, and walls; it took hours and by the time he had finished it was late. He went back for the Jeep and saw Sheena still working as he walked past Brew. Jones thought about going back in, but he didn't want any more coffee and he wasn't looking for a new friend. At best, he had only four days left with the ones he already had.

The late hour meant all the parking spaces near his place had been taken. Jones circled the block, looking for the scraps. He found a spot three blocks away in front of a vacant home that, if the neighbourhood gossip was true, had previously been rented by a group of college kids. Word on the street was the kids were paying their tuition by dealing prescription medication. They probably started small and sold off their extra Adderall one pill at a time. The kids either got too greedy or too sloppy because they soon got themselves evicted; their moving trucks were black and white and they were in the back seat. The house sat empty for months and eventually some of the neighbourhood kids took advantage and started sneaking in to have parties. Someone at the last party got careless with a cigarette butt and the drapes went up in flames. The fire department got there fast and they were able to put out the blaze before it got up the stairs. The house was left with all of its curb appeal intact and none of its contents.

Jones checked his phone before he got out of the car, opened the mail app, and saw Norah's name. The email had four words and three attachments. Jones paused on the words *Please bring her back* before he scrolled down and saw Lauren for the first time. She was just a kid. The first picture was of Lauren at Christmas. She was holding up a stocking and it looked like she had just finished laughing about something. The second shot was from the summertime. Lauren's dark hair was a little longer and the sun had made her skin a little darker, but she was still smiling. The last picture was taken while Lauren was on stage playing guitar in front of a small audience. Lauren was singing, and although she wasn't smiling like she had been in the previous pictures, you could tell that she was happy on stage. It was a good picture.

When Jones turned onto his street, he heard a familiar sound coming from an open garage. He nodded at the group of men watching a game of cricket on an old television that had been set up next to the central vac.

"Hey, Kumail."

Jones got a noncommittal nod from Kumail, his neighbour from three doors down, and nothing from the other four men standing around lawn chairs. The nod was unusual; usually Jones got an invite for a beer. Jones had agreed more often than he turned the man down, and he had a passable understanding of cricket to show for it. There was something else about the nod that was strange, and it took Jones a few seconds to pick up on it. Kumail hadn't nodded—he had jerked his head to the right too much for it to be a nod. He had also said nothing back—a decision as calculated as the nod. Kumail had given him a warning, and Jones thanked him by taking it. He changed course and started across the street, aiming for the house that had not yet put up a fence and offered a path to the street behind it. Jones put a foot on the street and then he heard his name.

"Mr. Jones."

He stopped and turned to see that the group watching the game in the garage had lost one member. The man who had said his name had been standing farther back from the street and Jones hadn't seen him, until he stepped into the street light. His wrinkled suit set him apart from the other men in sweatshirts and identified him as a cop as well as any badge ever could. He took a swig from a beer bottle that was the same rich brown as his skin and pointed the neck toward Jones. "You're a hard man to get a hold of."

"Do I know you?"

"Not yet."

Jones glanced over the cop's shoulder, and saw Kumail watching them out of the corner of his eye. "I thought there was a rule about drinking on the job."

The cop considered the beer before taking a swig. "What tipped you off?"

"The suit."

The cop looked over his shoulder and Kumail quickly turned his head toward the TV. "You sure it wasn't Mr. Haddad?"

"I don't follow."

The cop smiled. "Really? You were just crossing the street so you could appreciate your house from the other side of the road?"

Jones jutted his chin toward the end of the street. "Just realized that I was out of milk and thought I would walk over to the corner store , Officer—"

"Detective. Detective Scopes." The cop's age was hard to pin down. His thin body didn't have enough flesh to spare for wrinkles and there was no sign of grey creeping into his hairline. Jones thought about the number of years it would take a decent cop to make detective and came up with mid-forties.

Scopes didn't mind Jones looking him over; he was doing the same. He finished a second behind, but he spoke first. "I hear you were in the army. I guess this is where I thank you for your service."

It wasn't a question, so Jones didn't answer. It didn't matter because Scopes wasn't waiting for one.

"I looked you up, but the records were vague about the details. Purposefully vague, if you know what I mean. Like most police departments, we have some ex-military on the job, so I ran what I found by them. Some of them thought maybe you got into some trouble. A few others went the other way. They thought you might have been some kind of badass." Scopes tilted his head to the right and glanced down. "So which is it?"

"Bit of both," Jones said.

"That how you lost the appendage?"

If Scopes was trying to rattle Jones, it wasn't working. "I didn't lose it. I know exactly where it is."

Scopes barked out a laugh that drew stares from everyone in the garage. "And where is that?"

"Iraq."

Scopes took another drink and changed the subject.

"Did you know that you are the first PI I have ever met? Twenty-five years on the job and I have never met one. That's saying something. I met a Nobel Prize winner once, but not a PI. Do you know what a Nobel Prize is?"

Jones didn't have time to answer.

"It's this big award. This guy, he won for science, but you can win them for all kinds of things. They give out six a year. Just six, and I met a guy who got one of those before I met a PI."

"Is that what we're doing?"

Scopes smiled again and Jones saw white teeth that were just a bit crooked. "What?"

"Meeting."

"Have we met before?" Scopes asked.

"No," Jones said.

"Then I guess that is exactly what this is."

"Feels more like playing," Jones said.

"Playing what?"

"Good cop," Jones said.

"For that, I'd need a partner to be bad cop."

"A cop can pull off both if he knows what he's doing," Jones said.

Scopes rubbed his chin with his free hand. Jones could hear the stubble scrape against his palm. "I wanted to be a PI when I was a kid, but then when I got older I decided I wanted to be a real detective." Scopes squinted at Jones again. "Did you ever want to be a real detective, Mr. Jones?"

And just like that Scopes was done with good cop. The

change to bad cop didn't scare Jones—he knew how things were going to end for him. What he didn't know was how close he was to the credits. He was sure he could get the answer out of good cop, or bad cop, if he could just keep them talking.

"Sure," Jones said. "I wanted to be Serpico."

"That's a movie detective. The real job is nothing like that. A real detective is busy every minute of the day." Scopes tapped Jones' chest with the lip of the bottle. "I mean it. You need a goddamn daytimer to make sure that you get everywhere you're supposed to go. I don't suppose it works like that for you."

"Nope," Jones said.

"That's too bad. Because it's your calendar that I'm interested in, so a daytimer would have been helpful." Scopes smiled. "But you have the next best thing. You have a secretary. I bet she knows your schedule."

"I don't have a secretary, Detective. I employ a service to answers my calls and book meetings for me."

"That sounds a lot like a secretary to me."

"Someone calls her and she calls me. I take it from there."

"Still sounds like a secretary."

"'Fraid not."

"I guess we will just have to rely on your memory. If you're any kind of detective, you must have a decent memory."

"Sure," Jones said.

"Mind using that great memory to tell me where you were two days ago, between the hours of three p.m. and seven p.m.?"

"Meeting with a client," Jones said.

"The whole time?"

"No. Some of it was spent driving there and some driving back."

"Can I get the name of this client?"

"That's not the way it works," Jones said.

Scopes smiled again, but it was all teeth. "I'm sorry. Like I said, you're the first PI I ever met, so I'm not exactly familiar with *the way it works*. The way it works for me is I ask questions and people give me answers. You know what I do with those?"

Jones lifted an eyebrow.

Scopes lifted his arms and turned his palms to the night sky. "I weigh those answers," he lifted his right hand, "against a big pile of bullshit." He shook the left hand and mimed holding an incredible weight. "Whenever one of those answers sends that bullshit up in the air, I ask more questions in a room down at the station."

"I didn't give you an answer."

Scopes let his hands drop and stepped in closer to Jones. "What's that now?"

Jones could smell beer on the cop's hot breath and sweat on his clothes. Jones had at least fifty pounds and five inches on the cop, yet Scopes somehow appeared menacing. Jones wasn't put off by the proximity or authority—that cherry had been popped overseas by far more powerful men who answered to far fewer people. Besides, he didn't think Scopes would take a swing at him in the middle of the street in front of a garage full of witnesses. That would be stupid, and Scopes didn't seem stupid. Jones also didn't think Scopes had any plans to bring him in, not tonight anyway. If he wanted to make an arrest, he wouldn't have come alone and he wouldn't have accepted the beer. This was something else.

"Seriously, tell me that again."

"I told you that wasn't how things worked. That was not an answer to your question."

"Let me ask you again then, and let me preface the question with the fact that I don't give a shit how things work for a detective who has a business card instead of a badge. Two days ago, late afternoon, where were you?"

"Can't say."

Scopes stood chest to chest with Jones. "Can't or won't?"

"Won't."

Scopes smiled ugly again. "Another answer that isn't really an answer at all. So, let me ask you a question that is most definitely a question. How did I find you so fast?" Scopes took a step back so he could watch Jones think about it. "Interesting question isn't it? Got an answer?"

"No."

Scopes showed Jones his crooked teeth. "Because you can't give me one or because you won't?"

"Can't. I have no idea what this is about, Detective."

Scopes drained what was left in the bottle. "Hard way it is, then, Mr. Jones. You won't tell me where you were two days ago between the hours of three and seven. Fine. Where will you be tomorrow at one o'clock?"

"Not sure."

"That's where you're wrong." Scopes let the bottle slip through his fingers until the neck was in his hand. Jones glanced at the bottle; it didn't have any beer left in it, but it was full of violent intent. A minute ago, Jones had been sure the cop was just playing bad cop, but now he wasn't so sure. The cop grinned at the look. He liked Jones looking at the bottle and wondering about his intentions. It kept him off balance.

"You will be at the station to meet with me and my partner. There, you will give us an official statement as to your whereabouts on the date and time in question. Should you again clam up, or, worse, should you decide to skip the meeting, I will arrest you."

"For what?"

"I'll think of something." Scopes tapped Jones' shoulder with the base of the bottle. "It's easier than you think. Now, if you'll excuse me, I think I'm going to watch the end of the match with my new friends."

Jones watched as the men in the garage noticed the cop coming back toward them. They communicated their discomfort with body language that Jones had no trouble deciphering. Kumail met Jones' eyes for a split second as Scopes passed him, and then he turned and followed the cop into the garage. Behind his back, Kumail jabbed his finger in the direction of Jones' house.

Jones did as he was told and walked away.

18

JONES PUT ON A POT OF COFFEE AND BROUGHT THE HOT MUG OUT ONTO THE deck. It was just after a quarter past eleven and most of the houses he could see were dark. Jones' body wanted sleep, but his mind was nowhere ready to shut down; the coffee would sync the two. Scopes had waited for Jones to come home because the detective knew something, but he didn't know enough. He had wanted to rattle Jones a little bit. Jones understood the desire; that was what he had wanted to do with Kevin McGregor. It was a good tactic, and Scopes was one hell of an interrogator, but the confrontation on the sidewalk didn't work: Jones had a shelf-life of less than a week before his freedom expired—a terse conversation with a cop wasn't going to spook him.

Jones drank some of the coffee and spent a minute pondering the taste in his mouth. He didn't know if he could taste the hints of citrus and cocoa that the bag said were there, but there was something he liked about the beans. The night air was cold and it found its way down his neck, but the warmth in his belly kept it from digging any deeper.

The cold air on his skin and caffeine in his blood chased his exhaustion away and allowed Jones to focus on the question that had been nagging him since he left Kumail and his friends in the garage with the interloper— how *had* Scopes found him so quickly? There hadn't been enough time for forensics to turn up anything that would link Jones to the murder. That meant Scopes' had someone do his homework for him.

"The old man," Jones said.

Jones had started his investigation into the disappearance of Adam Verne by going over copies of the case files. Ruth was the kind of rich and powerful figure that was usually only found in movies. Ruth expended a few of the countless favours owed to her to get everything the police had on the disappearance of her son. The Adam Verne case had little in the way of physical evidence; without any science to go on, the detectives directed their efforts toward anyone who had crossed paths with Adam or his mother in the preceding six months. Jones under-stood the logic; the stats pegged the abductor as someone in the family's orbit. There was a hint of desperation in the heavy-handed approach detailed in the interview notes. The lead detectives put a spotlight on a gardener after they discovered several previous arrests for public indecency. The notes gave some context on the arrests; apparently, the gardener had been caught having sex with another man in a park late at night. There was never any mention of the sex being non-consensual or with anyone underage, but the detectives clearly thought the gardener was a person of interest. Even after his alibi checked out, the cops refused to rule him out.

Once he had gone over the material, Jones sought out the detectives. His efforts were not appreciated; one of the cops took a swing at him, the other refused to answer with anything other than yes or no. With no way past the detective's gold shields, Jones was forced to get Ruth involved. She made a call to the chief of police and Jones was granted another opportunity to speak with the two men who led the investigation into Adam's disappearance. Ruth's influence was not a balm that soothed the bruised egos of the two detectives. The cops were just as pissed the second time they saw Jones, but they did as they were told and played ball.

"There was nothing to go on," a detective named Doyle said. "The kid was there one minute and gone the next. We had nowhere to go."

"Why the interest in the gardener?" Jones said.

Doyle's shoulders tensed. "What, you think it was because he was gay?"

"Crossed my mind," Jones said.

Doyle took a drag on his cigarette. "You meet the gardener?"

"I've just seen the case file."

"There's something off about him," Doyle said. "I can't explain it, but I felt it. I was never interested in who he slept with. I was more interested in his job. The guy spent a lot of time around the house. Stands to reason if anyone could sneak a kid off the property, it would be him."

"He had an alibi," Jones said.

Doyle shrugged. "He could have killed him and hid the body somewhere on the property. You ever seen that place?"

Jones nodded.

"You think a guy who spent all day there couldn't find a place to stash a small body?"

Jones thought about it and then shook his head. "The alibi was too solid. The timing wouldn't work."

Doyle snorted.

Jones met with Doyle's partner, Tom Fontana, and got nothing more than *yeahs* and *nos* for the cup of coffee he bought the detective. Jones considered it a step up from the punch he got the last time they had met.

After he spoke with the detectives, Jones tracked

down every suspect and every person mentioned in the case file. When Jones met with Ruth to tell her that he had spent almost a year going through the case and had nothing to show for it, he expected to be fired. Instead, Ruth nodded and said, "Keep digging. My son is out there and someone knows something."

The press came next. Jones met with every major reporter who had written an article on the abduction. The journalists were chattier than the police, and Jones found he didn't have to work hard to get information from them; he attributed that to Ruth. Ruth owned a large interest in one of the major papers and she had used her position to keep articles about her son running. It didn't take long for the reporters to figure out who Jones was working for; after that they were happy to share. Print was dying and Ruth Verne's good books was a good place to be. Jones picked up names and insights that weren't in the police files and he ran every single lead down. Jones wound up with nothing to show for another year of work.

Again, Ruth accepted Jones' report with a nod. The lack of progress did nothing to dissuade her. "So you know where everyone else has looked. Look where they haven't. He's out there, Samuel. Find him."

Jones spent years chasing Adam. It was his job whenever he wasn't on a job. Ruth paid him a flat fee every month and she never asked for anything but a face-to-face meeting on the last Friday of the month. At the meetings, Jones would tell Ruth what he had learned or what he still needed to find out. During each meeting, Ruth sat erect in an antique chair that didn't look at all comfortable and listened. Ruth had the bearing of an Egyptian queen and Jones had always instinctively felt compelled to use his manners around her. She never demanded control over the investigation or Jones' efforts. Ruth listened and then she asked questions. The questions were intelligent and they were often seeking colour or context. Ruth wanted to know how Jones felt about the people he had met and what his instincts told him.

After Jones had finished telling Ruth what he learned, her butler, Peter, would bring coffee for Jones and dark rum for Ruth. She drank it every time they met. Ruth never offered Jones the spirit. The drink was a ritual and something deeply personal. Ruth did not speak a word when the glass was in her hands. She drank the rum in three long sips and exhaled loudly as she put the glass down on the tray Peter left behind.

Ruth concluded each meeting by rising from her chair to meet Jones in the centre of the space that separated them. She would clasp his hands in hers, and Jones marvelled at the strength of her grip every single time. Ruth would pull him close and speak the same words with breath that smelled of rum. "My heart is lost, Samuel. Find it and bring it back to me."

Jones spent years looking where the police and the press had not. His search eventually brought him to Kevin McGregor.

McGregor's name had come up in some old paper-work Jones had been working his way through. Jones had not come across the name before in the police records or press files, so he ran it against the databases he subscribed to. Kevin McGregor had lived at the same address for twenty-six years and worked as a city building inspector for thirty. He didn't have any debt collectors after him, and there weren't any warrants out for his arrest. The data-bases didn't paint much of a picture, so Jones made a few calls to the contractors who had completed projects on Ruth's home around the time of Adam's disappearance and something strange happened. Everyone remembered Kevin McGregor. The recollections of the project man-agers were all similar: they said McGregor had a habit of showing up unannounced and more often than most other building inspectors. They also said he was a huge pain in the ass. McGregor made a habit of thoroughly checking everything, and he was quick to shut things down for even the smallest infraction.

Jones wanted to know more about Kevin McGregor, not because the man set off any alarm bells in his head, but because he was someone who no one else had spoken to over the course of the investigation. Jones called the city first, and after several attempts he found out that McGregor was visiting job sites all day. Jones did his best to get the location out of the woman who had answered the building inspection office phone, but she was a hard-ened city employee with a healthy immunity to guile.

Jones hung up the phone, checked his watch, and saw that it was well after lunch. He decided to drive out to McGregor's neighbourhood and start asking around about him. He figured he could get some information about the man before he knocked on his front door after he got home that afternoon.

Kevin McGregor was in his early fifties and he lived alone in a bungalow close to the part of Greektown known as the Danforth. The home was pre-war and in the kind of impeccable condition you would expect from a man who spent his days finding faults in other people's work. The people who lived on either side of Kevin McGregor were happy to talk with Jones, but the old man who lived across the street preferred to ask the questions. The first one was out of his mouth before Jones had finished knocking.

"Who the hell are you?"

Jones lowered the hand that had been prepped for a third knock and extended it in the form of a handshake. The old man ignored the open palm, but he did shoot a glance at Jones' other arm.

"I saw you at the neighbours, but you skipped the house across the street before going to the next. That means you're not a salesman. So, who the hell are you?"

The nosey old man was short legged and barrel chested. The thin undershirt he wore tucked into his wrinkled pants exposed spindly arms and thick white body hair. The man's oversized head matched his body and gave him the wild look of a great ape; he would have been intimidating if he weren't so short.

"I'm a reporter, sir."

"Show me your press credentials."

"Freelance," Jones said. The lie spilled out of his mouth quickly, the way all good lies do.

"And you're interested in Kevin?"

Jones shook his head. "I already spoke with Mr. McGregor. It's his story after all."

"What story?"

"He contacted me about building inspectors shaking down people who have added to their homes without the proper permits." Jones leaned in closer as if he were sharing a secret. "Apparently, there is a group of inspectors using images stored on Google Earth to compare properties to their current appearance. They are able to see where decks, sheds, and pools have been put in without the proper paperwork. They approach the homeowners and take cash for looking the other way. For example, let's say you put in a shed—"

"I know how blackmail works."

Jones stepped back. "Good to know. Any chance a building inspector has approached you or your family about additions you might have made to your home?"

"No."

Jones nodded and made a production of looking at the house across the street. When he looked back at the old man, he saw that he was definitely not making a new friend. Signs of annoyance were written across the dinner-plate-sized face.

"Can I ask you one more question?"

The old man rolled his eyes. "I thought you'd never get around to what you really wanted."

Jones ignored the jab. "Mr. McGregor's story has the potential to be something big. It has all the hallmarks of a great story." Jones ticked off his fingers as he said, "Crime, corruption, greed, and regular people being taken advantage of. There is so much potential, but—" Jones glanced back at the house.

"What?"

"I need to know if I can trust my source." Jones stepped in a little closer. "I need to know if Mr. McGregor is someone trustworthy, or if he is someone who has an axe to grind."

The old man bit hit cheek and looked Jones up and down. "Un hunh."

"Have you ever heard Mr. McGregor complain about his employer?"

"No."

"Is there anything you can tell me about him? Nothing personal, of course. I just want to know what kind of person he is."

The old man rubbed at the stubble on his chin. Jones guessed it had been more than a few days since he last shaved. The white hairs against his palm sounded like a wire brush scouring metal.

"No," he said, and then he shut the door.

Jones walked to the next house, knowing the old man had seen through him. He wasn't sure where he went wrong; perhaps a steady stream of salesmen had fine-tuned his bullshit detector. Jones didn't have time to dwell on it; the woman who lived in the house next door was much older than her neighbour and much more interested in talking to a complete stranger. Jones talked to three more people before he walked back to his Jeep. The grumpy old man from across the street was walking on the opposite sidewalk and he made it a point to ignore the polite wave offered to him. Jones had assumed the old guy was just crotchety, but he now knew better. The old man had been waiting on Jones: he had tailed him to the Jeep and got the plate number.

Jones had planned on dealing with the cops after he found the girl and after he spoke with Ruth, but the cop waiting for him on the street changed things. In less than twenty-four hours, Scopes expected Jones to show up for an interview. Jones knew that Scopes was setting him up and that whatever he said, truth or lie, would get him the same cell.

_19_

JONES KNEW THAT SCOPES SMELLED THE MURDER ON HIM. HE HAD A
witness who could put him at Kevin McGregor's home
the day before he was killed. The only thing Scopes
probably didn't understand was the why—the why was
just as important as the who because without one, you
couldn't get the other. Scopes had given nothing away;
he hadn't even mentioned the second body. He had
wanted to push Jones to see if he would talk; maybe say
something that he could use to tie him up later. Jones
understood; he had done the same thing more times

than he could count and it usually worked. . Most people overcompensated, to hide the bad things they had done. Most people, but not all. There were some people who had done enough bad to not worry about it anymore. Jones was one of those people.

He sat down at the kitchen table and traced the grooves in its surface with his fingers. From his seat, Jones could see a business card adhered to the fridge with a magnet. Jones had used Jeff Pembleton's name with Norah because it was legit and would have stood up to a quick internet search. Ruth had introduced him to Pembleton years ago and Jones did work for the lawyer from time to time. Jones knew him to be smart and he could tell he was good by the way his fancy cheques cleared. In the morning, he would call Pembleton and bring him to the meeting with the cops. Scopes would see the call to the lawyer for the admission of guilt it was, but Jones had no other card to play. He had murdered a man and there was a witness. Jones thought about the word *murderer*. He thought about Kevin McGregor and waited to see if any feelings would show themselves. He waited five seconds, ten, thirty, but nothing came. He didn't think anything about McGregor; all his thoughts were of Adam.

Jones dug into his pocket for his phone. Before he spoke to the lawyer, he had to talk to Ruth, and it couldn't wait any longer. He dialled from memory and waited for the familiar voice to pick up.

"Verne residence." The voice showed no sign of the

late hour. It was the exact same voice that answered when he called at eleven in the morning.

"I need to speak with her."

"I am afraid Ms. Verne is sleeping, Mr. Jones."

Jones drank some more of the coffee and spent a second searching for the citrus. "I need to speak with her, Peter."

His voice broke and Peter had to clear his throat before he spoke again. "Have you come to the conclusion of your investigation?"

Jones stared out the window at the darkness created by sleeping houses. "No," he said. "Not the conclusion."

A heavy sigh that sounded close to relief came from the man in the large house. "Then I am afraid you will have to wait until tomorrow, Mr. Jones. I will inform Ms. Verne that you wish to speak with her, and she will contact you at her earliest convenience."

It was Jones' turn to sigh. "Fine, Peter. Please ask her to call me tomorrow morning."

"I will do no such thing. I will inform her about your call. Ms. Verne will call you when she wishes. Goodnight, Mr. Jones."

"Goodnight, Peter."

Peter had been Ruth Verne's butler for decades. He accompanied her everywhere and assisted her with everything. Ruth has never displayed the faintest whiff of formality with the man while Peter has never wavered in his dignified approach to dispatching his duties. Ruth and Peter were the two closest people Jones had ever met despite the fact that he had never once seen them touch.

Jones put down the phone and suddenly felt every minute of the day all at once. He planted two hands on the table and forced himself to his feet. On the way to his bed, he pulled his shirt over his head and balled it in his hands before throwing it toward the hamper. His phone rang just after the shirt landed on the floor. Jones pulled the phone from his jeans and looked at the screen. The number was blocked. Jones swiped his thumb and put the phone to his ear, expecting Scopes looking for another way to spook him.

"Hello?"

"I saw your poster."

The voice was female. Young and a little bit raspy. The girl was either tired or a heavy smoker. Jones heard her take a drag before she spoke again.

"I saw a bunch of them actually. They were all over the place."

"Lauren," Jones said.

"How do you know my name? How do you know me?"

Jones stepped back into the hallway and leaned against the wall. He barely noticed the cold surface against his skin. "Norah told me about you."

"Did she put you up to this?"

"No," Jones said.

"Living with her feels like such a long time ago."

Jones wondered if teenagers measured time differently or if she had just lived more than two years since she left Norah.

"She loves you," Jones said. "She wants you to come home."

"She'd say that. She would. She probably believes it too. But she's wrong. She wouldn't want me back. She doesn't know me."

Jones didn't have a counter; he felt like anything he said to the contrary would blow up in his face, so he changed the subject. "I saw the messages you left in Brew."

Lauren went quiet. Jones would have thought she hung up on him if it weren't for the faint crackle of a cigarette slowly disappearing one breath at a time. "I was high when I wrote that. I was in a bad place."

"And now?"

"I'm not high," she said.

"But you're still there?"

"In the bad place?" Lauren laughed. "Home sweet home."

"Doesn't have to be."

"You never told me who you are."

"I'm a private investigator."

Lauren laughed loud into the phone and for a second she sounded her age. "Those aren't a real thing."

"I keep hearing that from people."

"So you take cases and find bad guys?"

"I help people," Jones said.

"Is that what you're doing now? Helping me?"

"If I can," Jones said. "If you'll let me."

"Sounds like bullshit. What do you really want from me?"

Jones thought about it. He had an answer, but he lied instead. "I don't want anything from you."

"Now I know you're lying," she said.

"I'm not."

"You are because you're a man and men always want something."

"I want to help you."

"Un hunh." The sound was delivered with a snort and a heavy dose of attitude.

Jones felt the conversation starting to break apart like an asteroid entering the atmosphere. He took a shot and pushed back. "Why'd you call?"

Lauren laughed. "Someone left a pretty clear message meant just for me. I wanted to know who would go to all that trouble."

"Un hunh," Jones said. He didn't try to match the snort; just the attitude.

"You don't believe me?" Lauren jumped from mellow to angry at a speed that would make a race-car driver jealous. "Fuck you. Or is it the other way around? That's it isn't it. You want to fuck me. You want to save me so I can show you how grateful I am?"

Jones thought about how old the girl on the other end of the line was. There was no hesitation or self-consciousness in her words. She wielded them like a razor and thought there was enough truth in them to make them cut.

"There are easier ways to get a date," Jones said.

"Doesn't mean you don't want one," Lauren countered.

"I don't want to use you."

"Bullshit. You're a guy—using women is your default. Some guys are just honest enough to admit it."

Jones wanted to tell her she was wrong, but the sharp words had drawn blood. "You're right," he said. "I am trying to use you."

Lauren snorted.

"Not the way you think. I don't want to sleep with you."

She snorted again. "Right."

"It's not about sex."

"It's always about sex. Especially when it's not. What is it you want? You looking for me to call you Daddy?"

The words turned his stomach. "No," Jones said. "Nothing like that. I want to save you."

"Save me?" Lauren sounded amused. "So you are just a pervert." She wasn't angry anymore. She was taunting him.

"There was someone else," Jones said.

"There's always one of those."

"Someone I couldn't help. I'm trying to make up for that."

Jones heard something in the background and Lauren said. "I gotta go."

Jones quickly said, "Call me again. Please."

Lauren laughed. It was a kid's giggle. "Easy, tiger. I'll call you again sometime."

Lauren hung up and Jones put the phone down on the kitchen table. The clock on the microwave said it was 2:14. Jones put water into a kettle and set it on the stove. He needed to think more than he needed to sleep. In less than twelve hours, Jones was expected to meet with Scopes—but the call from Lauren had changed things. Jones couldn't sit down with Scopes anymore. He had to keep moving.

20

JONES HAD FALLEN ASLEEP WAITING FOR THE PHONE TO RING AGAIN. HE ATE
breakfast waiting for the phone to ring. He showered
waiting for the phone to ring. When his cell finally made
a noise, it wasn't Lauren.

"Where are you?" Mel asked.

"Kitchen."

Mel didn't think the joke was funny. "I called you
yesterday and you didn't answer. Where were you?"

"On the road. I'm working on something."

"I run your schedule. If you had something, I would know about it."

Jones dropped a spoon in the sink. "I don't tell you everything."

"Obviously."

"What's going on?"

"The police called. A detective had questions about your schedule and what cases you've been working on lately."

Jones put his elbows on the counter and closed his eyes.

"What did you tell them?"

Jones heard Mel exhale like a bull readying itself for a charge. "Nothing. I don't give out information about clients unless there is a warrant telling me I have to."

"Good."

"Not good. It was the police. They can get a warrant. What is going on? If this was about a case, the detective wouldn't have asked about *your* schedule. He's interested in you." Mel's voice went soft. "Are you in trouble?"

"Nah," Jones said. "I just stepped on some toes, working on a case."

"This case that you never told me about."

"Like I said, Mel. I don't tell you everything."

"That's what I'm afraid of. Jones, I looked this guy up. He's a homicide detective."

"I know. He got in touch with me yesterday and I have a meeting with him this afternoon."

Mel switched into work mode and all the worry left her voice. "How long are you going to be tied up?"

"They don't tie people up. They use cuffs, and I'm hoping to avoid them."

"Funny."

"It shouldn't be more than a couple hours."

"Should I be worried about you?"

"No more than usual," he said.

Mel said, "Fine," in a tone that said it was anything but. "There was something else I wanted to talk to you about."

"Shoot."

"You said not to bill Irene Hogarth."

"It was just a consultation."

"So why do I have five messages from her? Each, by the way, is nastier than the last. She does not sound like a woman who was happy with her consultation."

"Can you forward them to me?"

"Way ahead of you. Just don't say I didn't warn you."

"Thanks."

"Jones—"

"Yeah?"

"Be careful."

Irene's first message was standard enough. "I would like Mr. Jones to call me. This is in regards to a private matter discussed during our recent meeting. *Please* have him call me."

The please seemed to have edges that were as sharp as broken glass, and it sounded like it hurt coming out of her mouth.

The next message had the same details as the first, but it was delivered with fewer words and none of the niceties. Each following voicemail continued to reduce with the final message, consisting of barely more than her name and a hell of a lot of contempt.

"This is Irene Hogarth, again."

Jones glanced at his phone and saw that Mel had sent him a text with Irene's contact information. He touched the number and the phone automatically dialled.

"Hello?"

"Ms. Hogarth, this is Sam Jones."

"It's about damn time. I left several messages."

"Five," Jones said.

"Yes, five. I should not have to leave five messages to get in touch with you."

Jones adjusted the volume. "What can I do for you?"

"You can start by returning your messages."

Jones waited.

Irene got sick of the silence fast. "Are you still there?"

"Yes."

"Well, don't you have something to say?"

"How does goodbye sound?"

"What?"

"I don't work for you, remember?"

"My father is still missing," Irene said.

"I believe when we last spoke you had decided to take the advice of the police and wait for him to come home."

"He hasn't."

"It's only been two days."

"On top of the week he has already been missing."

"He's not missing. He's on a trip," Jones said. "He packed a bag and took his toothbrush with him."

"Something could have happened to him while he was on this *trip* of his. Something could have happened and no one will know because he's—"

"Eighty," Jones said.

"Do not mock me."

"Did you call the police again?" Jones was hoping she had. Maybe this time they had listened to her and they were already on the case.

"No."

Jones swore with only his lips.

"The police made it quite clear that finding my father is not a priority for them. I want you to do it."

Jones said nothing.

"Did you hear me?"

"I did," Jones said. "I'm thinking about it."

"What is there to think about?"

"If I have the time," he said.

"Two days ago you had the time. What has changed?"

Jones thought about Scopes waiting for him outside his house. "Something came up."

"Oh," Irene said. "I see what this is. This is about money. You see that I am desperate and you want to cash in."

Jones heard a faint double pulse in his ear, notifying him that he had another call. Jones took the phone away from his ear and put it on speaker so he could look at the screen while he spoke.

Irene took the momentary silence as a confirmation of her accusation. "I knew it. I knew it."

Jones said, "I will find your father."

Irene snorted. "Sure, for what? Double what you charged me the other day?"

Jones heard the pulses again. "I didn't charge you anything the other day." Irene was about to say something else, but Jones cut her off. "I need to call you back."

"Don't you dare hang up on me."

Jones ended the call and his phone immediately began to ring. He put the phone on the table and watched it call out for him, realizing he still couldn't tell her. After three rings, the call went to voicemail and the phone went quiet. Jones waited two minutes and then he unlocked the phone and called his voicemail. He had one message from Ruth.

"Samuel?"

Jones hated his first name, but he always liked it when Ruth said it with her Trinidadian lilt. Her voice was soft and rich; Jones thought Ruth had the voice of a singer despite never having heard her even hum a tune.

"Peter told me that you called. It must be something important if you called in the middle of the night. Do you have something for me?" The hope in her voice was the saddest thing Jones had ever heard.

She sighed. "I don't like this. It isn't like you not to pick up."

The line went quiet and then Jones heard Ruth swallow. Whatever she was drinking fortified her. When she spoke again, she sounded more like herself. "I have a few more matters to attend to before I fly home tomorrow. Call me as soon as you get this message. I will let Peter know that I am waiting for your call. Call me, Samuel." She sighed again and said, "I don't like this," before she hung up.

Jones deleted the message and leaned back in his chair. Last night he had everything for Ruth, but that was before Lauren called and changed things. Now everything he had for Ruth would leave Lauren with nothing. He needed a little more time to help her. Just a little more time outside of a cell to bring Lauren home.

The phone rang again and Jones looked at the screen, expecting Ruth.

"You hung up on me. Just who the hell do you think you are?" Irene said.

Jones thought about it. "I'm not sure anymore."

21

JONES ARRANGED TO MEET IRENE AT THE OFFICE. WHEN HE GOT THERE, HE found her waiting for him at the top of the stairs using a wad of tissue to carefully dab at her eyes. When she saw him, she balled the tissue up and threw it into her purse. Jones unlocked the door, and Irene stepped past him without a word. The smell of perfume and cigarette smoke lingered as Jones deactivated the alarm and turned on the lights. Irene draped her coat over one of the chairs and walked to the window to examine the street. The blouse and jeans she was wearing had both been tailored to fit her body very well. Jones found himself wondering what would happen to Irene's wardrobe if she gained three pounds.

After appraising the view, Irene looked over her shoulder and gave Jones a hard stare that tested the Botox. "You said he would come back."

Jones took a seat and leaned back a few inches. "I still think he will."

"When?"

Jones spread his hands. "You might be asking too much of a man who spent a quarter of an hour in a bedroom and maybe twice that much time talking to some of the other residents."

Irene turned and crossed her arms. "I didn't see you talking to anyone."

"You wouldn't have. You didn't bother to look back after you stepped off the elevator."

"Why didn't you tell me about it?"

"Because you didn't seem to care," Jones said.

"How dare you? I am the only one who gives a shit about that man."

"Your father."

"I know that."

"Sorry, it's just most people don't refer to their father as *that man*. They usually go with something a little more traditional, like dad."

Irene went to her purse and slipped out another piece

of tissue. Jones watched her expertly remove all signs of emotion. "Do you enjoy mocking me?"

"No," Jones said. He meant it.

Irene looked for a garbage can and then put the tissue into her pocket. "I guess it's easy for you to just sit there and make jokes at my expense. You have no idea what it's like to lay awake at night, wondering if someone you care about is safe or not."

Jones had been down this path before. He knew the way, so he took the lead. "I will find him," he said.

Irene walked back to her purse. "I insist on paying you this time."

"That's good because I insist on being paid."

"I assume the fee is the same?"

Jones nodded.

Irene put her chequebook on the table and began to write. "I am free for the rest of day. Where do we start?"

"Finish writing that cheque and go home. I will call you when I have something."

Irene didn't like that. She cocked an eyebrow and gave Jones a look that probably weakened the knees of waiters and sales associates. Jones had seen combat, so the look made him sweat only a little. "I don't need a gal Friday," he said. He was proud that his voice didn't crack.

"I'm not asking to be *your* gal Friday. First of all, I am no one's gal, and secondly, I am paying you, so if anything, I am Robinson Crusoe and you are Friday."

Jones grinned. "You are hiring me because I have a skill set that you do not possess. I will not be as effective at employing my skills with you along for the ride."

"And why is that, Friday?"

"Because you're scary."

Irene put her hands on her hips. "I'm scary?"

Jones leaned back in his chair. "You didn't know? I thought that was what you were going for."

Irene looked at the wall. "I'm not scary. I'm really not. This isn't me at all. It's just what I am when I'm with him."

Jones opened a drawer and extended a tissue to Irene. She took it and dabbed at her eyes. "I spent so long without him in my life. I learned how to do everything without him. I got to where I am today all by myself, and then, poof, he is suddenly there again. He's just back in my life, and I'm responsible for him because someone has to be. Do you know how frustrating that is? He should have been the one taking care of me, not the other way around."

"Sometimes prison punishes families more than it punishes the inmates."

Irene's head swung toward Jones. "How did you find out about that?"

"The other residents told me."

"So everyone knows," Irene said. "Great. Just great."

Jones shrugged. "It's not so bad. I get the impression that your father is kind of a rock star at the retirement home."

Irene shook her head. "How nice for him."

"They also told me about your father's girlfriend."

Irene's eyebrow rose again. "What did they say?"

"Let's just say your father might be a convicted felon, but his girlfriend seems to be the real thief."

"Excuse me?"

"Her name is Charlene, and she seems to be something of a local attraction. She dates a lot of men and then usually tires of them when they run out of money."

Irene spoke through her teeth. "My father doesn't have any money. I have money."

"Willy has a credit card, so he technically has his own money."

"I hate when people call him that. His name is William."

"No one calls him that but you."

Irene crossed her arms and telegraphed her displeasure. "You knew all this and you didn't say anything?"

Jones nodded. "I learned most of it after you dismissed me."

"And you didn't think I should know?"

"I wasn't sure whose side I was on."

Irene put two hands on the desk. "Because I'm scary."

Jones looked at the hands. "Also because I thought he would be back by now."

Irene lifted her hands and ran them through her hair. "God, I am so done with people making me out to be the bad guy." She pointed at Jones with a dark red fingernail. "You know what kind of bad guy I am? The kind who pays his rent. The kind who makes sure he has nice clothes. The kind who makes sure he has spending money. That's the kind of terrible person I am. I am also the only one who seems to care that my father is gone at all." Irene picked up her pen and quickly scribbled in the rest of the details on the face of the cheque. "He doesn't want me around and neither do you, and that is fine because I am done with this shit. I am done." She tore the paper free and slapped it on the desk. "Do whatever it is you do and call me when you find him."

Jones watched Irene gather her things and waited for her to slam the door behind her before picking up his phone. He retrieved the photo he had taken of William Greene's credit card bill and called the one eight hundred number typed in large bold font at the top of the page. It took him eight minutes to traverse the automated receptionists maze and to outlast the instrumental Springsteen tracks meant to turn away all but the most determined callers. Eventually, Jones was greeted by Brian and told that his call might be monitored for quality assurance.

"Good morning, Brian. I seem to have misplaced my credit card."

Brian gave every indication that he was sad to hear that William's card had gone missing and he pledged to do everything he could to rectify the situation. Brian asked a few questions to confirm Jones was who he was pretending to be. The bill in his hand and the information Irene had given him was enough to pass for William Greene.

"Mr. Greene, is there any reason to believe that your card may have been stolen?"

"I would hate to think that someone had taken it," Jones said. "But it is possible. I live in a retirement community, so there are many people in and out of my apartment every day."

"I see," Brian said. "Well, I can pull up your information if you just give me a moment."

"That would be wonderful, Brian."

Brian stopped typing just long enough to say, "It's no problem."

"I'm just so embarrassed. It's a new card and I tried to be careful with it. I remember having it last week," he said. "I know that much."

"Let's see. I have several charges attributed to a hotel in Niagara Falls. There are also charges to the Fallsview Casino."

"Which hotel?"

"The Hilton."

"I didn't stay at the Hilton."

"And what about the charges to the Fallsview Casino?"

"The only gambling I do is a regular card game with some of my neighbours."

"Do you remember the last charge you made?"

"Like I said, it would have been no more than a week ago and it would have been in Toronto."

"So the dinner at TOCA was you?"

Jones knew the restaurant in the Ritz-Carlton. Willy definitely had style. "Yes, Brian. I had dinner there."

"I also have charges to a gas station in Toronto six days ago."

"That was also me," Jones said.

Brian said, "Hmm. It is likely that is where your card was either lost or compromised because the charges in Niagara Falls come after that. Well, I can flag those charges and cancel the card as well. You should receive a new card in the mail within the next seven days."

Jones thanked Brian for his help and ended the call as he stepped outside and locked the office door. He got back into the Jeep and drove straight for the highway. The meeting with Scopes was in a few hours, but Jones wasn't thinking about the sit-down with the detective; he was thinking about what would happen after the meeting—after the cop realized that Jones wasn't going to show. The Falls wouldn't be the worst place to be when Scopes set the dogs after him.

22

IT TOOK JONES ALMOST TWO HOURS TO GET TO THE HILTON. HE SPOKE WITH a young kid working the desk and persuaded him, with two twenties, to tell him which room William Greene was in. Jones checked the room, but no one answered the door. He spent some time examining the automated lock and after he came to the conclusion that he had no chance of bypassing it with anything more subtle than his right foot, he turned his back on the room and went back to the Jeep.

Jones still had the picture of Willy stored on his phone. Irene's plan to paper the streets with flyers would have never worked. For one thing, William Greene wasn't even in the city; for another, the man in the picture looked nothing like the real William Greene. The man sitting at the poker table on the other side of the room was much older and thinner than the man in the picture on Jones' phone. The name on the flyer would have been wrong too. Jones could tell just by looking at the man that he was no William. The eighty-year-old retirement home resident might have been William Greene to his daughter, but the man in the tailored suit casually flicking chips toward the dealer was Willy Greene.

There were three other men seated at the table; their sweatpants and the way the freely bantered back and forth made Jones think they were regulars at the casino. Willy, leaning back in his chair in an expensive looking suit and what looked like alligator shoes, was disinterested in the conversation. He watched the cards as they were turned up by the dealer and never consulted his hand to determine how they helped or hurt his chances. When it came time to bet, Willy picked up a stack of chips without a glance and tossed them into the centre of the table. He won and folded with the same sly smirk on his face. Things got interesting on the seventh hand. Willy showed no signs of interest until the river card was placed on the table. Two players tossed in chips and the third made a joke that died in his throat when he saw Willy slide everything he had toward the centre of the table. The game had changed to business and the other players all suddenly forgot they were in dirty sweatpants. If Willy minded the hard stares, Jones couldn't see it. Only one of the men decided to stay in the game and show his cards. Willy smiled at the challenge and then presented a flush that beat the man's two pair. The regulars seemed to take Willy's win as a slight and they dropped the banter. The three men were suddenly united and out to bleed Willy of every piece of plastic in front of him. After an hour, the three men stood and left behind everything they had shown up with. One of the regulars flipped Willy off before he turned and walked away. Willy laughed at the finger and then tipped the dealer with enough chips to raise her eyebrows.

Jones caught up to Willy an hour later at the bar. Willy glanced at Jones on the next stool and took a sip of the single malt he had been getting to know. "I was wondering when you'd finally make your move."

"Are those alligator shoes?" Jones asked.

Willy smiled. "They are indeed gators." He looked down and appraised his loafers. "It's been too long since I had proper shoes."

"The suit is nice," Jones said.

Willy shrugged. "Not nice enough, but it's a start. You're not with the casino. If they wanted to watch me, they would just use the cameras."

"I'm not with the casino."

"You're not a cop either. They don't hire amputees."

Jones laughed. "Not a cop."

"So what are you?"

"Private investigator."

Willy glanced a Jones and snorted. "Bullshit."

"I get that a lot. Mostly it's taking pictures and watching eighty-year-old ex-cons gamble."

"Irene put you up to this?"

Jones nodded.

"I'm surprised she cares."

"You're her father," Jones said.

"She calls me William."

"Sounds like her," Jones said.

"What does she want?"

"She wants me to bring you home."

Willy took another sip and swirled what was left in the glass. "How'd you find me here?"

"Credit card," Jones said. "I found a bill in your apartment."

Willy put down the glass. "So it's no coincidence my card was declined." He turned and looked Jones in the face. "What did she tell you? That I'm some old man who can't take care of himself?"

"Those weren't her words," Jones said.

"But that's what she's thinking."

Jones shrugged. "She was worried about you. Then she found out about the credit card and Charlene."

"Charlene?"

"Your poker buddies told me that she has a habit of hanging around until the money runs out."

Willy thought that was funny. "You mean she's a bad girl. The kind your mother warned you about?"

"Sure."

Willy laughed again. "So you think I'm some fogey caught up in a honey trap. Did my poker buddies happen to mention that Charlene has a car?"

"They didn't."

"They wouldn't. That's because they can only think about what they would do with a woman like Charlene. They have no idea what a man like me might do."

"And what did you do?"

Willy smiled and Jones saw two rows of large white teeth. "I got her to let me drive her car to a nice hotel. I took her out for an expensive dinner, and then we hit the town and had some real fun."

"And where is she now, Willy?"

He shrugged. "Probably back home."

"She didn't stay with you?"

"Nope. Turns out she wasn't so bad after all."

Jones chuckled. "Not like you."

The smile stayed on Willy's face, but it wasn't in his eyes anymore. "You got that right, kid." Willy signalled to the bartender for another drink. "You want one?"

Jones shook his head.

"You sure? You're buying."

"Am I?"

"After that credit card stunt you pulled, absolutely."

"I saw you play remember? You've got cash."

"Doesn't matter," Willy said. "It's the principle. Besides, you don't want to risk causing a scene in this nice place, do ya?"

Jones did a poor job hiding his grin. "You're eighty. I don't think anyone's worried about you causing a scene."

Willy started to say something and then stopped himself. He lifted the glass and Jones heard the ice tinkle as he tilted it. Jones let the old con enjoy his drink and decided he would pay for it. It was the least he could do. Willy put the glass down on the table and broke one of the melted ice cubes between his teeth. Jones looked over at the older man beside him and saw Willy staring back. As soon as Jones met his eyes, Willy tossed the heavy lowball glass up into the air. Jones watched the glass as it went into the air and he instinctively extended his hands to catch it before it shattered on the polished bar. It was about this time that he realized his mistake; the realization wasn't fast enough to allow him to prepare for the elbow already most of the way toward his nose.

The impact made a sharp crack that originated from inside Jones' face and his vision immediately blurred with tears. The elbow was a hell of a surprise and meant to disorient him long enough for Willy to set up something more unpleasant. It was a good plan and it would have worked if Jones' nose hadn't already been broken four times before. Jones had been here before, and he knew what to do. He ignored the nose as he stepped off the stool and brought his hand up. His right hand brushed his eyes on its way to a position next to his jaw. The wipe was enough to clear his vision and he swung his head back and forth and got a second surprise. Jones had expected to see Willy coming at him, but the old man was still seated on the stool and he was holding the glass in his hand—he had managed to catch it after he broke Jones' nose. Willy's reflection in the mirror behind the bar told Jones that he thought the whole thing was pretty funny; at least, he did until Jones kicked the stool out from under him. Willy tried to use the two stools on either side of him to break his fall, but it didn't work. He went down with a grunt followed by a loud clatter from the toppled stools.

Jones waited for the old man to untangle himself, but Willy didn't move. Jones noticed the thin pale shin exposed by a pant leg that had ridden up and immediately regretted what he had done. Jones bent to start clearing the stools away and his head caught the heavy whiskey glass Willy had somehow managed to hold onto. The glass shattered against Jones' skull and put stars in his eyes.

Willy wrestled his way out of the stools and pulled himself to his feet using the bar for support. Jones braced himself against the bar and ran his hand through his hair; it came away red. Jones cursed and started toward the old man while the bartender yelled, "Hey," again and again from the safety of his spot on the other side of the counter.

Willy jabbed and then stepped in with a mean hook meant for Jones' chin; neither punch landed. Jones swatted the jab away and stepped inside the arc of the hook, leading with his forehead. The headbutt sent Willy stumbling back and one of the upended stools caught his leg and sent him back to the floor. Jones took a fistful of Willy's hair and was about to do something mean when two strong arms wrapped around his neck. Jones was forced to let go of Willy as a second security guard took hold of him and dragged him away. Jones stopped resisting and the guards shoved him toward a door marked exit. They forced Jones through the door and shoved him back a few feet. When they saw that Jones had no intention of rushing at them, they turned their backs and went back inside. The door opened again a second later and the security guard who had first grabbed Jones popped his head out. "We called the cops, asshole. You should get out of here before they show."

Jones watched the door close and then took a scan of the alley. There were two green Dumpsters and the pavement bore signs of the sloppy job the garbage truck did the last time it had emptied them out. The door that he had been forced out of had no handle and there was no intercom. Jones wasn't getting back inside. The security guards read the situation like anyone else would have and assumed that a drunk asshole attacked an old man. Willy was probably getting some first aid while the staff waited for an ambulance to arrive. Jones looked up and down the alley trying to gauge the fastest way back to his Jeep so he could follow the ambulance to whichever hospital it took Willy to. He settled on going left and took two steps in that direction when the door opened again. The guard who had shoved Jones out was holding Willy by the torso while the other guard held one of the old man's legs. Willy's other foot was pushing against the guard's face.

The guard looked up and saw Jones still standing there. "What are you still doing here? We gave you a pass because we know what a pain this asshole is."

"Why don't you put me down, Marty, and try saying that to my face?"

"Fuck you, Willy. Don't come back inside. If you do, we'll have you arrested for trespassing."

Willy thought that was funny, and he looked like he had something to say about it, but he suddenly realized that Marty and his partner had cleared the door and were starting to swing Willy's body back and forth. They threw the old man into the air and he landed five feet away on the pavement.

Willy rolled onto his back and stared at the sky as the guards went back inside and slammed the door. When he saw Jones in his line of sight, he smiled and said, "Still think I can't cause a scene?"

Jones took a fistful of the man's jacket and pulled him to his feet. "Did you do all of that because I called you old?"

Willy yanked his lapel free and tried to smooth it out. "I did all of that because you cancelled my credit card."

He gave up on the wrinkles in his jacket and spent a few seconds examining a stain his clothes had picked up from the pavement. Willy licked a thumb and rubbed at his suit. "So I guess this is the part when you drag me home."

"I'm not here to drag you anywhere."

"Bullshit."

"I'm a detective, not a kidnapper."

"So you're just going to take my kid's money and do nothing?"

Jones laughed. "So now you're mad I'm not dragging you back."

Willy poked at Jones' chest. "I don't like anyone taking advantage of my daughter."

"Unless it's you," Jones said.

Willy made a show of making a fist. "You want to go another round?"

Jones heard a siren. "I'd rather get out of here before we get picked up."

"Fine," Willy said. "Let me buy you a drink. It's the least I can do for kicking your ass."

23

THE BAR WILLY CHOSE WAS ON A SIDE STREET WITHIN WALKING DISTANCE
of the casino. It was a place for career drinkers who
moonlighted as professional gamblers. Everyone seemed
to know everyone else, and they mixed drinking with
casino shop talk. Jones listened to conversations about
hot tables and which machines were paying out while he
waited for his drink at the bar.

"You pick up hustling cards when you were inside?"

Willy took his eyes off the poker game playing on a
television mounted above the bar. The question lifted his

brow and made deep lines in his forehead. "Irene told you about that? She hates talking about that."

"Not her. Your poker buddies told me that you spent some time away."

Willy shrugged.

"They also said you were a cheat."

Willy smiled.

"They ever say they caught me cheating?"

"Nope."

Willy checked the TV again. "Then I guess I wasn't cheating." Willy took his eyes off the poker game when the bartender came back with their drinks.

"Here's your whiskey, Willy. On the rocks, like you like it."

The bartender was in her fifties, but the dim bar lighting tried its best to shave some time off.

She put Jones' water down and leaned over a little farther than necessary to slide Willy's drink in front of him.

"Donna, you might be the only friend I got in this town."

Donna rolled two mascara shrouded eyes, but the grin on her face said she liked the line. She leaned in closer and touched a bruise that had already started to swell under Willy's eye. She looked at Jones with none of the warmth she gave the older man. "This one giving you trouble?"

Willy laughed. "Other way round, darlin'. Who do you think busted up his nose?"

Donna surveyed the damage on Jones' face and then rubbed the old con's forearm. "Willy, you are something else."

Jones said, "I gave him the mouse."

One eyebrow raised and did a hell of an impression of a middle finger. "You're a real tough guy, pal."

Donna leaned toward Willy again and talked him into some ice wrapped up in a bar towel for his eye. She didn't offer Jones a thing.

When the bartender walked away, Willy said, "I'm not going back."

"Fair enough. I never told Irene I would bring you back. I only agreed to find you."

"How much is she paying you?"

Jones looked at his nose in mirror behind the bar. It would likely need to be set. "Not enough."

"Bullshit. How much?"

Jones told him.

Willy shook his head. "For that much, you should have to drag me back."

"You know the moral ground you are standing on would be a lot higher if you didn't run away and cause this whole mess."

"I'm still her father. I look out for her no matter what."

Jones put his phone on the bar. "You can look out for her by calling her."

Willy slid the phone away with the side of his glass.

"She's worried sick about you."

"It ain't worry, kid," Willy said. He took a drink and gave himself a moment to let it linger on his tongue before he swallowed. "Irene has been getting hurt by me for most of her life. All those years and all of those hurts changed what she sees in me."

"What does she see?"

"At first, I was a disappointment. I didn't know it then, but I had it good when that was all I was. After that, I became an asshole. Now, I'm a burden. My little girl went her whole life without a stitch of help from me. Fuck, I was pulling her down the whole time and she still made it to the mountaintop. She made something of herself in spite of me and what does she get for all her trouble?"

Jones knew, but he let Willy say it.

"She feels like she has to take care of me. There would be irony in there somewhere if it wasn't so god-damn sad." Willy finished his drink and pushed the glass toward the other side of the bar. "I was inside a long time. Long enough to finally understand where the blame really lies. I know what I am and I know it ain't anything good. I wasn't good then and I'm not any better now." Willy looked at Jones with two hard blue eyes. "I can't change who I am, but I can change what I am. I won't be her anchor anymore." Willy ran a hand across his smooth chin. "I thought she would be happy if I just walked away. I thought if I made the first move, she would finally be able to put all the blame where it belongs, on me, and move on." Willy looked at Jones again, but this time the hard eyes were sad. "But instead of letting me go, she finds someone to bring me back. She's not going to let herself be happy. That is what I did to her. My kid. She is going to make herself suffer until I die, maybe longer, and there is nothing I can do about it."

Jones pushed the phone in front of Willy again. "You can start by calling her."

Willy got loud. "Did you not hear a thing I just said?"

"I heard it all. It was mostly about you. If you really want to stop being Irene's burden, a phone call is a good place to start."

"And what if I won't do it?"

Jones shrugged. "I pay for your drink and drive back to the city. I'll tell your daughter what I found out. After that—I'm guessing she'll drive out here herself and start looking for you."

Donna stopped in front of the glass Willy had pushed away. "Another, Willy?"

He nodded.

"She won't stop," he said.

Donna snorted as she finished the pour. "You stop paying and I will."

"I meant my daughter," Willy said.

"You have a kid?" Donna put the bottle down. "You got any pictures?"

Willy shook his head.

Donna frowned. "Willy, you should always have a picture of your kid with you."

Willy looked to his drink for an answer and found only a way to forget. He took a drink and looked up to see the bartender still standing in front of him. She took a second to get her phone out of the back pocket of her skin-tight jeans.

"I mean, I get not having pictures because who has pictures anymore. I wouldn't even know where to get them developed, Walmart maybe, but you should at least have a picture on your phone." Donna turned her phone so that Willy could see the small child on her home screen. "That's my daughter Angela and my grandson Trevor."

Willy nodded. "He's cute."

"Yeah." She turned the phone and stared at the picture for a few seconds; it took effort for her to put the phone away. "Sometimes that picture is the only thing that gets me through my shift. That's why you gotta have one, Willy. I mean, you care about your kid, right?"

There was something in the question; like the last word was heavier than the others and it was a struggle for Donna to get it out. She was afraid of what the answer might be.

Willy heard it too and he was slow to answer. The old man who had picked a fight with Jones and tried to kick two of the casino bar bouncers without hesitation was now struggling to meet the eye of the bartender.

"He hasn't met his daughter yet," Jones said.

The lie earned Jones his first non-threatening look from Donna. Willy turned on the stool and looked at

Jones too. His look wasn't threatening either—he looked afraid of what Jones was going to say next.

"I'm a private investigator—"

Donna turned and playfully slapped Willy on the forearm. "Is he for real, Willy?"

Willy, still unsure about where Jones was going with his story, risked a quick glance down the bar. Jones saw Willy's worried eyes ruin an otherwise good poker face. He tilted his head a fraction of an inch and saw Willy's face relax as he registered the message. "Yeah, he's a real dick."

Jones ignored the insult and launched into his story. "After her mother died, Willy's daughter found that she had not been completely forthcoming about the identity of her father. Willy's daughter, Irene, hired me to track him down."

Donna looked at William. "Is that true, Willy?"

Willy glanced at Jones, hesitated, and then nodded.

Donna put a hand on top of Willy's. "That is amazing, Willy! All these years and you really never knew?"

Willy shook his head without looking at Jones. The movement seemed natural and the answer honest. Willy had his some of his swagger back.

"You need to go see her."

Willy smiled. "I plan to."

"And then you need to come back and tell me all about it." Donna put her palm on top of Willy's hand. "With a picture." The smile on Donna's face made it obvious that she wanted to hear the story when she was off shift.

"I'd like that, Donna."

The bartender's hand lingered long enough to make Jones feel awkward about watching, and then Donna slowly slid her palm away and walked down the bar.

Willy said, "Thanks," to Jones without taking his eyes off Donna.

Jones was about to tell Willy not to worry about it when his phone rang. He checked the display and saw that it was Scopes. He thought about letting it go to message, but there wasn't anything to be gained from pissing the cop off even more.

"You gonna get that?" Donna said from the other end of the bar. Her voice was loud and it turned everyone's eyes toward Jones.

Jones lifted the phone to his ear and nodded.

"Take it outside."

Willy laughed. "You heard the lady."

"I'll be right back."

Willy lifted his glass. "I'll be right here."

Jones answered the call as he opened the door. The bright light of the midday sun gouged his eyes and stalled him in the doorway.

"Close the door," Donna yelled.

Jones took a blind step forward and said, "Would you believe something came up?"

"Nope." Scopes sounded calm. The kind of calm that came after furious. "I gave you a chance to play it straight, and you turned it down. That tells me everything that I need to know about you, Sam Jones. You are now officially a suspect in the murder of Kevin McGregor."

"Because I missed a meeting?"

"Because you ran."

"Scopes."

"*Detective* Scopes," Scopes barked. "We ain't friends, Sam."

"Detective—" Jones got only the word out before the phone was snatched from his hand. Willy had come out behind him and now he had Jones' phone in his hand. The old man leaned back against the wall and shielded his eyes. One alligator shoe left the pavement and took up residence against the worn brick exterior. The tailored grey suit looked like it had been made to lean against the brick wall of a dive bar in the middle of the day. Willy had every ounce of his swagger back.

"Hello?" The voice was Willy's, but it didn't belong to the Willy who had broken Jones' nose. This man sounded old and frail.

"What are you doing?"

Willy waved him off. "My name is William Levine. Mr. Jones saved my life earlier today, and I understand that in doing so, he might have neglected an important appointment he had today. Were you the police officer he was supposed to meet?"

Scopes said something Jones couldn't make out.

"Oh, a detective," William said. He rolled his eyes when he said the word *detective*. "You see, I was crossing the street when a bicycle ran through the crosswalk without stopping. Tell me, Detective, do you handle bicycle crimes?" Willy said, "Oh," and "I see," while Scopes explained that he did not handle bicycle crimes. "A homicide detective." Willy laughed. "I guess you can tell we won't need you because I'm talking to you on the phone. Dead people don't do that too often, do they?" Willy paused long enough to allow Scopes to laugh politely. "Could you put me in touch with who I would need to speak with about a crime involving a bicycle? I would like to press charges once I am out of the hospital."

Jones watched Willy while he listened to Scopes again.

"This young man found me on the ground and drove me to the hospital himself. He saved my life. Have you ever called an ambulance?" Willy didn't give Scopes a chance to answer. "I can tell you that when we call one at my apartment complex, we might as well call the funeral home to send a hearse to follow behind. The wait times are just ridiculous. Now, you're a homicide detective, right? That's what you said. Tell me, is there a way we could charge the paramedics with murder for taking so long? I bet their lateness has killed more people than some of those serial killers you read about in the paper."

Willy listened for half-a-minute and then said, "Well, that is too bad. I bet things would be a lot faster if the paramedics thought they would be held accountable." Willy paused for a second to listen to Scopes. "Well, I've taken enough of your time, Detective. I just wanted to tell you that this young man saved my life. I don't know how I could ever repay him. He won't even let me pay to have the blood cleaned off the seats of his car. Apologizing to you on his behalf is the very least I can do. He didn't want me to say anything, but I insisted. I even had to steal the phone away from him. If you can believe it." Willy laughed himself into a coughing fit. When he finished, he looked at Jones and smiled. "Please don't be upset with him, Detective. He is a good boy."

Scopes spoke for a minute and then Willy held the phone out toward Jones. "He wants to talk to you."

Jones took the phone and Willy leaned in close so that he could whisper in Jones' other ear. "That makes us even, dick."

Jones nodded. "Detective Scopes?"

"Don't for a second think that helping an old man who couldn't cross the street earns you any points with me. I'm not the Boy Scouts. I am the police. I meant what I said. Every single word. I want you here tomorrow at noon. I don't give a damn if Mother Teresa falls down the stairs and lands at your feet. You leave her where she is, understand?"

"Mother Teresa is dead," Jones said.

"Then you have no reason not to be here," Scopes growled.

Jones hung up the phone and walked back into the bar. William was back on his stool with a fresh drink to help him hit on Donna. From the way she was leaning, Jones could tell that she was buying whatever he was selling.

Donna saw Jones coming and smiled at him before giving Willy's arm a squeeze and moving down the bar. She walked away with a saunter that drew Willy's eyes exactly where she wanted them to be.

"Does Donna know about Charlene?" Jones said as he took a seat on the stool next to Willy.

Willy drank and admired the bartender. "There's nothing to know. Charlene left two days ago."

"So you broke up?"

"We were never together. We had an arrangement. She wanted my money and I wanted a ride."

Jones narrowed his eyes and Willy elbowed him.

"A ride to the casino." He paused with the glass near his lips. "I don't pay for it."

"A gentleman," Jones said.

"Not even a little bit. Charlene got tired of me pretty quickly once she figured out that there wouldn't be any money coming her way. There wasn't much for her to do if she had to pay for it herself, so she took her Toyota and drove home to find another mark. At this very moment, Charlene is making some guy very happy before she makes him very poor."

"She sounds like a real charmer."

"She doesn't need to be. She has a fast car and very few morals." He finished what was left of his drink and slid it to the other side of the bar. "So when are you going to talk to Irene?"

"On the way back to the city."

"What are you going to tell her?"

"She paid me to find you. I will tell her that I did and that you are safe. If she has questions, I will answer them. What she does after that is up to her."

"I think I'd rather tell her myself," Willy said.

"I'd rather that too," Jones said. "You want a lift?"

Willy nodded and jutted his chin toward Donna. "Pay up and we'll go."

"I thought the drink was on you."

"That was before I smoothed things over with the cop. Now, you owe me."

Jones got out his wallet.

"And don't even think about forgetting a tip."

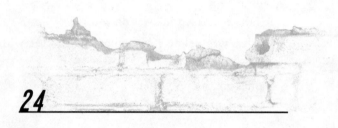

24

JONES AND WILLY MADE IT TO THE JEEP WITHOUT GETTING INTO ANY MORE trouble. Willy got in while Jones opened the trunk. He yanked out the first aid kit and set up shop in the driver seat. Looking at his reflection in the rear-view mirror, Jones could see his nose had a new angle. He reached across the front seat, opened the glovebox, and rummaged for a pen. Willy was clearly interested in what was happening, but he kept his mouth shut while he watched. Jones stuck the pen up his nose and leaned closer to the mirror as he began to apply pressure. He grunted as he felt his nose shift back into place. The pen came out messy and Jones wiped it on the back of his knee before he put it back in the glovebox. Willy, seeing the interesting part was over, turned his attention to the radio while Jones prodded his nose and inspected his work: the break was relatively minor and he might just walk away from his trip to Niagara Falls without two black eyes. Jones pried the end of the tape loose and used his teeth to peel back a strip. He adjusted the roll and tore the tape free. He applied the tape and slowly worked it across the bridge of his swollen nose. He tested out his work with a few sharp inhalations and found that he could breathe through it again.

"You look pretty yet?"

Jones looked over and saw Willy still playing with the stereo. "I don't think anyone will ask me to prom anytime soon, but I won't scare any kids, so it should be fine."

"You think that cop will think that it's fine?"

"I think he already has his mind made up about me. What I look like won't change that."

"Spoken like a man who has nothing figured out. If I had known you were going to be this clueless, I would have said you got hit by the bike."

"That would sound better if it wasn't coming from a man who can't work a radio."

"There are too many goddamn stations on this thing," Willy said. "For Christ's sake, you have a channel for every fucking decade. Every car I ever owned just had

AM and FM. There was none of this satellite bullshit. We had a rock station, a jazz station, country, and couple for whatever the kids were into. AM had sports, weather, and music no one listened to."

"Which was your station?"

William sat back in the seat and smiled. "Jazz. Not that smooth garbage. Real Jazz. The stuff on the radio wasn't always good, but if you were patient, Miles would come."

Jones hit one of the presets and put the Jeep in gear.

Willy nodded his approval. "It's not Miles," he said. "But I'm a patient man."

Jones stopped just before the road and scrolled through his phone. He jabbed at a button on the steering wheel and drove out of the parking lot as *Miles in Berlin* slowly filled the cab with sound.

"Show-off," Willy said.

Jones smiled.

Willy gave Miles a few minutes of quiet respect before he said, "You set that nose pretty well."

Jones grinned. "I could do it with one hand tied behind my back."

"That's not what I meant," Willy said.

"I had a lot of practice."

"Medical school?"

"Army," Jones said.

"Medic."

"No. The army just taught me how to tape things together until someone with better training showed up."

"Where did you serve?"

"All over," Jones said.

"See anything interesting?"

"A lot of broken things," Jones said.

Jones' ringtone interrupted Miles' solo. Ordinarily, Jones would have been upset, but the call ended a conversation he didn't want to have.

Jones glanced at the phone. "I gotta take this," he said.

"Is it Irene?"

Jones shook his head. "Do me a favour: let me handle this call myself."

"I'll only step in if you start drowning again."

"I mean it."

Willy lifted two palms in submission. "Alright. It's your show. I'll just watch from the front row." The old man dipped a hand to his right and sent the seat back into a forty-five-degree angle.

Jones answered the phone. "Hello?"

"I was just about to hang up on you, tiger."

"I didn't think you'd call again."

"Why?" Lauren's voice came out loud from the car speakers. Jones adjusted the volume and glanced at Willy, but the old bank robber was looking out the window.

"Maybe I was just afraid you wouldn't."

Lauren laughed. "Because you wouldn't be able to save me?"

"I want to help you," Jones said.

"Nope. Nuh-uh. You said you wanted to *save* me because you couldn't save someone else. Who couldn't you save?"

Lauren's teenage voice was flirty, and the words spilled out of her mouth. She was on something.

"Just someone I knew."

She took a breath as though she were underwater and coming up for air and said, "Oh, no. That's not how the game works. If you want me to tell you about my life then you have to do the same."

"His name was Adam."

"What happened to him?"

"Someone took him."

"Who?"

"A man."

"Did the man hurt Adam?"

"Yeah. He hurt him."

"Tell me about it."

"No."

"Then I'm going to hang up."

Jones waited. Lauren didn't hang up.

"You're no fun, tiger."

"This isn't fun, kid."

Lauren changed the subject. "I found another one of your posters. I stopped to look at it, and Tony thought I wanted a cat."

"Who's Tony?"

"He's my boyfriend."

"You guys serious?"

Lauren laughed. "Yeah. He loves me. We're going to move away together."

"Where to?"

"I want to go to California. I've always dreamed of going Hollywood."

"Norah said you were a singer."

"She said that?" Lauren went quiet and for a second Jones thought the call had dropped. "I don't sing much anymore."

"What do you do?"

"What?"

"You don't sing anymore, so what do you do instead?"

"I work a lot." The energy in her voice had drained away.

"What kind of work?"

"I work for Tony."

Jones looked over at Willy and saw the old con looking back at him.

"I thought he was your boyfriend."

"He is."

"What kind of work does Tony do?"

Lauren didn't answer and Jones knew pressing her would be a mistake.

"He loves me," Lauren said.

The words interested Willy, and he brought the seat out of its lean. Jones could tell that he wanted to say something, but he didn't want Lauren to know that there was someone else on the line. He put a hand up and Willy reluctantly nodded.

"You mean Tony?"

"Yeah. He calls me his baby girl. He's always getting me things. New clothes, make-up. He always wants me to look nice when we go out."

"But you didn't tell him about the posters."

"What?" Lauren suddenly sounded unsure of herself.

"You said he thought you wanted a cat."

"Doesn't mean I didn't tell him the rest."

"Did you?"

Another silence that Jones knew better than to break first.

"He loves me."

"So I hear."

"You're a jerk," Lauren said. "You talk about wanting to save me, but then all you do is put down my boyfriend. You aren't looking to save me. You just want to fuck me. All that bullshit about saving people is just a way to get close to me. You know what I think? I think you're probably a stalker. We had a date once and now you're trying to get into my head so you can get into my pants again. Wait until I tell Tony. He's going to find you and mess you up. You are gonna be so sorry."

Jones had miscalculated the effect his probe about her boyfriend would have. The pin was out of the grenade and he was worried it would explode before he could get it back in. "Do you really believe that, Lauren? Do you really think I tracked Norah down and put up all those posters because I'm stalking you?"

"Do you think a normal person would do all that for someone they never met?"

Jones didn't have an answer.

"Y'know what? This was supposed to be fun, but now it's just a drag. I gotta go."

Jones took one last shot at putting the pin back in the grenade. "Adam was murdered by a man named Kevin McGregor."

Lauren didn't hang up.

"He took Adam from his backyard on a Wednesday afternoon while his mother was on the phone. She had no idea what happened to him."

The admission got everyone's attention. Willy turned his head to the left and watched Jones with two cold blue eyes that betrayed the sharp mind wiles that were hiding just under the swagger.

"Kevin had befriended Adam. He had been *nice* to him." The word nice tasted like bile on his tongue. "Nice enough to make a seven-year-old think it was okay to walk off his lawn and get into the back of a van. Adam trusted Kevin because he thought they were friends." Jones swallowed and cleared his throat. "But there was nothing that resembled a friend in the back of that van."

Jones took a breath and said, "Adam fought back. His house was just across the street. His mother was in the kitchen. Being so close to home gave him the courage to say no to a man more than twice his size. He kicked, he punched, and then—he screamed. Kevin put his hands around Adam's throat to keep him quiet, but he wouldn't stop screaming. Adam died twenty metres from the edge of his front lawn." Jones inhaled slowly. "His mother didn't know he was missing until almost an hour after he had died. By the time she realized he was gone, Kevin McGregor had already started entombing him."

"Entombing?" Lauren said the word slowly as though its meaning may reveal itself in the dissection of its sounds.

"Kevin was scared. He hadn't planned on killing Adam. He took his body home and brought it down into his basement. He wrapped Adam's body in a tarp and wound tape around his neck, waist, and ankles. He put Adam's body against the wall of his cold cellar and spent the night laying bricks until there was a wall hiding what Kevin McGregor did."

Jones and Willy heard a sniff amplified through the expensive speakers.

"Adam's mother spent years looking for her son, believing he was out there somewhere. She said good night to him every single night. That is the God's honest truth. She was terrified that her son was somewhere without someone who cared enough to say those two simple words."

It was Jones' turn to sniff.

"Adam's mother hired me to investigate the investigation. So many people had looked for her son over the years and no one could find a trace of him. She was sure that someone had missed something."

"They did," Lauren said. "You found him."

Jones sighed. "I looked for Adam for six years."

"And you found him." Lauren said it as though Jones should be proud of the accomplishment.

"I was too late."

"That wasn't your fault. You know that, right? He died before you even started looking."

"The thing about searching for people is they become real to you before you ever find them. Everything you learn about them and all of the things people tell you about them feed this belief you have deep down inside that you will find them. The people you search for are born in your mind. They exist and feel as real as memories. Living things that never really lived."

"What did you do to the man who hurt him?"

Willy put a hand on Jones' arm. Jones looked at the old man and mouthed the word, "Easy." Jones had heard it too. There was fear in the question.

"I was hired to find Adam," Jones said. "That was what I did."

"But didn't you want to, like, hurt him or something?"

"Baby girl, it's time to go to work." The male voice had lost a lot of its distinction as it travelled through whatever barrier separated Lauren from Tony. But Jones could still mine a few details from what he heard. The voice wasn't as deep as his own, but it possessed an air of authority. There was no anger in the command; it wasn't necessary because Lauren responded right away with a voice stripped of her teens. "Coming, Daddy."

Jones shuddered at the word *daddy* in the manufactured little girl's voice. "Will you call me again, Lauren?"

"You still want to save me, tiger?"

"I want to help you, if I can," Jones said.

"What are you doing in there, baby girl?" The voice was closer and louder.

"Lauren," Jones said.

"I'll call you," she said and then she hung up.

"WHO HIRED YOU TO LOOK FOR HER?" WILLY ASKED WITHOUT TAKING HIS eyes off the passenger window.

"No one. She left a note on a bathroom door." Jones said the words without taking his eyes off the road. "'He's going to kill me, and I think I want him to.' She had no one to say the words to—not one soul. I figured that kid deserved more than a bathroom door."

A brief silence followed the last notes of "Stella By Starlight," then Willy said, "What did you do to the man who killed that boy?"

Jones didn't answer.

"People are funny," Willy said. "Two people heard the same story at the same time, and at the end of the story they had the same question, but they're not looking for the same thing."

"She wanted to know what I did to Adam's killer," Jones said.

"That's what she asked and that's the answer I'm interested in, but that wasn't what she wanted to know."

"She was wondering what I would do to Tony."

"Bingo. She's smart enough to know that any way out for her leads straight through her pimp. She's worried about what will happen to him. You know why, right?"

"She was telling the truth," Jones said. "She loves him."

"Bingo again. Like I said, people are funny. They should hate the ones who hurt them, but it hardly ever works out like that. I have some experience with this." Willy took his eyes off the window and put them on Jones. "You know what you're doing, right?"

"I know what I'm doing."

Willy looked at Jones for a long time. Jones didn't turn his head.

"So what's next?"

"I wait for her to call again," Jones said.

"While you dodge the police," Willy said. "Why are they interested in you exactly?"

"Parking tickets," Jones said.

Willy turned down the stereo a little bit and smiled over his shoulder at Jones. "That wasn't a traffic cop. That was a murder cop."

Jones shrugged.

"Do you know what I went away for?"

"Sure."

"You know how I got caught?"

Jones glanced at Willy. "No."

Willy smiled. "I robbed thirty-seven banks in my life."

Jones whistled.

"Thirty-seven, but they nailed me only for the last two. I did 'em both on the same day. Thirty-six was as smooth as the thirty-five before it. Thirty-seven started off the same way, but on the way out of the bank a woman hit me as she was backing out of the handicap parking spot near the door. She didn't check her blind spot." Willy chuckled. "A couple minutes later, the cops showed up and found me lying on the ground with a broken femur and a shattered elbow. Two banks in one weekend was stupid. I told myself it was about the money, but, like most things, it's never really about what we tell ourselves it's about."

"I know what I'm doing," Jones said.

"I'm not talking about you, kid. I hurt a lot of people because I wasn't capable of being honest with myself. I wrecked my life and did a hell of a job messing up my kid's life too. That girl on the phone is no different than I was. She is a wrecking ball in motion. You ever see one of those things?"

"She's not a wrecking ball. She's a kid in trouble."

"She is both and you're trying to catch her. You don't catch a wrecking ball, kid. It hits you."

25

JONES LET WILLY OUT AT THE CURB IN FRONT OF PACIFIC HEIGHTS AND drove north. He knew better than to go anywhere near his place or the office. Scopes had given him another day, but he wasn't about to take the cop at his word. Were the roles reversed, Jones would already be staking out Scopes' house and waiting for him to come home. Jones checked his watch—he could still make visiting hours.

Laverne smiled when she saw Jones sitting next to his father. "Back again so soon?"

Jones turned his head away from his father and smiled at Laverne. "I was in the neighbourhood."

Laverne winced at the sight of him. "What happened to your face?"

"Fist fight."

"Looks like you lost."

Jones held up his arm. "I was outnumbered."

Laverne frowned. "That is not funny. You are far too old to be getting in fist fights."

"Now that's not funny," Jones said.

Laverne giggled and Jones smiled. Her laughter was infectious and Jones was glad that it was a sound his father heard often. She checked on his father and made a few notes on the clipboard stored in the sleeve attached to his bed. "Your father is a popular guy. Your brother was just here the other night."

"Did he stay long?"

"The usual."

Jones nodded and thanked God for Tom. He had every reason to be distant, but he kept showing up. Twice a week for an hour at a time, like clockwork, Tom sat with his father, fed him, and then read him the day's sports section. Jones loved his brother and he was grateful for the knowledge that his father's care was something he would never have to worry about.

When Laverne finished, Jones transferred his father to his wheelchair. He wheeled his father outside and paused on the sidewalk to button his coat. These days, his father always felt cold—years of soft food had tenderized his body. The once hard contractor's muscles had vanished, and his skin hung like wet laundry on fragile bones that had never been so close to the sun.

"I heard Tom came to see you yesterday."

Jones stopped his father beside an empty bench and clicked the brakes with the toe of his boot. He heard his father exhale as he sat down beside him on the bench.

"You and me are lucky to have him."

Jones didn't hear a breath this time. "I don't want to hear it. Whatever you think about how Tom lives his life, he is family."

Jones heard another breath; in his head, it sounded like it came out in a huff. "Listen, Pop, I tried to stay out of things between you two when I was growing up. I like to think it's because I knew there was no way to make you see that you were wrong. I gave up on changing you and tried instead to keep the peace. I was wrong. You have no idea how lucky we are that Tom didn't decide to walk out on us. It sure as hell would have been easier for him than staying. And while you might have been happy if he had left us, I can tell you that you wouldn't have felt that way forever. I've seen what the lost do. They carve a deep wound that never scars. You might have hated him, but you would have felt it eventually and then you wouldn't be able to stop feeling it."

Out of the corner of his eye, Jones caught the movement of his father's head as it began to drift back. He slipped the crook of his elbow around the old man's head and eased it back to where it had been.

"I was wrong and I don't have any more time to spend keeping the peace."

His father said nothing.

"Listen, I want to talk to you. I might not be around for a while."

Jones gave the words time to sink in.

"I got into some trouble, and I'm not going to be able to find my way out of it. It wasn't bad luck, Pop. I earned the trouble. I earned every inch of it."

Jones didn't hear a sound from the man sitting next to him.

"It's hard to understand. I know."

Jones heard a short breath that might have been an attempt at a laugh.

"Tom is going to take care of you when I can't. I haven't talked to him about it, but I know he will. I wanted to tell you myself because you should hear it from me, not anyone else. I also wanted to tell you that you need to get past whatever bullshit you have with Tom because he is going to be all you have and he deserves better than he has ever gotten from you."

Jones watched his father watching nothing and tried not to read anything into it. He got off the bench and unlocked the wheels. "Why don't we see if we can sneak a little dessert before dinner."

26

JONES STAYED WITH HIS FATHER UNTIL THE STAFF TOLD HIM HE HAD TO GO.
He smiled at the nurse to let her know he was on his way
out and waited for her to leave. He put on his coat and
stopped at the side of the bed. Jones took his father's hand
and felt his cool skin slowly begin to warm in his grip. He
said, "Bye, Pop. Remember what we talked about," and
then he walked out the door.

In the Jeep, Jones dialled Irene before he put his foot
on the accelerator. She answered with a voice that was
more pleasant than anything he was used to. "Hello?"

"It's Sam Jones." His name was the real test, and Jones waited to see how she would react.

"Mr. Jones, I can't thank you enough."

"He called?"

"He did. He called and we talked. We really talked."

"I'm happy to hear that," Jones said.

"My father really liked you."

Jones glanced at his nose in the mirror. "Not at first."

"What?"

"Nothing. Listen, you have my number. Call me if you need anything."

"I will," Irene said. She blurted out, "Mr. Jones," in an effort to catch him before he hung up.

"I'm still here."

"What did you think of him?"

Jones pulled to a stop at a red light and thought about the question. "I don't follow."

"Do you think he's a bad person?"

The light changed and Jones was slow to accelerate.

"I mean," Irene said, "he did some terrible things. There were the banks, but there were other things. Things he won't talk about—at least, not with me."

"What do you think?" Jones said.

Irene sighed. "Some days, I think he is the worst person in the world. Other days, I think he is an old man with a past everyone has forgotten about except me."

Jones thought about it for a block. "I met a man trying to be better than he was. I don't know if he will ever put down the baggage he's lugging, but he might get better at carrying it if he gets some help."

"What if I'm never ready?"

"You chased him when he ran."

Irene thought about it. "Thank you," she said. "Oh, and my father told me to tell you to call him if you needed any more help with your parking tickets. What does that mean?"

"Inside joke," Jones said.

Irene didn't sound convinced, but she said, "Okay," before she thanked him again and hung up the phone.

Jones had barely slept the night before, and this night had barely started. He felt exhaustion wash over him as though it had been waiting in the back seat for a quiet moment to grab him by the throat. Jones yawned and turned up the air conditioning in an attempt to force his body to rally. Three yawns later, Jones admitted to himself that he needed more than cold air—he needed sleep. Jones found a movie theatre close by and killed some time sleeping through the last half of a deserted showing of a big budget rom-com that couldn't shake the stench of the rotting tomato it had earned. When the house lights came up, he woke feeling less groggy but nowhere close to rested. He headed to Brew to find something more effective than a nap.

Jones opened the door and saw no sign of Sheena behind the counter. He ordered a coffee and a sandwich and picked up a newspaper someone had left behind on his way to a vacant corner table. The coffee shop was busy, and Jones had to buy another sandwich and a few more coffees to keep his claim on the table. When he finished the paper, he noticed an old crate that had been refurbished and stocked with used paperbacks. Jones instinctively wrote off the novels as donations that wouldn't be worth the fraction of a calorie that would be spent flipping the pages, but a glimpse of a name on an orange spine that barely had a crease told him he was wrong. Jones picked up John D. MacDonald's *Darker than Amber* and killed a few hours reading about another PI's troubles.

When the staff at Brew started to close up, Jones drove around until he found a motel that would accept cash for a room. The place was small and dirty, but Jones had spent more time in worse surroundings. Jones lay down on top of the covers and put his phone down on his chest. Whoever was next door was playing music and they had the speaker turned up loud enough to vibrate the wall. Jones ignored the sound and closed his eyes; in a few seconds, he was asleep.

The phone woke him an hour later. The number on the screen read private again.

"Lauren?"

"Did I wake you?" She found the question funny. She was high again, he was sure.

"Where are you?"

"Work. My next client is late, so I figured I'd call you

because Tony is in no mood to talk. He hates it when people are late. He says its screws up the whole schedule. I can't talk to him when he's like this."

The words came at Jones fast and he had to concentrate to understand her.

"I can talk to you, right?"

"Sure," Jones said. "Can I ask you something?"

Lauren laughed. "Sure, tiger."

"What do you do?"

"What?"

"You work for Tony, I know that, and you schedule appointments with clients at one in the morning. I just want to know what line of work you're in."

Lauren didn't think anything was funny anymore. "You're the detective. You tell me." Her tone was sullen and made her sound every bit like the teenager she was.

"I think you're a call girl," Jones said. He waited for Lauren, who was suddenly much less chatty, to say something.

"Call girl." She said the words with a bit of a snicker. "Call girl. No one has ever called me that before. How old are you?"

"Forty-two."

Jones' age brought some of the levity back into Lauren's voice. "You're old."

"Second time I heard that today."

"The name doesn't even make sense," Lauren said. "Nobody calls me."

Jones had been worried that the question would spook her, but she hadn't denied it and it didn't seem as though she was going to hang up on Jones for suggesting it. He pushed his luck a little more. "Who do they call?"

"They? You mean the men I fuck for money?"

Jones made a fist. Now he had stepped on a land mine, and he wasn't sure how to get off it. He tried to slowly back away. "The guys you meet."

It was no good. "God, you can't even say it can you? The *guys* I meet are men, and I meet them to fuck. Say it."

Jones saw that there was no getting out of it, so he doubled down. "Who do they call?"

"Who? The men I fuck? Tell you what, tiger, I'll answer your question if you say it."

Jones stared at the smoke-stained motel ceiling. In the dim light cast off by the parking lot, he could see a spot that had gone brown from water damage. He realized that the music next door had stopped, and now he could hear two people arguing. Lauren had picked up on his discomfort like a predator smells blood and she was attacking his weakness with something sharper than teeth.

Jones had no other move to make, so he said it. "The men you fuck." The words came out quiet and slow.

Lauren giggled. The sound was full of the juvenile cruelty of a schoolyard bully. "Website," she said. "Tony puts up an ad in the personal section. The part for people looking to hook up."

"Where do you meet up?"

"This doesn't feel much like a conversation. It's more like an interview. I don't want to talk about me anymore. It's my turn to ask you something."

"Okay."

"What did you do to the man who killed Adam?"

A car started in the parking lot and beams from the headlights easily penetrated the membrane-thin curtains and lit up the room. "I told you—"

"I know what you told me. I want you to tell me the truth. I didn't lie to you. Don't lie to me."

Jones remembered Willy's hand on his arm when Lauren had first asked about what he had done to Kevin. Willy had warned him to go *easy*. Jones sighed, knowing there was nothing *easy* about what he had done. "I killed him."

"You lied to me." She didn't sound surprised.

"I'm sorry," Jones said. He meant it.

"You're a murderer." The word sounded strange in her teenage voice. She wasn't scared or disgusted. She was interested. "You're a murderer."

The car headlights moved on and the room was dark again. "Yes."

"How does it feel? To have killed someone."

Jones thought about it and admitted the truth. "I haven't really thought about it much."

"Are you for real? I mean you killed someone. A person no longer exists because of you. Do you really expect me to believe that you don't think about it?"

Jones didn't know what to say to the girl.

She went quiet while she thought and then she quietly said, "Was it hard?"

"No."

"Do you feel bad about it?"

Jones thought about it and then he thought about lying to Lauren. He told the truth. "For this one—no."

"Because he deserved it. He deserved it for what he did," she said.

Jones sat up and swung his foot off the bed. He was angry with himself for reading the girl so wrong. He had assumed that she wanted to protect her pimp, but that wasn't what she was doing. She was working up the nerve to kill him, and Jones had just told her murder was as easy as it really was.

"Kid, you are in an impossible situation, but killing Tony isn't the answer. I can help you."

Lauren snorted. "I don't want to kill Tony."

Jones leaned against the wall and let his head loll back until it hit the wall. The argument on the other side of the wall had become a screaming match, and the loud noises vibrated the drywall against his skull. Jones pushed off the wall and crossed the room in five steps. The distance did little to muffle the sounds of the people next door. Jones could make out the hard-edged consonants of curse words, and he stared at the wall thinking he would rather hear those instead of what he knew was coming.

"I want to kill myself."

27

"I LIED TOO," LAUREN SAID. HER VOICE WAS QUIET.

Jones pressed the phone harder against his ear to hear her over the couple next door.

"About what?"

Lauren sniffed. "About Tony. He was my boyfriend, but we broke up. He doesn't want to be with me anymore. He says I'm only good for one thing—making him money."

Jones walked into the bathroom and shut the thin door behind him. "That's not true," Jones said.

Lauren sniffed and Jones heard her voice waver. "No? Tell me one thing I'm good at. Just one thing."

"Singing," Jones said.

The answer made Lauren angry. "That's just something someone told you about me. You don't know me at all."

"You're right," Jones said. "You're right. I don't know you, but you know something? I don't think Tony does either, not if he said something like that to you."

"It was my fault. I broke his trust."

"Money or sex?"

"Jesus! So, because I have sex for money it must be about money or sex?"

"It has nothing to do with your job and everything to do with mine. In my experience, most problems are about one or the other. Sometimes it's both."

Lauren quietly admitted, "It was about money. We had this plan. We were saving money so that we could move to California together. I was going to sing and Tony was going to manage me."

"What happened?"

"We needed money to get to get out West, so I started looking for a job, but everything was minimum wage. It would take twenty years of flipping burgers to earn enough. We needed to make some real money."

"Let me guess, Tony got an idea."

"No," she dragged out the word sarcastically. "I had the idea. Tony had a couple of girls working for him and they were making good money. Better money than

McDonald's was offering. I thought it would get us to California faster."

"What happened?"

"Things were good at first. I only worked a couple times a week and I was making good money. Real money."

"And how was Tony with all of this?"

"He was fine with it," she said. "I had been doing some gigs around the city and Tony was managing me, so he just managed this too. He set up my appointments, got me there, and made sure I was safe."

"For a cut," Jones said.

"Managers don't work for free." Lauren said the word in a sing-songy way that made Jones think she was parroting something she had heard Tony say often.

"What happened next?"

"Things were going fine, and then I screwed it all up. As usual because that's what I do. It's what I always do."

"How did you screw things up?"

"I got into some things."

"What kind of things?"

"Popcorn mostly."

The answer was not what Jones had been expecting.

Lauren laughed at the sudden silence. "Drugs, tiger. Popcorn is drugs."

"What kind?"

Lauren blew out a stream of air. The conversation was starting to bore her. "Fentanyl and heroin. And before you say it, yes, I know it's dangerous."

"I wasn't going to say anything," Jones said.

"Bullshit."

"Maybe," Jones said. "Where did you get the popcorn?"

Lauren spoke in a sigh that told Jones he was pushing his luck. "One of the other girls who works for Tony gave it to me one night. One thing led to another and after a couple of weeks, I was hooked. I tried to hide it from Tony, but I ran out of money pretty fast."

"The money for California," Jones said.

"All gone. I told you. I screwed everything up."

"How did Tony take the news?"

Lauren quietly said, "Bad. He called me a junkie. He hates junkies. He said I ruined our dream. After that, he didn't want to be with me anymore."

"Are you still using?"

Lauren hesitated. "Yeah." She waited another beat and then added, "Tony gets me what I need."

"Uh hunh."

"He says he wants to make sure I don't do too much, and he wants to make sure that I don't buy anything dirty."

"How do you afford it?" Jones asked the question though he already knew the answer.

"I work."

"Still a couple of times a week?"

"More."

"Why not just walk away?"

"And go where?"

"Anywhere."

"With you?" Lauren put on a little girl's voice that was stained with adult sexuality. "Are you going to be my big strong protector instead of Tony?"

"I'm serious, kid. Why not just walk away?"

"That's what I'm going to do."

"No, you said you want to die."

"If that ain't walking away, I don't know what is."

"That's not what I mean."

"You want to know why I don't walk away? It's because wherever I go, I'll still be me. I'm no good."

"That's—"

"Don't, okay! I didn't call you to talk about this. This was supposed to be fun, but it's not. It was nice to have someone to talk to, but I don't need to talk about this. I know what I am and it's shit. I'm not a good person. I have ruined every relationship I have ever had. Me, not someone else. It's been my fault every time. I don't know how to be good, I sure as hell don't know how to be happy, and I am so tired of feeling bad." Lauren sighed. "You know what? I gotta go."

"Lauren wait." Jones' voice ricocheted off the cramped walls of the bathroom.

She didn't hang up. "What?"

"What if I told you that there is a way out?"

"I just told you there is."

"Another way," Jones said.

"Is this where you tell me you're going to save me again? Let me stop you right there. After I screwed up,

Tony changed, or maybe he just stopped pretending. He's not with me anymore. I'm with him and he will never let me go. I've seen what he does to people who try to leave. You have no idea what he's like. I do, and that's how I know there is only one way out for me."

"What about through?" Jones said.

Lauren said, "What?" as though she thought she had misheard him.

"A way through instead of out."

"Through to what?"

"Home. Norah said you could go home to her."

He had expected the offer to stun her. He had expected tears and agreement. He got laughter.

"I bet Terry would love that."

The name threw him. "Who's Terry?"

"Norah's brother. He liked to take me out on *dates*. Norah thought it was all cute and innocent until I told her it wasn't. Terry said I was lying. He told Norah that I had been in the system my whole life and I thought every guy was looking to abuse me. Norah was the first real mother I ever had, and she didn't believe me. She turned out to be just like everyone else. So, no, I'm not going back to her." She snorted. "At least now I get paid when a man touches me."

"I didn't know."

"I told you. There is nothing better out there for me."

"Lauren, you wrote on that door. You called my number. You aren't ready to go out. You're holding on for something. I was wrong about Norah, but not about this. Some part of you knows that there is something better out there."

Lauren went quiet and Jones thought that he might have gotten through to her. The growl of frustration that came out of her mouth next told him he was wrong.

"This was a mistake. Talking to you was supposed to be fun, not like this. I don't want to talk anymore."

Jones said, "Lauren," but she was already gone.

JONES OPENED THE BATHROOM DOOR AND FELT COOLER AIR TOUCH HIS SKIN.
The relief was short lived. If the argument next door had been a thunderstorm before, it was a hurricane now. He could hear an angry exchange peppered with every word his mother had once told him not to say. Jones walked to the bed and sat down with his eyes on the wall. Lauren was supposed to be the one he could save—the one who would go home and have a life. Someone on the other side of the wall slammed a door hard enough to buck the picture frames and Jones was blessed with a moment of quiet. He lay back on the bed and felt his back complain.

He had spent years looking for Adam, and in the back of his mind, in a place he had never told Ruth about, he had harboured wild dreams of being able to find him, and reality stabbed through his fantasy when he did. Jones never had a chance—he had failed before he started; then, he saw Lauren's message. Part of him, the part that had thought he could have found Adam, wanted to believe that it might have been about Lauren all along—that maybe Adam was meant to lead him to Lauren. It was a ridiculous thought, but that didn't mean it hadn't taken root deep inside his head. But when Jones hung up the phone, that silly fantasy met the same fate as the one he had about finding Adam. He had no other moves to make and no one left to save, not even himself.

Through the thin wall, Jones heard the bathroom door in the other room open and bounce off the spring doorstop that matched the one on the baseboard in the bathroom in Jones' room. He could make out the voice he heard as male and it intensified in sync with the other guest's thunderous footsteps. Jones heard a woman yell and then a loud *thump* shook the wall. The drywall shook again as it attempted to redistribute the energy of whatever she threw against it. Jones pinched the bridge of his nose as the argument began again in earnest on the other side of the wall.

"Liar!"

Thump.

"Asshole!"

"Whore!"

Thump.

"I hate you."

"I hate you more."

Thump.

Thump.

Thump.

Jones sat up and stared at the wall. A few feet away in a room that matched the one Jones was sitting in, two people were at each other's throats. Two people hell-bent on hurting each other. Why didn't one of them just leave? Why couldn't one of them just walk away from the words and whatever was flying around in that tiny room.

Jones stood up.

Thump.

"Fuck you!"

"Fuck you!"

Thump.

The sound was coming from the other side of the wall. Jones took two fast steps and punched the wall. He didn't hear the sound his fist made going through the cheap layers of low-end drywall because he was screaming. He hit the wall again and again. As he lost steam, it was harder to say the words and Jones realized what he was screaming. "Why won't you just leave?"

Panting, Jones braced himself using his elbow and pulled his arm out of the wall. He left his blood on the powdered edges of broken gypsum. Through the hole, Jones could see them. Two people suddenly quiet, but standing together. Jones looked at the woman and said, "Go."

She stepped toward Jones and yelled through the hole in the wall, "Fuck you, you psycho!"

Jones turned and threw the nightstand at the wall. The small piece of furniture made a great deal of noise as it exploded. Jones whirled toward the other wall and splintered the dresser with his boot. Two more kicks reduced the motel prop to kindling.

The cops found Jones sitting on the floor with his back against what was left of the wall. The motel room dimensions were the only thing left intact.

28

IF JONES HAD ANY QUESTIONS ABOUT THE KIND OF COP SCOPES WAS, THE detective's response time answered them. Jones had been arrested, booked, and put into a holding cell with five other men who had likely been picked up for offences linked to their varying degrees of intoxication. Two of the men had passed out and a third was on his way to joining them. The fourth man was in a business suit that looked like it had weathered a busy day at work and an even busier night out. Jones watched the man nervously look around the cell and figured it was his first time; it was Jones' first time too, but he couldn't manage to work up any feelings about it.

He opened and closed his hand and judged his success to be a sign that nothing was broken—nothing physical anyway. He wondered if the same was true for his head. Sitting in the cell with nothing to do but think, Jones could not remember how far he had taken it; he had even less of a recollection of the arrest and drive to the station. He had seen soldiers break. The battlefield would damage the reinforced mental structures created by the army's relentless drilling and the soldier would collapse in on himself. Jones had always thought that he had left the army with all his scars on the outside, but now, sitting inside a cell, he wasn't so sure.

Jones was given two hours to cool off in the cell and then he was brought to an interview room upstairs. Jones was led to a chair that gave him a view of the door and told to sit down. Twenty minutes later, Scopes walked into the room, holding two cups of coffee. He put one of the cups in front of Jones and then took his seat opposite him.

"I don't know how you take it, so I just said regular. Hope that's okay."

Jones nodded. "Back to playing good cop?"

Scopes flashed a smile and Jones saw his crooked white teeth. "Good cop left town when you blew off our meeting. You're fucked now, big boy. Totally fucked. I checked on that accident you told me about and you know what I found?"

Jones tested the coffee and found it lukewarm and bitter. He took half of it down before he answered. "What?"

"Nothing, that's what. Your story was bullshit. And right then and there, good cop walked away because good cop hates nothing more than getting shit on his shoes." Scopes drank some of the coffee and then opened the file that had been under his arm when he opened the door. He scanned a few pages before sliding a paper clip off a small stack of pictures. He turned the pictures around and slid them one by one toward Jones, until they were in a line that ran like a film strip.

"Know what these are?"

Jones looked at the pictures, knew that he did, and said, "No."

"They are part of a case that I'm working on. Seems someone killed a man in his basement. Interesting thing about this murder isn't the man. The interesting thing is the basement."

"Got a nice pool table?"

"Funny." Scopes stared at him with no humour in his expression. "No, there isn't a pool table. The interesting thing about this basement is that there was a second body—a kid. One that I have been told was murdered decades ago. We've had our people go over the scene. People with degrees and computer skills that go beyond surfing for porn, and do you know what they came up with?"

Jones waited.

"Nothing. We don't know who the body belongs to. What we do know is how it was found." Scopes stared at Jones as he drank some more coffee. He put the empty cup down hard and said, "The second body had been hidden inside a wall for those decades I spoke of. Best we can tell, our other victim was forced to open up the wall with his bare hands before he was shot while he was on his knees. There were powder burns on his palms. Do you know what that means?" Scopes didn't care if Jones had something to say. It wasn't a conversation; it was more of a soliloquy. "It means he had them up when he died. He was begging for his life."

Jones waited.

"Want to know what I think?" He leaned in close and whispered his hypothesis to Jones. "I think our victim was a murderer himself. I think he killed that kid, and he sealed him up in the wall like in that story by the Nevermore guy."

"The Cask of Amontillado," Jones said. "Edgar Allan Poe."

Scopes slapped the table and the empty cup jumped a few centimetres.

"That's the one. The name has been on the tip of my tongue for days." Scopes breathed a sigh of relief. "How did you think of it so quick?"

Jones shrugged. "I like to read."

Scopes smiled. "Maybe you had more time to think about it. Anyway, our vic was a killer and someone knew about it. Now, pay attention, because this is where it gets interesting."

Jones waited.

Scopes flipped a few pages in the file before extracting a thin stapled stack of sheets. Scopes took his time turning the papers around with his index finger. "This is all we have on our murder victim slash killer. This is it. He's lived in the same place for twenty-five years. He's had the same job for almost thirty. He is not currently married and he doesn't own a dog. He pays his taxes and doesn't have so much as an unpaid parking ticket on his record. All the neighbours said he was a great guy. He kept his lawn clean and in the winter, he cleared off other people's driveways."

Jones could feel Scopes was getting closer to the point, and he knew the cop wanted to make it sharp, so it would hurt when he jabbed it at him.

"On paper, this guy is no one. He is boring and he is clean. That's what the paper says, but the basement." Scope shook a finger at Jones. "That basement says something different. This man has a body wrapped up in a tarp hidden inside a wall in his basement. The body has been there for years. I don't know how many yet, but the techs will know soon enough. They have all kinds of tests they can do with their fancy equipment, and one of them will give me a number." Scopes leaned in closer and whispered across the table. "But to tell you the truth, I'm not interested in what the techs have to say about the kid in the wall. Do you know what I'm interested in?"

Jones shook his head.

The cop lifted a single finger. "That first body. Kevin McGregor. A sixty-two-year-old man who, on paper, appears to be the most law-abiding son of a bitch who ever abided. That is what I am interested in. Those crime-scene techs are all about the body in the wall. They're running all kinds of tests through all kinds of fancy machines, thinking that they are going to come up with something that breaks the case. *CSI* has gone to their heads. They think computers have all the answers." Scopes smiled and shook his head. "Those eggheads don't realize they're all looking in the wrong place. That first body has more to say about what happened than the kid in the wall. Someone broke into that man's house, walked him down to his basement, and then made him knock down a brick wall without tools." Scopes paused to observe how Jones felt about this part. When he saw nothing on Jones' face he went on. "Someone hated that man, and it looks like they were right to, and they made it ugly. After our killer broke McGregor's body, he put him on his knees and shot him while he pleaded for his life. My question is, how did our killer, well our second killer, technically, know what had been hiding behind that wall?" Scopes paused for an answer, and when Jones didn't bite, he said, "I don't need a computer to tell me about the kid. I just need to find the man who killed Kevin McGregor. That guy knows the whole story."

The cop stared at Jones and his eyes betrayed a sadist's amusement. He had gotten to the point and he was ready to shiv Jones with it.

"Now, I'm not going to lie to you, Sam. When I saw the scene, I thought this thing was a dud." He ticked off his fingers as he spoke. "No evidence left by the killer, a second unidentified body that had been there for years, and no clear evidence of a motive. Cases like that usually end up in a box in the basement, unless we get a lucky break." Scopes smiled. "Guess what happened?"

Jones said nothing.

"Not gonna guess? Okay, I'll tell you. We got a break. A witness came forward and told us about an odd conversation with a man who, and you'll find this interesting, only had one—"

"Lawyer," Jones said.

"Eureka."

"That's not his name."

Scopes closed the file and folded his hands on top of the paper. He was smiling wide enough for Jones to see his sharp discoloured canines. "People cry lawyer the same way they cry uncle when someone has them in a headlock. They say the word like they think it will make everything stop." He leaned back in his chair and slid the folder back and forth a few times with the fingers on his right hand. "I get it and I don't take offence. I really don't. I blame TV. Every cop show has it play out the same way. Some crook, no offence, says lawyer, and

241

a few seconds later his attorney walks through the door and says something stupid like, 'No more questions, Detective.' Cut to the next scene and the bad guy, again no offence, is walking out the front door of the station. You know that's just TV, right? You've been around long enough, and seen enough, to know that isn't how this is going to play out."

Jones lifted a hand. "You're going to get up and take me to a phone so I can call my lawyer."

"No," Scopes said. "What's going to happen is—"

Jones lifted his hand again. "Lawyer." He looked at the camera mounted in the corner of the room and said, "Lawyer."

Scopes sighed. "Listen, I know I came down hard on you, but you have to know that I'm on your side. That animal killed a kid. You did the world a favour and there isn't a cop in the world who would say different. Talk to me. Let me help you."

Jones watched Scopes watching him. The cop was looking for a reaction that he could use like a compass to get inside Jones' head. Jones gave him nothing. "I don't know what you are talking about, Detective. The only thing I know is that you have concocted some elaborate story in your head that somehow includes me, and I want no part in it. I want to call my lawyer."

Scopes stared at Jones with his jaw set. When he finally spoke, it was through clenched teeth. "If that's the way you want it. But you're making a mistake.

Forensics moves slower than investigators. I thought I would do you a favour and give you a shot at saving yourself because of the circumstances. But if you want to roll the dice on science, that's fine. Just know that the lab is the hardest bitch I've ever met, and I have two ex-wives. It might take some time, but she will find something, something microscopic you didn't even know you missed, and seal your fate in one typed page. It won't matter that you killed a monster because science doesn't see monsters. Science just sees ones and zeros. Guess which one you'll be."

Scopes stood and put the folder under his arm and then made a grand gesture of checking his watch. "Four a.m. Let's go wake your lawyer up." He smiled at Jones. "At least that will be fun."

Scopes brought Jones to a desk that had pictures of three little girls positioned in the far corners. He handed Jones the receiver and hit a button to get him an outside line. "You know the number, or do you need to look it up?"

"I know it."

Scopes waited, so did Jones. Finally, Jones said, "Could I get a bit of privacy while I speak with my lawyer?"

"You need privacy to leave a message?"

"He might pick up."

Scopes snorted and took a seat at a desk out of earshot. He put his feet up and spoke loud enough for Jones to hear. "This enough room for proper confidentiality?"

Jones turned one of the frames. "Maybe you should make your own call to your wife and ask her why none of the kids look like you."

Scopes barked a laugh. "Not my desk. Not even my precinct." An empty cup on the desk caught his eye and he put his feet back on the floor. "I'm going to hit up the coffee machine, so you can have a little more *privacy*." He used air quotes for the word privacy just in case his tone didn't properly convey his distaste. "Tell your lawyer I said good morning, and don't think I'm bringing you back any coffee."

Jones dialled Ruth's number. She had told him that Peter would be waiting for his call. He hoped she had been telling the truth.

29

DAN PEMBLETON WAS AT THE PRECINCT BY SIX. THE LAWYER LOOKED exactly like a television actor playing a high-priced attorney. His body had the build of the university rower he had once been, and his hair had just the right amount of grey to look wise without appearing old. The locks on his briefcase popped loudly, and Pembleton removed a yellow legal pad from inside. He closed the case and put it on the floor before he took a seat in the plastic chair opposite Jones. Pembleton dipped a tanned hand into the inner pocket of his suit and took out an expensive looking pen. He turned the pen, wrote the date at the top of the page, and then finally looked at Jones.

"It's good to have friends in high places," he said.

Peter had answered the call from the station, and after he had listened to what Jones had to say, he woke Ruth. "I only have the one."

"Lucky for you that one friend is the only person who could get me out of bed before the sun came up."

Jones answered every question Pembleton asked. He went through what had happened at the motel and then made Jones go through it again. He didn't ask how a damaged motel room related to one of the richest women in the city, but he was interested in why a homicide detective had been the one to interview him. Jones told Pembleton just enough, but he never mentioned Adam. That story was for Ruth first. Pembleton knew Jones was holding back information and he was not happy about it. Jones sat through a serious lecture fueled by the lawyer's frustration from the early morning wake-up call, but he kept his mouth shut. When Pembleton was done blowing off steam, he told Jones to sit tight and let him handle things.

At eleven, Jones was in front of a judge and at eleven forty-five, he was in the parking lot standing next to Pembleton's Bentley, talking to the lawyer through the driver side window.

"How much did you have to offer the motel to drop the charges?"

Pembleton didn't look up from his phone. "Enough to renovate the whole place."

"That's a lot of money."

"Not really. That place is a shithole. I expensed the shoes I was wearing when I went over there. I wouldn't even bring them into my car after I set foot in that place." Pembleton turned the rear-view mirror so that he could check his hair. "That your kind of place, Jones?"

"I was trying to lay low," Jones said.

"Because of that detective?"

Jones nodded.

"I would say you accomplished your goal then because there is absolutely no way you could have gone lower." A melodious chime rang and Pembleton took a moment to glance at his phone. He looked back at Jones and gave him his full thousand-dollar-an-hour attention. "I spoke to that detective. He was a serious customer. I know I said it once, but I am going to say it again, so pay attention. You were holding back with me and that was stupid. I can't defend you if you're treating me like the enemy. That cop likes you for something and he's a homicide detective, so it can't be anything good."

Pembleton waited for Jones to give him the standard "I'm innocent" rap. One well-groomed eyebrow arched when he realized it wasn't coming. He picked up his phone and quickly opened an app. After a few quick swipes with his index finger, Pembleton said, "I want you at my office tomorrow at four. I think we have more to discuss, and I want to be prepared to do something about that cop who wants to arrest you so badly." He typed the appointment into his phone and then looked at Jones. "I mean four in the afternoon. I don't care if it is a favour to Ruth Verne. I won't be coming to save you this early again."

"Thanks, Dan."

He pointed at Jones. "Tomorrow at four. Got it? The only reason it's not today is because Ruth told me she wanted to talk with you first."

Jones nodded and Pembleton gave the phone a final glance before putting the Bentley in gear.

"Can I get a lift?"

Pembleton put on a pair of sunglasses and looked at Jones with a smile on his face. "A call from Ruth Verne gets you a lawyer, not an Uber. Stay out of trouble and don't forget about tomorrow." The Bentley purred as it began to accelerate away from Jones. "And good luck with Ruth."

30

JONES BOOKED AN UBER TO GET HIM BACK TO THE MOTEL AND THEN dialled the same number he had called from the police station. Peter answered faster this time, and Jones wondered if he had been sitting beside the phone ever since he put it down.

"Verne residence."

"I'm out, Peter."

Peter went quiet and Jones heard a faint sniff through the receiver. "I will tell her that you are on your way."

The Uber showed up two minutes early, and Jones was

glad that the driver wasn't interested in talking. When they got to the motel, Jones saw the driver double-check the destination. When he looked over his shoulder and said, "We're here," Jones could see from the look on his face that he wondered why anyone would want to be.

Pembleton hadn't been kidding about the payoff because the motel manager actually smiled and waved to Jones when he saw him get out of the Uber. Jones picked up the Jeep and drove home to eat, shower, and change. Twenty minutes later, he was back on the road two days early for his end-of-the-month appointment.

Ruth Verne lived in a house that Jones thought of as a mansion, but that was only because he didn't know a word for something bigger. Jones had been to the house more than seventy times, and he had only set foot in two rooms—the living room and Adam's room. On his first visit, Ruth had interviewed Jones in the living room. After Jones had agreed to take her case, she forced herself to allow Jones to go through Adam's things. The room had already been scoured countless times by the police, but that had been years before, and the fresh invasion stung. Jones could see the pain on her face as she led him to the room and he heard it in her heavy footsteps when she walked away. Jones was careful, and respectful, but he was also thorough. When he was finished, he eased the door shut and then sat down on the hallway floor with Ruth while she cried. That first time in Adam's room was his last; every visit that followed took place in the living room. The space was large and bookcases surrounded the furniture like guards at the ready. Jones had walked the perimeter of the room many times while he waited for Ruth, and he found that the rarest books in her collection were those with creaseless spines. Ruth said she had stopped sleeping after Adam disappeared, and the onslaught of TV reporters and seemingly around-the-clock discussion of Adam's disappearance had left her with a distaste for television, so she read anything she could get her hands on.

Jones was buzzed through the gates and he found Peter waiting for him at the door. The butler led Jones to the living room without a word or a look over his shoulder. Ruth was seated in a chocolate brown leather chair. The chair was positioned in the corner of the room next to a bookcase and a window. Jones knew that the chair was where she spent most of her nights, reading and watching the street. The chair was old and the leather soft and creased. Ruth had a habit of tracing the lines running across the arm with her finger whenever she sat in the chair. Today, her hands were folded white-knuckle tight in her lap. Peter stopped next to the chair and quietly asked Ruth if there was anything she would like. Ruth shook her head without taking her eyes off Jones.

After Peter left, Ruth said, "You look like shit."

Canada may have been her home, but Trinidad had never left her voice. Jones walked to the desk on the other side of the room and retraced his steps holding an antique wooden chair. He placed the chair across from Ruth and gently reintroduced it to his weight. The chair creaked loudly, but it shut up once Jones was seated.

Ruth, in a plain black t-shirt and faded jeans that hugged her legs, ran a hand through her white hair. Her hair was healthy and it defied gravity, like the plumage of an exotic bird.

She took off her red round-framed glasses and used her shirt to dry the tears that had fallen on the lenses. When she put the glasses back on, she took another look at Jones and said, "You really do look like shit."

Jones nodded.

Ruth took a deep breath. The air made a loud noise as it entered her nose and she held it there like a diver refusing to surface. Eventually, Jones heard a loud reluctant exhale. "Peter told me that you know everything."

Jones nodded again.

"You found him?"

Ruth was smart enough to know that good news wouldn't show up like this, but she was hopeful. The sound of the hope in her voice made Jones wince: he knew he'd be the one to put an end to it.

"I'm sorry—"

Ruth put her face into her hands and began to weep. Sound lurched out from somewhere deep inside her. The noise had no harmony or soft notes. It was the bellow of a great beast left caged for so long that it had forgotten what it was and called only for an end. Peter heard the sound and came rushing into the room. Ruth rose to meet him and their bodies collided hard enough to force the breath from Peter's lungs. Jones turned his head from the pair; witnessing their moment of intimacy made him feel like an interloper.

Jones shifted in his chair and Ruth's back went rigid at the sound. She dragged her face away from Peter's chest and aimed two red eyes at Jones. "I want to know—I want to know what happened."

Peter said, "Ruth—"

Jones had never heard the man ever call her anything but Ms. Verne. Witnessing the pair grieve in front of him dissected their relationship and exposed the parts they kept most private. Jones felt the shame of his intrusion in the pit of his stomach.

"No," Ruth said. She placed an hand on Peter's chest and slowly pushed him back. "I need to know."

Peter nodded and stepped back. He slowly extended his hands and lifted the glasses off her face. "I will make you some tea."

Ruth used her sleeve to dry her eyes. "Only if tea means rum."

"I mean tea." Peter looked at Jones and then back at Ruth. "Rum will come later."

After he left, Jones said, "Ruth—"

She waved her hand and cut him off. "Save it. I know you're sorry." Her chin quivered and her voice faltered. Ruth looked at the wall and cleared her throat. When she looked back at Jones, her chin was steady and her eyes were wet. "Tell me who murdered my son."

"His name was Kevin McGregor."

Ruth turned her head and cried into her fist. Jones waited as her sobs became less intense and her formidable will took over again. When Ruth looked at Jones again, she said, "Kevin McGregor." Jones watched Ruth sift through years of police reports and newspaper articles in her head. "I've never heard of him."

"He wasn't in any of the reports and his name wasn't in the news until recently."

"Recently?"

Jones ignored the question. "He was never a person of interest."

"Then who was he? How did he—"

"He was a building inspector for the city," Jones said.

"Building inspector?"

"He met Adam when you were building the pool house in the backyard. There were some issues with permits and McGregor showed up on your property three times." Jones paused for a second and then he said, "Officially."

"Officially?"

"He talked to Adam the first two times he was in your yard. Just a hey and a high-five. After that, he made it a point to check the job site when he could. He would watch Adam from his van. On his third official visit, he spoke with Adam about a tree house after he saw him trying to nail a board into a tree to make a ladder rung."

"I remember that," Ruth said. "He got a tick on his leg when he was back there. I panicked. I had never seen one before. I was sure that he was going to get Lyme disease, or an infection. I told him he wasn't allowed to go back there anymore. It was—"

"'Too dangerous,'" Jones said. "That was what Adam told Kevin McGregor."

"He told him about that?" Ruth's jaw hung slack. "Why would he tell him about that?"

"He wanted a tree house and he was mad that his mother had said no."

Ruth shook her head. "No, no. The pool house and backyard renovations were finished months before Adam was taken. It couldn't be this person. No, you're wrong." The prospect of Jones being wrong about what had happened to Adam made Ruth sound relieved and a little manic.

Jones hated ruining the tiny sliver of hope she had created for herself. "You're right, *your* renovations ended months before Adam was taken. Other people in the neighbourhood started their own renos after your yard made the life and style section of the paper. Your contractor did similar work at two of your neighbours' houses. Both projects required—"

"Permits," Ruth said.

Jones nodded. "The permits gave Kevin a reason to be around. To the contractors, he was a nuisance; to Adam, he was a safe adult with an official truck, an ID badge, and a bunch of tools that he said he would let Adam use."

"He never told me about any of this."

"He wouldn't have. Kevin convinced Adam that it should be a secret. Adam told him what he wanted his tree house to look like and Kevin said he would draw up plans. They made a deal to build it together when no one was around."

Ruth was horrified. "They made plans. He never told me. He never told me any of this. Peter, did you know?"

Jones looked over his shoulder and saw Peter standing in the doorway with a tray in his hands. He slowly shook his head and Ruth began to cry.

"How could no one know, Peter?"

Peter rushed to Ruth and set the tray down before taking her hands. He began to apologize over and over again while Ruth cried. Eventually, she pulled away from him and said, "I'm okay."

It was not convincing and Peter didn't budge.

"I am," Ruth said. "Let me go. I need to hear all of it."

"Are you sure?"

Ruth squeezed Peter's hand. "I am."

Peter nodded and stood. He smoothed his clothes and then poured two mugs of tea. He added milk to Jones', the way he liked it, and placed a mug on the table next to Ruth before passing Jones his. Peter stood, collected the tray, and left the room without another word.

No one touched the tea.

"Get on with it." She knew that the story was nearing its end; that everything was nearing the end.

"Kevin showed up one day when no one was on-site working. He had been planning it for a while. He told Adam that he had drawn up some blueprints for the tree house and that he had them in his van."

"Did he have the plans?"

The question surprised Jones, and he had to think about what Kevin had told him when he was on his knees with a gun to his head. "I don't know."

"Adam hated it when people lied to him. He always saw the best in people, and it hurt him when they disappointed him." Ruth shook her head and looked out the window. "God, I sound so stupid."

"No, you don't," Jones said.

"What happened next?"

"Adam got into the back of the van with Kevin."

Ruth sniffed and Jones paused. She was staring at the window, but she sensed Jones looking at her. She nodded her head and Jones kept talking. "Adam said he wanted to get out. Kevin said no."

Ruth began to cry.

"Kevin said no, and then Adam began to yell for help."

"What did he say?"

Jones knew who Adam had called for in the small cramped space twenty feet from his front lawn, but he said, "I don't know."

Ruth nodded.

"Kevin was worried someone would hear Adam, so he covered his mouth. Adam panicked and they fought. Kevin—killed Adam."

Ruth shook her head and wiped her eyes. She looked at Jones and spoke through bared teeth. "Goddamn you. Do your job and tell me exactly what happened to my son."

"He strangled him in the back of his van," Jones said. "He strangled him and then he panicked. His first instinct was to drive away, but then he got scared that someone might have seen his van across from your place. He was terrified that he was going to get pulled over with Adam's body in the back of his van, so he drove home and put the van in his garage. Then he wrapped Adam's body in a plastic sheet and carried his body down to his cold cellar."

Ruth tilted her head and stared at Jones, trying to comprehend what he had just told her. "Cold cellar?"

Jones nodded. "He placed Adam's body against the far end and put up a brick wall so that no one would ever be able to find him."

Ruth was horrified. "Adam has been cold and alone in the dark for all these years?" She stood. "No. Not for a second more. Take me to him."

Jones stayed in his chair. "He isn't there, Ruth. Not anymore."

"What? You said that he bricked Adam inside the cold cellar." Ruth's eyes were wild with fear. "Where is he? Where is my son?"

"His body is at the morgue," Jones said. "The police found him."

"How—how can that be? The police never contacted me."

Jones shook his head. "They wouldn't have. They don't know that they found Adam."

"How could they not know? Why didn't you tell them?"

Jones struggled to hold Ruth's gaze. "I wasn't there when they found his body."

"You didn't stay with him? How could you not stay with him?" Ruth's face was equal parts rage and disgust. "How could you leave him there with that monster?"

"I didn't leave Adam there with him."

"But you said the police found his body in his basement."

"They found two bodies," Jones said.

31

"YOU KILLED HIM?" RUTH BIT HER CHEEK AND STARED AT JONES. TEARS welled in her eyes and she pushed them off her cheeks with her fingers in two swipes. "I want to know what happened. Everything."

"I had spent years going over police reports and articles in the newspaper—all of it went nowhere. So I started from the beginning and went looking for what the police and the papers missed. I found everyone interviewed by a cop, or a reporter, and I talked to them myself. That was how I eventually found out about the building inspector.

The Seattle Public Library
Central Library
www.spl.org

Checked Out On: 2/26/2022 13:03
XXXXXXXXX9496

Item Title	Due Date
0010101270592	3/19/2022
Running from the dead : a crime novel	
0010102096681	3/19/2022
The unspoken	
0010103515341	3/19/2022
The silenced women	

# of Items: 3

Renew items at www.spl.org/MyAccount
or 206-386-4190
Sign up for due date reminders
at www.spl.org/notifications

It was just something one of the contractors happened to mention. The guy who did the electrical in the pool house said he remembered the job well because the building inspector was such a fucking hard-ass. I hadn't come across any mention of a building inspector in the police records, so I followed up on it. On paper, Kevin McGregor was clean. There was nothing there that raised any alarms, not even a parking ticket. I wondered how many other people had missed this guy because he flew under everyone's radar. The first time I showed up, he wasn't home, so I talked to the neighbours. The people I met described Kevin McGregor as a quiet, pleasant man who kept to himself and did the occasional neighbourly favour. When I showed up the next day, McGregor wasn't there. I saw a couple kids playing street hockey and I brought up McGregor. They said he was quiet, but they didn't think he was pleasant and they sure as hell weren't interested in any of his favours. The kids stayed away from that house. It was an unwritten rule that everyone understood, even if they didn't exactly know how they all came to know it."

"They never told their parents about him?"

"I asked that. One kid told me that his parents said McGregor was harmless and only interested in them because he didn't have a family of his own."

"What happened to his family?"

"They moved away years ago. The divorce was quick and McGregor's ex-wife got full custody of their son. As far as I can tell, Kevin didn't fight her and in exchange she didn't come after him for alimony or child support."

"He had a son?"

"Brian McGregor was eight years old the last time he saw his father."

Ruth put a hand to her mouth. "Adam was eight."

"I tracked Brian down," Jones said. "I told him that I was a lawyer writing up a will for his father and I needed to send him some forms to sign. McGregor's son told me to never call him again and then he hung up."

"Did he—" Ruth didn't want to say the words.

"I don't know," Jones said.

Ruth wiped away a stream of tears with her thumb.

Jones sighed. "I had run out of ways to play it sly, so I broke in while McGregor was at work."

"And?"

"I found things." The memory turned his stomach and Jones swallowed hard. "He lived alone. There was no one to hide his true self from, and it made him lazy. There was probably more there, but I stopped searching. I couldn't look at it anymore." Jones shook his head. "I should have called the cops right there, but I couldn't."

"Why not?"

"I hadn't found Adam."

Ruth stared at Jones and waited for what was coming.

"I waited for him to come home. In that house, surrounded by everything that I had found and the things I was afraid to look for. I waited for hours for him to open the door."

"What happened?"

"He came home just after five. He walked in and took off his coat and boots. He didn't notice me sitting at the kitchen table when he walked into the kitchen with his lunch box. He was humming, "Walk Like an Egyptian," He put the lunch box under the sink just as he started doing the whistling part of the song when he turned and saw me. The whistle trailed off and he just stood there with his lips puckered."

"What did he say?"

"Nothing. I spoke first."

"What did you say to him?"

"I said *his* name."

"Adam?"

Jones nodded.

"And what did he do?"

"For a second he just stood there with his mouth like that while he tried to process the strange man sitting in his kitchen and the name no one had ever said to him. Then, panic set in and he started looking around frantically for cops he imagined were going to jump out and arrest him. When they didn't materialize and he realized it was just me, that confused him more. It took him a beat to get his head around the situation. He had two choices, fight or flight."

"What did he choose?"

"Flight. At least, that was what I thought it was at first. He ran for the hallway and I figured he was trying to get out the back door, but he passed the door and went into the bedroom. He was fast for an old guy and he got the door shut and locked behind him. I thought it was strange until I hit the door with my shoulder and it didn't give an inch. He had put in something custom and he had put a serious lock on the door. He wanted to make sure nothing could get in—or out."

"My God," Ruth said.

"I hit the door again and bounced right off it."

"What did you do?"

"I went through the wall," Jones said.

Ruth stared at him.

"He had fortified the door. He didn't do anything to the walls. I had thought he was going for a phone or maybe out a window." Jones shook his head. "He was going for a gun. I didn't know he had one. It wasn't registered and I hadn't found it because I stopped looking after I found—what I found. I should have known better."

Jones shook his head at the memory.

"The gun was in his nightstand. A small-calibre revolver that hadn't seen any love but would still do as it was told. Revolvers are good at that. He was faster with the gun than I was with the wall. He could have killed me; he probably considered it, but he needed answers. After all, I had said *his* name."

Ruth whispered. "Adam."

"The upper hand gave him a chance to show his teeth. I was bigger than what he was used to hunting, but the role came natural to him and he figured it out as he went along. The problem with a gun is you might have to use it. He realized that it would be too loud in the bedroom, so he took me down into the basement. The gun made him confident, but Adam's name made him desperate. He wanted to know how I found him and who else I had told about him. I told him what he wanted to know and waited for him to get sloppy. When I said that no one else knew about him, he believed me. I think it was easy to accept because he wanted so badly for it to be true. He thought he had gotten away with it again. The relief was euphoric, and right then, he started looking at me differently. I had been a threat at first, then I had been a puzzle that he had to solve. All of a sudden, I was something to be disposed of—but not right away. McGregor had ideas, a gun, and no one to stop him. He slipped into a familiar role. He was used to using people to get what he wanted. He knew what I was after, and so he asked what the story was worth. What would I do to find out what happened to Adam?"

"Jesus," Ruth said.

"McGregor told me that he would tell me where Adam died if I undid his pants."

Tears ran down a face as still as a statue. She closed her eyes tightly and inhaled sharply. When she was able to look at Jones again, she said, "Please, tell me the rest. I need to know."

"McGregor was feeling his way along, but he was finding his rhythm fast."

"He was talking about Adam and the first time they had met. At first, I thought he was taunting me, but then I realized he was enjoying himself. He was getting off on the memory."

Ruth closed her eyes again.

"He pointed the gun at my head and told me to get on my knees."

Ruth turned her head and began to cry again. When Jones paused to let her, she shook her head. "What did you do?"

"I did what he asked. He was used to making people scared, and he knew that scared people do as they're told. I wasn't scared, I was just waiting."

"For what?"

"For him to get close. When he did, I took the gun away from him, and after a few minutes of—persuading, he was ready to have a conversation. Now he was terrified, so he did as he was told and he told me everything. I thought I had been ready for it, but then he told me where he had buried Adam."

"Don't use that word," Ruth said. "That man didn't bury my son. He locked him away to rot. I will bury my son."

Jones nodded. "When he told me what he had done, I made him take down the wall with his bare hands."

This got Ruth's attention.

"It took him half an hour to get through. I don't know for sure, but I think he broke his shoulder trying."

"Good."

Jones nodded again. "McGregor had wrapped Adam in a plastic sheet and wound duct tape around his neck, waist, and ankles."

Ruth began to sob.

"I wouldn't let him touch Adam again," Jones felt his eyes well up. "The Adam inside my head, the one I had been chasing, died right there in that basement, when I reached into that hole and picked up your son." Tears soaked Jones' cheeks at the memory. "I knew everything about your son. I knew his favourite Blue Jay. I knew every scar on his body and how he got it. I knew the names of everyone in his class. I knew everything about him, but none of that made me ready for how he felt in my arms. I didn't expect him to feel so light. I stared down at him. This boy wrapped in a sheet. After everything I had learned about him, after all those years of searching for him—I wasn't ready for how he would feel in my arms."

"What happened next?"

"I made a mistake."

Ruth had rested her jaw on top of her laced fingers. The knuckles were white and her eyes were red. "What was your mistake?"

"I took my eyes off Adam, and I looked at McGregor. He saw me looking at him and he knew. He knew what

I was thinking. He started to cry and then he began to beg. First to me, then God." Jones, still mystified at what he had heard, shook his head. "That basement was closer to hell than it was to heaven. He should have known that God wasn't listening, not in that place. I pulled the trigger until the gun was empty."

"And then you left my son in that basement. In a place that was closer to hell than to heaven."

32

"HEARING THE SHOTS SOBERED ME UP. I KNEW A LOUD BANG THAT SOUNDED
like a gunshot could have been written off for one reason
or another by anyone who had heard, but not six. I
couldn't stay there."

Jones felt Ruth's anger on his face like a sunburn. "You
should have come straight to me," she said.

"I couldn't. I was too hot. I went into the city and found
a place where I could be invisible until things died down."

"And when things did die down—" Ruth's lips curled
as though the phrase left a bad taste in her mouth, "you

called. You called my home and told Peter you *needed* to speak with me. You said you *needed* me, but when I called, you didn't pick up. Why, Samuel?"

"It's complicated," Jones said.

Ruth clicked her tongue. "It is anything but. You should have talked to me."

"I was trying to find a way to work things out."

"By keeping me in the dark and my son in the morgue. Don't lie to me. All of this was about saving your own skin."

Jones shook his head. "No, I climbed those basement steps knowing there was no way I was walking away from this. I just thought I had more time before it all fell apart. At first, I told myself that I was giving you a little more time to live with the hope of seeing Adam again before I had to snuff it out. I thought it was a mercy to live a little longer with the idea that your son was alive after burying your mother. But I was lying to myself. Part of me, a bigger part than I had ever realized, had thought I could bring him home. Finding him there. Finding out that I had been too late, that I never could have saved him from that man, hurt me. I had failed Adam. I wasn't ready to fail you too."

Jones and Ruth stared at each other until their tears got in the way; then, they cried together about some of the same things.

"I'm sorry." Jones dragged his sleeve across his face. "I used the cops as an excuse. I used your mother as an excuse. I used Lauren as an excuse."

"Who is Lauren?"

Jones thought about the kid who had run from a home hundreds of kilometres away and wound up confessing to bathroom walls. "A kid I thought I could help. At first, she was a distraction. Then she became something else."

"What?"

"Someone told me that hope is the worst kind of torture because hope goes on forever and it won't let you die."

Something in Ruth's eyes told Jones that she understood exactly what Norah had been saying.

"Do you know what I told her?"

Jones saw the awful truth that Ruth had learned minutes ago roll across her face. "There's something worse than hope," Ruth said.

"Knowing," Jones said. "Knowing is worse than hope. I learned that when I found Adam. When the hope I was carrying was taken from me." Jones sniffed and ran his knuckles across his face. "The girl, Lauren, gave me some of it back. The idea that I could save her—I—I needed that. I chased it. Away from you. Away from the cops. Away from Adam and what I knew." Jones shook his head. "It was stupid."

"And did you save her?" Ruth couldn't hide the emotion in her voice.

"Some people don't want to be saved," Jones said. "Not until they're ready."

"No. I don't believe that," Ruth said. "Tell me about her."

"Ruth—"

"Shut up. Just shut up," she snapped. "After what you did, you owe me. I want to know about the girl."

Jones opened his mouth to speak and Ruth cut him off with a raised palm. "Wait." She raised her voice and Jones heard it crack a little. "Peter, bring me a real drink, and don't argue with me about it. I don't care what time it is." She looked back at Jones and said, "Tell me."

Jones told her about the girl who had left the note in eyeliner on the back of a bathroom door. He told her about Norah and finally talking to Lauren. He even told her about Irene and William. Ruth didn't interrupt him again. She listened and she drank. The rum softened her face and weakened her defences. While Jones spoke of a young girl determined to run away, Ruth began to cry. Her sobs began as strained jerks that slowly birthed sounds that eventually became wails. Jones sat quietly until Ruth was able to quell her misery with the help of more rum. Thirty minutes later, Ruth knew everything.

Jones pointed to the glass. "I could use a drink."

Ruth lifted the glass and drained what was left in one gulp. "No."

Jones understood. He had no right to ask her for anything. He had taken too much from her. He stood and felt his back complain after sitting for so long in the uncompromising chair.

"You have too much to do."

Jones forgot about his back. "What?"

"You don't have time to be drinking." Ruth's heavy tongue had trouble with the suffix on the last word. She either didn't know her speech was slurred or didn't care because she filled her glass again. "I won't let my son's bones spend another night in a morgue. He will not be away from me for another minute." Ruth had more of the drink. "That should give you a day, or two at best."

"To do what?"

"To find Lauren. When that detective finds out that I have taken my son home, he is going to have some questions for me. I won't make it easy for him to find me, but he will get to me eventually. If the detective has half a brain, and I hear many of them do, it won't take him long to learn that you have been working for me for quite some time. When he learns that last piece of the puzzle, he will come after you with everything he has." Ruth drank again. "So, that gives you a day, maybe two. That's not much, but it's something. Enough to give you a chance to do for her what you couldn't do for my son."

Ruth put down her glass and got to her feet. Jones followed. She took an unsteady step forward and used two fistfuls of Jones' shirt to steady herself. "Find her. Find her and bring her home."

Jones wrapped his hands around the fists holding onto him. Ruth lowered her head to his chest and Jones held her close while she cried. Minutes passed, then Ruth shook her head and broke away from the embrace. "Go."

Jones turned his back on Ruth and started down the hallway to the door. Behind him, he heard Ruth calling to Peter.

"Peter, bring the car around. We are going to bring Adam home."

33

JONES DIDN'T HAVE TO WAIT LONG FOR HIS COFFEE. SHEENA SAW HIM COME in and immediately started working faster to dispatch with everyone who was already in line. When Jones stepped to the register, Sheena passed a hastily made macchiato to a woman who clearly took her caffeine seriously. The customer shifted on expensive suede heels and made a face that telegraphed the complaint that was on its way. Sheena didn't notice the face; she was already turning to look at Jones. "Where the hell have you been?"

"Jail."

Sheena stared at Jones for a second and then she scrunched her nose and turtled her neck. "You look like shit. What the hell happened to you?"

"An eighty-year-old man beat me up," Jones said.

Sheena rolled her eyes. "Fine, don't tell me."

Jones looked to his left. Suede heels hadn't budged. She pushed the cup back toward Sheena. "This isn't what I ordered."

Sheena made no effort to muffle her sigh.

"I asked for—"

"I remember." Sheena picked up the cup and gave it to Jones. "Drink this."

"That's not what I want."

Sheena spoke over the grinder. "Shut up. She gets to say that, not you."

Suede heels clearly had an opinion about Jones and Sheena. He guessed it started with a hypothesis about their ages and then some quick math to confirm she had the right level of disgust. The jail comment probably didn't help.

Sheena spoke over her shoulder while she worked. "You're not drinking. I want to hear this story, and you need to be awake to talk."

Suede heels made a noise that was meant to be heard; Jones ignored her and took a sip of the macchiato. The espresso was strong in his nose and bitter on his tongue. Jones felt it burn on the way down and he smiled through the pain as he felt the fog of exhaustion immediately start to thin.

Sheena gave suede heels a drink that closely resembled what Jones had in his hands, and for a moment he wondered if Sheena was messing with her. Suede heels glanced at the cup and found nothing to complain about this time. Sheena hadn't waited around for a review; she stepped back to the machines behind the counter and returned with a cortado for Jones.

"Alright," she said. "Go."

"She called me."

Sheena grabbed Jones' shoulder and squeezed it harder than he thought she would have been able to. "Shut up."

Jones noticed a veiny forearm exposed by her t-shirt and resisted the urge to rub his shoulder. "She saw the posters I put up."

"Holy shit! I did not think thought that would work."

"Really?"

"I think I just expected more from a real-life private investigator than lost cat posters." Sheena grinned excitedly at Jones. "So?"

Jones shook his head.

Sheena's smile fell away. "Is it bad?"

Jones nodded.

"How bad?"

"Kid runs away from a small town to the big city with dreams of making it as a singer."

"I know that story," Sheena said.

"Then you know how it ends."

"Some of them make it."

"Most don't," Jones said.

"Most go back home."

"Lauren didn't."

"So what are you going to do?"

Jones drank the rest of his macchiato and gave Sheena the empty cup. "I'm going to go after her."

That made Sheena smile. "Good."

"I need to find her fast."

"She in trouble?"

"Other way around," Jones said.

Sheena smiled wider. Her teeth were straight and white. "Cops hot on your tail?"

Jones didn't smile. "They should have a murder charge ready by tomorrow morning."

"Jesus, I was kidding. I thought you were one of the good guys."

"No such thing."

Sheena wrinkled her nose while she considered what Jones had said. Eventually, she shook her head. "I don't buy that. You're a good guy, Jones." The sound of the door opening caught her attention and drew her eyes away for a second. She smiled at the man walking toward her to let him know that she saw him, but she stayed with Jones. "What do you need from me?"

"More coffee and your WiFi."

"Done."

34

SHEENA BROUGHT A SECOND CORTADO TO JONES WHEN THE LINE HAD
fizzled. "Any luck?"

"Not yet."

"Can I help?"

Jones finished looking at a page before he said, "No."

"What are you doing?"

"Lauren said that she gets dates through the internet,
so I'm searching for escorts online."

"Gross."

"You have no idea."

Sheena took the seat next to Jones and adjusted his phone so that she could see the screen too. "Gro-oss." She emphasized the word, but it still did not do justice to what she was looking at.

"This site is the most popular for escorts, so I'm starting here."

"How are you going to find her on this thing? None of the girls show their face."

There seemed to be a standard profile of a neck down shot of a woman in lingerie. Nine times out of ten the shot was either a selfie in a bathroom or a selfie on the bed.

"It looks like the posts are put up daily. Men and women put up a short ad with details about who they are, what they are in to, and when they are available that day. Anyone who is interested can call or message to arrange a time and place to meet up. The site archives old posts, and that lets me see the previous listings. Lauren called three times and each of those times she had been working that day. I'm looking for women who put up ads on each of those days. From there, I can check the descriptions for things that match what I know about Lauren."

Sheena stared at Jones for a few seconds and then the eye roll that had been waiting in the wings was exchanged with a smile. "That's actually not a terrible idea."

"Only if it works," Jones said.

Ten minutes later, Jones decided the site was a bust. None of the posts looked like they were from Lauren. Jones did a bit of research and found a newspaper article from earlier in the year about the escort industry in the digital age. The article mentioned the site that Jones had been on, along with three others. Jones was on his fourth site when Sheena brought him his third cup of coffee. Jones had applied the same logic and narrowed the field down to four posts. Each was a from a teenage girl looking to party with older men. Jones clicked the first link and discounted it because the girl was from Russia. The next link gave no personal details about the girl other than her age and her name. Jones clicked the link and saw that Chanel's first picture was a profile shot of her body in a full-length mirror. She was far too tall to be Lauren. Jones found the next post with the right dates and saw similar bra and panty shots of a girl who was shorter than Chanel. Jones read her post, and then read it again.

> 5'4" – 105 lbs – 34 B. 19-year-old student looking to have fun w an older man who knows how to treat his baby girl right. I'm open to trying new things if you are open to teaching me. Hotel hookups only. Appointments only. Texts only.

Jones read the post three times and then started going over the pictures. Like all the other pictures, the photographer had been careful to keep the girl's head out of the frame, so Jones enlarged each image as best he could and checked each shot for any reflections that may have made their way in. When he came up with nothing, he moved on to the obvious. The height matched the information Norah had given him in her reply email, but the weight was less—a lot less. The skin tone was similar and Jones checked the pictures for any scars or birthmarks. Norah had said that Lauren didn't have any—the girl in the post didn't either. A sound pulled Jones' attention away from his phone. A couple stood looking over his shoulder at his screen. Jones recognized them as the people who had been sitting behind him. They had noticed Jones' phone when they stood to put their coats on and what they had seen had rooted them in place. The woman, her coat only half on, had made the noise, and it was clear from the look on her face that it was meant to be an opening salvo. Jones put the phone face down on the table and looked first at the woman and then at her companion. The woman was dressed in a white t-shirt and distressed jeans. The purse on her arm was expensive and Jones had no doubt it was real. The man to her right was wearing skinny jeans and the kind of sneakers people stood in line for. His V-neck t-shirt was deep enough to almost show nipple. The clothing would have looked more at home on people in their twenties. The couple were at least twice that and it made the clothes seem a little silly.

Jones waited for the pair to leave, but it quickly became apparent that they were waiting for something to happen.

The purse shook as the arm it hung off jabbed the man's ribs. The woman, making no effort to hide her disgust, said, "Chris." There were expectations in the word.

When Jones opened his mouth to speak, he felt an ache radiate from his jaw and realized that he had been clenching his teeth while he went through the profiles. Jones was angry, and the couple gave him something to aim it at. He was surprised by his rage and barely able to stifle the urge to get out of his seat. It required effort to keep his voice level, but he managed.

"Walk away, before you can't."

He didn't bother to look to see if the two people took his advice. Jones turned his back on them and felt his molars find each other as his hand picked up the phone again.

"Boy, you pervs are jumpy." Jones lifted his eyes just as Sheena slid into the seat opposite him.

"I think I got something," he said.

She held out her hand and said, "Gimmie."

Jones handed over the phone and Sheena looked at the page that Jones thought was Lauren's and lingered on the message. When she looked back at Jones, her nostrils flared as though she were venting steam. "What makes you think it's her?"

"The dates match, so do the age and race."

"That it?"

"There's something else," Jones said. "Lauren mentioned that her boyfriend calls her his baby girl."

Sheena's nostrils flared again, and she looked at the phone another time. "That's in the ad."

Jones nodded. "It is. I think it's her."

"So what are you going to do?"

"See if I can get a date," Jones said.

35

INTERESTED IN A DATE, BABY GIRL?

Sheena reached across the table and turned the screen so that she could see it. Her nostrils flared again and she said, "Gross." She pushed the phone closer to Jones and sat back in her chair. "So what now?"

Jones looked at his watch. "Wait."

"Do you think she'll answer?"

"I don't think she decides. I heard her interact with Tony a little. He's the one in charge. The number probably goes to a prepaid cell that he bought."

"Tony?"

"Her *boyfriend*."

Sheena's tongue drifted over her teeth. "Ugh, boy-friend. He's her pimp."

"Not how she sees it," Jones said.

"Fuck Tony," Sheena said.

Jones nodded. "Fuck Tony."

"What are you going to do if he responds? You going to show up and take her?"

"It crossed my mind."

"What if she doesn't want to go?"

"That crossed my mind too."

"Do you have a plan for that?"

"Yeah."

"Care to elaborate?"

"No."

Sheena put her elbows on the table and leaned in. "Need help?"

Jones looked at Sheena. She might have been a hundred pounds, but her shoulders were wide and there were veins visible anywhere skin was exposed. There was something hard in Sheena's eyes, and Jones didn't doubt she could provide the kind of help she was offering. "Not yet, but maybe later."

Sheena took Jones' phone and keyed in her number.

"Whatever it is. I'm in."

"Can I get a sandwich?" Jones said.

"Not what I meant."

"I know."

Sheena stared at Jones until she was satisfied that he did, and then she got up from the table to get him some food.

Jones set his phone face down on the table and didn't pick it up again. When he got bored of people-watching, Jones got up to bring his empty mug to Sheena. The end of the workday brought a stream of people in, and Jones had to go to the end of the counter to find a place to leave his cup. The toe of his boot knocked against the crate of donated books, and Jones saw that *Darker than Amber* was exactly where he had left it. Jones picked up the book and waited with Travis McGee.

Sheena finished her shift and then occupied the table with Jones for a while. She kept stealing glances at the phone while they talked, as though she thought she had heard it ring. Eventually, she gave up on waiting and told Jones to call her if Lauren reached out. Jones said he would.

"You're lying."

Jones said he was.

She gave him the finger and punched him in the arm before she walked away.

The phone buzzed an hour later.

I'd love to see you. I've been so lonely. Tonight?

Jones turned the book over to save his page and texted back.

Definitely. Send me the details, baby girl.

Jones barely got through the next page before the reply moved his phone. He was exhausted and the message was blurry. Jones rubbed his eyes with his thumb and index finger and then blinked hard until the message was clear.

500 for the hour and ANYTHING you want.

Jones typed a response that contained none of his revulsion.

Sounds like we have a date. Where and when?

Jones got an answer within seconds.

Camelot Motel. Room 203. 10 p.m.

A quick Google search placed the motel just off the highway in Brampton, a suburb of Toronto.

Perfect. See you at ten.

A pair of red lips came back before he put the phone down. Jones got to his feet and put on his jacket. He had a few hours and he hoped they would be enough. Before he walked out of Brew, he put the book back in the crate, making sure to leave it at the top of the pile where it rightfully belonged.

Jones slid behind the wheel and drove to the Eaton Centre. Inside the mall, he bought new clothes and took money out of an ATM. Jones left the mall in what he bought and tossed the soiled things he had been wearing into the back of the Jeep.

Jones rummaged through the glovebox for a charging cable and plugged it in to a USB port in the dash while he made a call. Jones had done more than read while he waited for Lauren to text him back. He spent some time considering the other ads he had read and how the hook-ups seemed to work. If Lauren operated in a similar fashion, and there was no reason to think she wouldn't, Jones would need help. He was planning to separate *the girl* from her pimp without her knowledge, or consent. There was a high probability of violence and a low probability of success. He knew people who had left the army with a set of skills that weren't exactly transferrable and an itch for excitement that pick up hockey couldn't scratch. Jones had a few friends who were always up for danger pay, but none of them were close enough to sign on for this particular job. Jones went over his plan again and tried to work out a way he could make it work on his own. He gave up on the idea almost immediately. He needed help.

Jones opened Safari on his phone and found the website he was looking for after a quick Google search. He tapped contact information and touched the phone number. A receptionist answered on the second ring.

"Could you connect me with William Greene's room please?"

The receptionist was more cheerful than Jones had expected. "Sure thing. Please hold."

"Yeah?" Willy took so long to pick up the phone that Jones heard his voice from his lap as he was moving his thumb to end the call.

"You still looking for a little excitement?"

It took the old stick-up man less than a second to place Jones' voice. "You're calling me already? You must be worse at this than I thought, or in deeper trouble."

"I need to steal something and I don't know a lot of people in that line of work."

"Technically, I'm retired, but some skills you never really lose. What is it we are stealing exactly?"

"Not what," Jones said. "Who."

"The girl?"

"Yeah."

"I'm in."

"Just like that? You don't even know what I want you to do."

"Is it more exciting than sitting in this tiny room?"

Jones thought about it. "It's definitely more dangerous than sitting in your room."

"Even better. You know what you're doin'?"

"If we play it right, they won't find out what we did until after we're gone."

Jones heard William sigh. "I robbed thirty-seven banks, kid."

Jones whistled. "You told me."

"Do you know how many of those jobs I was able to do *just right*?"

"I know one of them didn't work out like you planned."

"Wrong. None of them worked out like I planned. Not a damn one, kid. I'm not saying this to talk you out of things, but you need to understand that in this type of work, things never go the way you think they will. You're dealing with people, and people always find a way fuck up your plans."

Jones glanced at his forearm. "I get that."

Willy grunted as though he understood what Jones meant. "Maybe you do."

"Can you be ready in half an hour?"

"I'll meet you out front."

36

SHEENA LAUGHED WHEN SHE HEARD HIS VOICE. "YOU'RE SMARTER THAN YOU look. I thought it would be at least another hour before you gave in and called me."

"I wasn't going to call."

"Oh, I know you didn't want to, but I also know you were full of shit when you said you had a plan if Lauren decides that she doesn't want to leave with you."

"Sheena—"

"Is this the part where you tell me it's going to be dangerous?"

"It is," Jones said.

"Next you'll tell me that I need to stay in the car."

"You will need to stay in the car."

"Let me stop you right there, righty. I'm not some damsel in distress who needs a big strong man to keep her safe. I can look out for myself just fine. Lauren needs help, not someone waiting in the car."

"I need you in the car."

"You don't listen, do you? I am not going to wait in the car like some fucking cab driver."

"I don't need a cab driver," Jones said. "I need a wheelman."

"I can't tell if you are being offensive or progressive."

"I need you to be our getaway driver, and if the need arises I need you to be plan B."

Sheena thought about it. "I've never done anything like that before."

"You ever drive a car?"

"Sure."

"You ever get a speeding ticket?"

"Tons of them."

"Then you're qualified. You in?"

"I'm in."

"I'll pick you up in an hour."

"I'll be ready."

"Sheena?"

"Yeah?"

"Righty?"

She laughed. "Too much?"

When Jones pulled up to Pacific Heights, Willy was already standing in front of the building in a pair of charcoal pants and a black jacket. The pants were a slim fit that looked good on the old man, and Jones decided that Irene must have picked them out for him. Willy nodded when he saw the Jeep and opened the door before Jones had even pulled to a stop.

"Drive," Willy said as he slid into the seat.

Jones checked his mirrors as he hit the gas. "Something wrong? I thought you were allowed to come and go as you please here."

Willy laughed. "I am. I just *borrowed* a few things before I left."

Jones glanced over at Willy, and the old man lifted his shirt high enough to show a gun in the waistband of his pants.

"What the hell is that?"

Willy smiled. "This is just in case things don't go as you planned."

"Where did you get that?"

"One of my poker buddies bragged that he had snuck his gun into his room when he moved in. I think he was trying to impress me because he knew that I had spent some time inside. After you called, I came up with a bull-shit reason to go knock on his door, and I lifted it when he wasn't looking. I must be getting old because he was on to me before I got on the elevator." Willy laughed. "You should have seen him running down the hall after me."

Jones gave the old man a look.

"What? It's not like he can tell anyone I stole the gun he had smuggled in. It's a victimless crime."

"Not for the victim," Jones said. "For you, either, if he kicks your ass."

"Let him try. If I could kick *your* ass, what chance does an eighty-year-old man with a cane have?"

"You didn't kick my ass."

"Sure, kid. Sure."

"You didn't."

"That nose says different."

Rush hour was long gone, but no one had let any of the other drivers on the road in on the news. Jones forced his way into the next lane and turned west onto Gerrard Street while Willy played with the radio. When he found a Bob Seger song he liked, he said, "You got a plan, or are we just going to wing it?"

Jones changed lanes and fished his phone out of his pocket. He used his thumb to unlock the phone and handed it to Willy.

"What am I supposed to do with this?"

"That's a street view of the motel we're going to."

Willy craned his neck back and began moving the phone back and forth in an effort to see it without his glasses.

"Put two fingers on the screen at the same time and move them apart."

Willy looked at Jones to see if he was kidding and then tried it out. He smiled when the image enlarged.

"Now look around back."

Willy flipped the phone over.

"What are you—no, use your finger to move the image so that you can see the back of the building."

"These weren't a thing when I went away. My apologies for not knowing what to do with your stupid phone."

"Do you see it?"

"No."

"You'll figure it out."

Jones drove while Willy caught up with the rest of the world. He remembered a story about an experiment where scientists had dropped tablets into an Ethiopian village. Within a few minutes, they turned it on. In a few days, they were using close to fifty apps. In under six months, they figured out how to hack the tablet. Willy should be able to figure out how to use a map before they got to the motel.

A minute later, Jones smiled when he heard Willy let out of a small squeal of delight after he discovered how to see the other side of the building.

"There is a service road running behind the motel."

"Already there," Willy said.

"The room is around back on the second floor."

Willy leaned in closer to the phone.

"Two fingers," Jones said.

Willy sighed. "I swear I will never get used to this shit." Thirty seconds later, he said, "I got it. No balcony, but there is a window."

"That's our way out."

"Your way out is a two-storey drop. Maybe you're interested in taking a swan dive out a window, but I don't think you're going to convince the kid to follow you. For that to work, we'd need a ladder or something."

Jones gestured up the road with his chin. Willy leaned forward and scanned what was ahead. It only took him a second to spot the orange Home Depot sign.

"You must think you're pretty fucking smart."

Inside the hardware store, Jones picked out an expensive ladder that folded up small enough to fit in the trunk with room to spare. It was something that he had seen on a late-night TV commercial. The guy from the ad was pictured on the box, standing on the ladder two storeys up with a shit-eating grin on his face. Jones wished he had the man's confidence. He put the box in the cart and went in search of a few more items that were harder to find than the ladder had been. Jones found a folding knife with a four-inch blade next to the boxcutter he had initially been looking for and put it in the cart. He found a glass cutter without having to ask for help and the suction cups he needed were right next to it.

Willy took them from Jones and inspected them. He shook his head and dropped them into the cart. "A little James Bond, don't you think?"

"James Bond always gets the girl." When he saw Willy roll his eyes, Jones said, "If Tony stands outside the door, we might have to be quiet about the window." Jones could see that his answer didn't satisfy the old man, but he didn't complain about it.

Jones paid for everything in cash and stowed the ladder in the back of the Jeep. He took the rest of it to the front seat and pulled off the packaging. Jones put everything into the inner pockets of his coat and then pulled out of the lot.

Willy craned his neck to get a look at the street signs when they entered Chinatown. "You're going the wrong way."

"We need to make one more stop."

"What else do you need to pick up, double-oh seven? Is it a watch with a laser in it? Because, that would go great with your glass cutter."

"Not what," Jones said. "Who."

"Who are we picking up?"

"Our driver."

"We have a wheelman?"

Jones glanced over at Willy. "Do me a favour. Say getaway driver instead."

"Why?"

"Trust me."

Jones pulled to the curb in a no-parking zone and watched Sheena walk to the car in the side mirror. She wore black boots with black jeans and a black leather jacket. The outfit looked like it belonged on the Ramones who named her. She got in the back seat and looked at Jones and Willy.

"You're late."

Jones said sorry to the reflection in the rear-view and pulled back onto the road. He glanced at the mirror again and saw Sheena looking at Willy.

"Holy shit, is this the guy that broke your nose?"

Jones said, "It's not broken," and Willy said, "Yes," at the exact same time.

Sheena laughed and Willy joined in. The bank robber turned down the music before turning to get a better look at Sheena.

"What's your name, kid?"

Sheena said her name as though she was daring Willy to say something.

"Nice to meet you, Sheena. My name is Willy Greene. I hear you're our getaway driver."

"I heard the same thing."

"You ever done anything like that before?"

"Nope. Most people usually try and get away from me."

Willy barked out a laugh and punched Jones on the shoulder. "I like her." The convict leaned into the gap between the seats and put a little sugar in his voice. "You'll do fine, and if you don't feel comfortable behind the wheel, you can switch places with me on the ladder."

Jones glanced at the mirror and saw Sheena smile. "Thanks. Wait, what?" she said.

Willy glanced at Jones. "He didn't tell you about the ladder. Well, it seems our damsel in distress is in a tower of sorts. Like that story. The one who had to let down her hair."

"Rapunzel," Sheena said.

"Bingo," Willy said. "Except there's no evil witch in this story."

"There's all kinds of evil out there," Sheena said.

Willy turned around and eased back into his seat. "On that, we can agree, kid."

"So tell me more about this ladder," Sheena said.

"After we eat," Jones said.

"Now?"

"Eat when you can," Jones said.

They got burgers and ate them in the parking lot, using the hood of the Jeep as a table. While they ate, Jones laid out the plan and Willy did his best to poke holes in it.

"You're overthinking this whole thing. We should just walk up to her pimp, put a gun in his face, and make him turn over the girl."

Jones finished chewing and shook his head. "We don't know how Lauren will react to something like that. She has feelings for Tony."

Willy rolled his eyes. "He's a pimp."

"Not to her," Sheena said. "She calls him her boy-friend."

"You gotta be kidding me."

"I need you to be my second-storey man, not a stick-up man," Jones said.

"I can be both."

Jones sighed. "Listen, I got enough to worry about in front of me. I don't have time to worry about my back. If you aren't down with the plan, I'll call you an Uber and you can finish your burger and go home."

"What's an Uber?"

Sheena laughed.

"In or out?"

Willy ate a fry and grunted, "I'm in."

They ate in silence for a few minutes. It was Willy who broke it first. "You got a plan if things go south?"

Jones jutted his chin toward Sheena. "We let Sheena take the lead."

Willy shook his head. "That's if she doesn't want to leave with us. I'm talking south." The bank robber mimed a plane crashing with his hand and supplied a long shrill whistle as a soundtrack. "That kind of south."

"If the plan goes off the rails, just follow my lead."

"With my gun?"

Sheena stopped chewing and stared at Jones.

"With your gun," he said.

Willy smiled. "Finally, we agree on something. Now, one of you tell me what an Uber is."

37

THE CAMELOT WAS A TWO-STOREY RED-BRICK BUILDING SHAPED LIKE A stunted capital L. The base of the L housed the manager's office while the longer portion was devoted to a long row of rooms—twenty-four in total. Jones had pulled into the gas station up the road to scout the motel and parked in the shadow of the tall Esso sign. The sign threw off just enough light to give the darkness a murky yellow tinge that made everything ugly.

Willy jutted his chin toward the motel. "Slow night."

Jones had been thinking the same thing. Most of the

lot was empty. He pointed to the farthest corner of the building where the light from the gas station was most diluted. "I'll park the Jeep by the office."

Willy thought about it. "Makes sense. No one will be able to see it from the rooms."

There were six cars parked close to the rooms and a seventh a row back. A BMW was parked across three spaces with the windows down and the stereo up. Jones could hear hip hop playing at the kind of volume and bass only a custom stereo could generate.

"I'm guessing that's our guy," Sheena said.

Willy took his eyes off the motel and looked over the car. A few seconds later, Jones saw Willy's head move as he started inspecting each of the other vehicles. Jones had already scanned the cars and knew them to be empty.

A heavy plume of smoke drifted out the driver side window. The cloud was too big to be from a cigarette.

"Of course he vapes," Sheena said.

A few seconds later, a twin cloud billowed from the passenger side.

"You see that?" Willy had finished looking at each of the cars.

Jones nodded. "Two of them."

"Maybe it's her," Sheena said.

"I doubt it. I figure the girl is in that room right there." Willy jabbed his index finger at the building. "It's the only one on the second floor with any lights on."

"I see it," Jones said. "Let's see who's right."

Jones pulled out of the gas station and drove down the street at a speed that told people he wasn't from the neighbourhood. He signalled way in advance of the parking lot entrance and drove around toward the manager's office. Jones reversed into the spot and killed the engine.

Jones reached up and turned on the dome light above the dash. "Give me ten minutes before you move." Sheena nodded; Willy didn't. Jones looked at the bank robber. "Not eight. Not nine and three quarters. Ten."

Willy reluctantly agreed without taking his eyes off the motel office window. "Sure, sure. Whatever you say, boss."

Jones lifted his phone and typed two words.

I'm here.

Jones got a reply within seconds.

C U soon daddy.

Jones reached up and turned off the interior light. He looked at Willy and said, "Keep your head down."

Jones looked at Sheena in the rear-view and said, "You ready?"

Sheena inhaled sharply through her nose and said, "Let's go."

Willy bent forward as Jones counted down from three. At one, he and Sheena opened their doors and got out of the Jeep. Sheena quietly shut her door and stepped past Jones so that she could climb into the driver's seat. Jones quietly said, "Ten minutes," and then closed the door.

Jones felt the cold night air frisk him with cold fingers that found their way into his coat and under his clothes; he felt the folding knife weighing down his pocket and hoped Tony didn't do as thorough a job. He walked toward the stairs without looking at the BMW that was still radiating bass. He was sure that his last message was relayed to the men in the car and that they would be watching him.

When Jones got within ten metres of the stairs, he suddenly stopped feeling the music in his chest. He glanced back at the BMW and the doors opened and two men got out. The driver was shorter than Jones and his body was thick from workouts that were heavy on the weights and light on the cardio. The driver's squat size was a direct contrast to the other man's long lean body. He was well over six and a half feet tall, and he moved with a fighter's grace that Jones could read as well as words on a page. The man's height and dark sunglasses made Jones immediately think of Kareem Abdul-Jabbar, not the Laker on the court, but the gangster in the Bruce Lee movie *Game of Death*.

Jones thought about using the stairs to reduce the chance of being swarmed, but he stayed where he was. He was supposed to be a john, not a threat.

The big man was in no rush, but his long strides put him in front of Jones before his partner was halfway there. He stood looking at Jones and slowly shifted his weight back and forth as though he was dancing to the music that had been playing on the car stereo. Jones looked up at his reflection in the man's sunglasses and put the proper amount of intimidation into his voice. "Can I help you?"

The tall man said nothing.

"He don't talk," Tony said when he finally caught up. Despite the cool night air, Tony was sweaty, and he kept his hand on his side as though the walk from the car had given him a cramp. Up close, Jones put Tony in his early twenties—too young to be that out of shape. Jones wondered if the vaping was to blame. "He can. I heard him scream once when he broke his collarbone. It was funny. His voice wasn't as deep as you'd think it would be."

The big man looked at Tony.

"What? It isn't."

He kept staring.

"Tell me I'm wrong."

When the big man said nothing, Tony smiled at Jones. "See what I did there?" Tony looked Jones over, and his eyes went wide when he saw his arm. "Holy shit, Marvin check it out. This dude only has one hand."

Jones saw the big man glance at his arm.

"Did it get cut off or something?"

Jones crossed his arms as though he was embarrassed. "I was born this way."

"That sucks," Tony said.

"I'm sorry, do you work here?"

The question made Tony smile and Jones saw that his two front teeth were stained yellow. It was probably one of the reasons he switched to vaping. "Sort of. We manage the business upstairs."

Jones pretended to think about it and then said, "Oh."

Tony smiled. "Yeah, we're in the O business. What room is she in?"

The question surprised Jones. He hadn't expected there to be more than one girl. He glanced over his shoulder at the second floor and saw the single room lit up. Maybe another room had looked like that before another kid like Lauren turned off the lights.

"You don't know?"

The tone brought Jones' eyes back to Tony. "Sorry. It's two oh three."

Tony brought his vape pen out of his pocket and took a long drag. He spoke through the dense plume. "Money up front."

Jones had expected this and he had already decided how to play it. He took a step back and hardened his voice just a little. "I don't think so."

Tony invaded Jones' personal space and shoved him. "You don't think so? Listen, you booked time with one of my girls and that means you owe me money. If you want to cancel, that's okay, but there's a fee."

"How much?"

"Four hundred."

"On the phone she said it was five. Is this a different girl?" The words came out fast. His panic was real.

"Tonight is your lucky night," Tony said. "There's a discount. Think of it like a garage sale."

"I don't understand."

Tony stepped closer and Jones could smell the artificial fruit on his breath from the vape pen. "It's cheaper 'cause it's used junk." Then, he smiled. "Relax, it's a good deal. It's not like there's anything wrong with her pussy."

Jones knew there was no point in arguing, but he made a show of being upset about the situation. Eventually, he pulled the money from his pocket and used his thumb and index finger to lift off five twenties.

Tony watched Jones slip the hundred dollars into his pocket and looked at Marvin. "You see how he does that? That is funny."

Jones held out what was left in the wad and Tony took it.

When Tony finished counting it, he looked at Jones. "You got an hour. You go over and it'll cost you another hour. Do you have the money for that?"

Jones shook his head.

"Then you better be on time."

Jones nodded and Tony started back toward the car. Marvin stared at Jones for a few seconds longer and then he followed the pimp.

Jones went up the stairs slower than he wanted to and forced himself to walk down the concrete landing to room 203. Jones passed the first two rooms and noticed that the curtains on the second were a warmer shade of red than the first; there was someone inside. Jones walked past room 203 as though he had missed it and checked the curtains on 204; the room was dark like the first had been. Jones made a show of craning his neck to look at the door he had just passed before shaking his head for the audience of two below and walking back to 203. The motel room door had once been the colour of a candy apple, but over the years the red paint had been chipped and scuffed so many times that the door now resembled a raw wound. Jones knocked twice and stepped back so that he could be seen in the peep hole.

Almost a minute went by before Jones heard the loose doorknob grind as it turned. The face that greeted Jones had the dimensions of a catcher's mitt. Her cheeks were swollen and her lips split. Jones took a small step closer and examined the girl. He wasn't sure if it was Lauren; her features were too distorted.

"Hey, Daddy."

The sound of her voice forced the breath from his lungs. It was her. "Hey."

She tried to smile and Jones felt his throat catch. Someone had hit her hard enough to break bones in her face. He had to clear his throat before he spoke so that she wouldn't hear the revulsion in his voice. The girl in the photograph had been broken inside and out, and there was nothing left that wasn't bent out of shape.

"Can I come in?"

She nodded and tried to look coy. "Sure." The words were slurred, but not from the beating. The men outside had beaten her and then doped her up until she couldn't feel anything at all. She backed up just a little, and Jones did his best to slide past her without making contact with her body.

Lauren leaned against the door in an attempt to close it with her back. She was unsteady on her feet and misjudged the distance; her arms went rigid when she realized she was falling backward and she was unprepared for the door when she hit it. Her head struck the wood with a loud thump.

Jones stepped forward and took her by the shoulders to keep her on her feet. She leaned into his grip and smiled.

"You got a name, Daddy?"

Jones let her go, and when he was sure she could stay on her feet, he stepped back. "My name is Sam, Lauren."

Jones waited to see if her name and the sound of his voice registered. It didn't.

"That's a funny name."

"What happened to you?"

She smiled again and her lip started to bleed. "I fell."

Jones shook his head. "Was it Tony?"

"No, Daddy. I fell."

"It's Sam."

"Men like it when I call them Daddy."

"I don't."

"Okay." Lauren stumbled past him and fell onto the bed. Jones could tell that she was trying to be seductive; it was the opposite. Her injuries and whatever she was on left her slow and disoriented, and it took her a long time to roll over. When she finally looked at Jones, he noticed the strap of her bloodstained white tank top had fallen off her shoulder.

She draped a bruised leg over her knee and dangled her cheap shoe. "What do you like?"

"I'd like to leave, Lauren."

"You don't like me, Daddy?"

"It's Sam."

"Sorry."

Looking at her and hearing her apologize made Jones sick. "It's okay, and I like you, Lauren. That's why I want to leave with you."

She shook her head. "Nu unh. That's against the rules. I'll do anything you want. Anything but that. Tony's rules."

"I don't care about Tony's rules."

Lauren's mouth formed a dark circle in her pink inflamed face. "Ooooh, don't say that around him. He gets angry. He is mean when he's angry."

"I see that."

Lauren rolled onto her side and propped herself up on her elbow. She winced and clumsily rolled onto her other elbow. "I made him angry." She said the words like they were a fun secret she was sharing with a friend.

"What did you do to make him angry?"

"I stabbed him." Lauren lifted her hand, pointed at Jones, and then turned the finger and dropped it onto her side. "Right there." She giggled. "He did not like it."

Jones remembered Tony holding his side. "Why did you stab him?"

"I was stupid."

"I don't believe that."

Lauren flopped back onto the bed and stared up at the ceiling. "I was. For a second, I thought there might be a way through instead of out." She shook her head. "It was stupid."

Jones heard her say the words, but they were his.

"That wasn't what I meant, Lauren." He kneeled beside the bed and quietly said, "I'm sorry, Lauren."

His proximity triggered something in her, and she turned her swollen face toward him. "Do you want to lay on the bed with me, Sam?"

Jones stared into her dull eyes. "No, thank you."

Lauren rolled over and lifted her ass on the bed. "How about now?"

Jones stood and took a step back. "I just want to talk."

Lauren sighed and worked her way back onto her elbow. "I bet we can find something more fun to do than talk."

Jones went back to the door and glanced out the window to the parking lot. Both men were still in the front seats of the BMW; the bass from music was back and loud enough to make the glass buzz. "I can think of something fun," he said as he started back across the room. The sparsely decorated space was surprisingly larger than Jones had expected it to be and it made him wonder if the motel had once been something more elevated than a pop-up brothel when it had opened. The cheap flat screen television on the dresser was the only obvious update—the dresser and wooden chair in the corner were both decades out of date and the picture frame above the bed had a hairline crack running across it that Jones noticed as he crossed the room to the large window overlooking the back lawn. He slipped his phone out of his pocket when he saw the Jeep parked on the service road.

"Oh yeah? What?"

Jones turned on the phone's flashlight. The paint on the sill had begun to peel and Jones could feel a draft weaving its way through the pane when he pressed the face of the phone against the window. "Leaving."

Lauren groaned. "I told you. That will make Tony mad."

"Lauren—"

"Wait. How do you know my name?"

It had taken a while, but the mental fog that had settled in was starting to lift. "Norah told me."

The name got her attention. She looked at Jones and then she pulled herself up and crossed her legs under her. "I called you."

Jones nodded as he put his phone away.

"I never should have listened to you," Lauren said. "I tried to go through instead of out and look what happened. I can't even kill myself. Tony took all my things away. I was stupid to think there was anything for me but this."

"What if I took you to my place." The words came out fast and desperate—like a scream from a man drowning close to shore.

She laughed again. "So I'll just exchange one pimp for another."

"I don't want to be your pimp."

"My john then? Let me guess, fucking me whenever you want should be just enough to cover room and board."

"I don't want that either."

Lauren shimmied back to the wall. "Sure you don't. You just want me to come live with you in your house. No strings attached."

"There aren't any strings."

"There are always strings."

"Not this time."

She shook her head and mimicked his tone. "Because you're different."

"Because I won't be there."

"What?"

Jones sighed. "The cops are going to pick me up tomorrow, and they don't plan on putting me down."

"Because you killed that guy."

"Because I killed that guy," he said.

"So you're just going to let me live at your place?"

"I'm going to let you *stay* at my place until you figure out what you want to do next. I know some people—a woman—who might be able to help with that if you'll let them."

That was it. Jones had offered all that he had and there was nothing left that he could do. Jones wondered if Lauren noticed the quiver in his voice.

She didn't laugh this time. Lauren sat motionless staring at Jones, trying to read something in his eyes. Jones didn't dare look away. He waited, holding his breath, and prayed for a single word. She saw whatever she had been looking for and opened her mouth to deliver her verdict. Jones never heard what she said. Lauren was interrupted by the sound of blunt force against cheap wood.

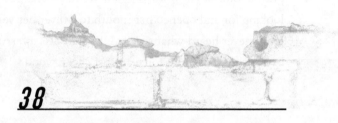

38

TONY'S AIR JORDAN PUNCHED A HOLE STRAIGHT THROUGH THE MOTEL DOOR.
The jagged perforation snagged his pants, and Jones
heard Tony swear as he tried to wrench his leg back
through the hole he had made. The second kick hit closer
to the door knob and sent the door swinging inward. The
door rebounded off the wall and Tony swatted it out of
his way as he stepped into the room. The climb up the
stairs and taking down the door had winded him again
and Tony paused with his hand on his side to catch his
breath. Behind him loomed most of Marvin; the bigger

man's eyes loomed above his partner's head and were staring at Jones. Marvin's chest showed no signs of his partner's exhaustion.

"You think I wouldn't figure out who you were?" Tony pointed a finger at Jones. "Did you really think I wouldn't know that you were the guy who got in her head?" Tony jerked his head in Lauren's direction. "This is him isn't it?"

Lauren lifted her palms up toward the red-faced angry pimp. She was terrified and her fear evaporated the rest of the fog she had been in. "I didn't call him, Daddy. I swear. I don't know how he found me. You gotta believe me."

Tony pointed a finger at Lauren. "Shut up."

Lauren nodded and closed her mouth.

"I thought I taught you a lesson. I thought you understood how things are, but I guess I was wrong."

"No, no you weren't. I learned my lesson. I did. He wanted me to run away. He did. He told me that I could live at his place, and I said no. I said no, Daddy."

Tony pointed at her again. "I told you to shut up." He moved the finger toward Jones. "You got in her ear and you know what she does? She stabs me." Tony looked at Lauren shaking on the bed. He shook his head and looked at Jones. "That wasn't her. My baby girl wouldn't do that. No, that was you. You stabbed me."

Tony stepped into Jones' personal space. The pimp's cologne was nauseating. "You—stabbed—me." He tapped his side to emphasize each word.

Jones looked at Lauren, but she wouldn't meet his eye. She hugged her knees and stared at the wall.

"I should fuck you up," Tony said. "I should. But the doctor said I had to take it easy. He said I could wreck my stitches if I wasn't careful. But that's okay. It's perfect actually. You got someone to hurt me, so it feels just right that I get someone to hurt you." Tony took a step back and spoke over his shoulder. "Marvin, come hurt this guy."

Marvin ducked his head and stepped into the room. Tony clapped him on the back as he switched places with the much taller man. Marvin brought his fists up and angled his body into a boxer's stance. Jones noticed the way he positioned his shoulders and the distinctive way he placed his lead foot and realized that he had been half right—Marvin was a Thai boxer. Jones began to back up slowly. Marvin read the movement as a retreat and began to follow.

"Get him, Marvin."

Marvin ignored Tony and slowly advanced. Jones stopped inside the bathroom and brought his right hand up to his jaw. He kept his left arm bent so that his elbow was out in front.

The door frame created an awkward buffer that limited the kickboxer's options. Marvin paused at the threshold and glanced left and then right. He understood what Jones had done and what he was suddenly unable to do. Marvin let Jones know how he felt about the restrictions with a jab into the bathroom that came at Jones faster than he expected. Jones parried the attack with his elbow and held his ground. There was no point in punching back—Marvin's reach kept him too far away.

Marvin sent another jab through the doorway and followed it with a right cross that hit Jones on the jaw and sent him stumbling into the toilet hard enough to crack the ceramic. Marvin used Jones' momentary disorientation as an opportunity to enter the bathroom.

"Now you're in trouble," Tony called from just outside the doorway.

Marvin took hold of the back of Jones' head and pulled him tight. Less than a second later a knee drove up into Jones' chin and set off fireworks in his head. He managed to get an arm in the way of the next knee and everything went numb below his left elbow. Luckily for Jones, there wasn't much below his left elbow. Jones drove his knee into Marvin's groin and heard a whoosh of air leave the big man. Marvin stumbled back and Jones wrestled free from the clinch. Jones grabbed hold of the top of the toilet tank and swung the ceramic rectangle as hard as he could against the side of Marvin's head. The ceramic exploded and the big man stumbled sideways. The low lip of the tub caught Marvin by surprise and he fell through the shower curtain. Jones reached up and yanked the rod down on top of Marvin. The man was a trained fighter and he was probably deadly in a ring with rounds and rules, but in a bathroom with no referee, he was average at best. Jones took advantage of the couple of seconds it took Marvin to get his feet under him to snake a hand inside his coat and then waited until his hands went low for the curtain. When Marvin took hold of the rod, Jones drove the knife forward into the long target. Jones heard a whoosh of air leave Marvin as the knife went in deep and then a gasp when he yanked the blade out. He was trained to aim better, and to keep going, but he didn't want the man dead; he just wanted him out of the way.

Jones wiped the knife on the only bathroom towel and stepped out of the room. Tony had moved to the bed and taken Lauren by the hair so that he could use the girl as a shield. The fistful of hair didn't make her cry out or cringe; she just stood there in front of him as though it were a regular Thursday night. Tony glanced at the knife without a trace of fear in his eyes. He wasn't afraid of a knife fight because he'd brought a gun.

Tony rested his elbow on Lauren's shoulder to steady his aim. "Look at all the trouble you caused."

"I didn't do this," Lauren sobbed. "I didn't. You gotta believe me."

Jones lifted his hand and arm. "I just want to get Lauren somewhere safe. That's all."

"Oh, that's all? And what about all the money she earns. Where is that going to go? You going to keep that safe for me too?"

"I told you, Daddy. I said no to him. I want to be with you."

Tony tightened his grip on her hair and Jones saw her lift to her tiptoes. "You hear that? She don't need saving."

"Lauren," Jones said. "I meant every word. You can be done with all of this."

Tony let go of Lauren's hair. She stumbled forward but didn't try to move any farther away. "Make your choice. Do you want to go with him, or do you want to stay with me?"

She didn't look back at the gun pointed in her direction. Jones watched her walk back to the bed. She looked up at Jones from the cheap mattress and said, "This is my life."

"There. It's settled. Well, it's almost settled." He gripped the gun tighter and a small tremor shook the barrel. "Get on your knees."

Jones looked at the girl. "I'm sorry, Lauren. I tried. I really did."

"I'm not going to ask you again," Tony said.

Jones remembered Kevin McGregor on his knees and stayed standing. "I know."

He was surprised to realize that he didn't think about whether it would hurt; instead, he wondered if he would hear the shot. He doubted it.

The sharp bang made his body tense. It took Jones a second to realize it wasn't a gunshot.

Tony, looking suddenly less sure of himself, was looking around the room for the source of the noise.

"Behind you," Jones said.

Tony turned just enough to see the Willy standing on a ladder pointing a gun at him.

"Drop the gun," Willy yelled. The window was thin and the sound carried through it just fine.

Tony began to move the gun away from Jones and toward the window and the next bang from the butt of the revolver broke the window. This time, Willy didn't have to raise his voice at all. "Maybe you didn't hear me. I said, drop the gun."

"Who the fuck are you?"

"A peeping Tom who didn't like what he was peeping. Listen, I'm standing here on a ladder with a gun in my hand. I don't have all night. Drop the piece."

Tony thought about it.

"This thing is wobbly as hell, so I need you to make a choice because if it comes down to shooting you or falling, I'm going to shoot you and get off this ladder."

Tony looked at Lauren and then dropped the gun. "This is all your fault."

"I guess we skipped plan B and moved right to plan C," Willy said. "Who could have predicted that? Oh, wait, I think I did."

Jones ignored the bank robber. He looked at the kid on the bed. "You ready to go?"

Lauren looked at Jones and then at Tony. Jones let out a sigh of relief when she got off the bed. The relief ended when she picked up the gun and pointed it at Jones.

"No."

Tony smiled. "I told you. She's my girl."

She pointed the gun at Tony. "No."

"Where is this going?" Willy said from the other side of the room.

"For the first time in a long time, anywhere I want it to."

"What do you want, Lauren?" Jones asked.

"I want to be done with this. All of this."

Jones was afraid she was going to kill herself right there in front of them, but the gun stayed pointed in Tony's direction.

"You want to be done with all of this? You want to go back to what it was like before you met me, is that it? You want to go back on the street? Because that's where you were. You want to go back to blowing guys in cars? Because that is what you were doing. I gave you a place to live. I gave you food to eat. You were on the streets starving, freezing, dying. You would have too, if it wasn't for me. You needed me to save you, and you still do—you just don't know it."

The last words punched Jones in the stomach. They could have been his.

Jones had wanted to think that he and Tony were nothing alike, but maybe that wasn't true. Like the pimp, he had thought Lauren needed saving, and he had thought he was the only one who could help her. Jones wondered how many people in her life had hurt her because they had felt they had the right to decide things for her? Tony had been out for himself and so had Jones. He didn't want to use Lauren for money, or her body, but he was using her. His intentions were good, but they were still his and not hers. Jones knew then that he couldn't save Lauren. It had to be her. She had to choose what she wanted for herself.

"If you want to be through with all of this," Jones said. "Walk away. No one will stop you."

Tony's laugh was a harsh bark. "Where are you gonna go? What are you gonna do without me looking out for you? You don't even have enough money to ride the bus."

Jones could tell that Lauren wanted to say something back that would prove him wrong, but she stayed quiet.

She looked at Tony for a long time and then she said, "Give me your wallet."

Tony bared his teeth and Jones heard him force his breath through the spaces. He turned his hip. "You know where I keep it. Come and get it."

Lauren didn't move. The gun in her hand didn't make her any less afraid of getting close to Tony.

Jones understood the play, so did Willy. From the window, he said, "As the only other person with a gun in this conversation, I think I should have a say. Why don't you let *him* get the wallet?"

Lauren looked at Willy and saw that he meant Jones. When she looked at Jones, he could tell that she liked the idea. "Do it."

Tony glared at Jones and drew his hip back. Jones walked forward and looked the pimp's jeans over. The artificially distressed pants were tight and Jones could easily make out the outline of the wallet. Sliding the wallet out of the tight space would require getting close to Tony; it would also provide several opportunities for Tony to change the odds. Jones stopped a foot away from Tony and reached for the pocket. He jammed four fingers into the opening and yanked back as hard as he could. The jeans ripped with a loud pop and Tony's wallet and phone fell to the floor.

Lauren snickered.

"What the fuck?"

Jones ignored Tony and kicked the billfold and phone away from the pimp.

"Keys too," Jones said.

"She didn't ask for my keys."

Jones looked over his shoulder at Lauren.

"Give him your keys," she said.

Tony didn't wait for Jones to rip his pocket. He pulled the BMW's keys out of his pocket and dropped them onto the floor.

"Oops."

Willy groaned. "I know you think you're being clever, but you're really just embarrassing yourself and keeping me on this ladder longer than I want to be. You pull one more stunt and I'm going to shoot you in the ass. Understand?"

Tony flicked a glance at Willy and smirked.

Willy thumbed back the hammer and the smirk vanished. "I'm going to need you to say it."

"I understand."

"Super."

Jones used the toe of his shoe to slide the keys across the floor toward the wallet and phone. He stepped back, picked everything up, and handed the items to Lauren. She hadn't thought everything through and she clumsily mashed Tony's things against her chest while she tried to keep the gun pointed at the pimp. Jones stepped around her and pulled a pillow case off one of the pillows. The material was so cheap it was almost transparent. He went to Lauren and held the bag open. "Put them in here."

Lauren dropped Tony's things inside and took the bag. Jones went into his pocket and pulled out his wallet. He extended his arm and saw from the look on Lauren's face that she was surprised. He shrugged. "Take it. There's not much cash, and I don't think I'll be needing my *ID* anytime soon."

Jones hoped Lauren was alert enough to have heard the emphasis he put on the word ID.

"Sit on the bed, Tony," Jones said.

"Fuck you."

Lauren jabbed the gun toward Tony. "Do it," she said.

"Fuck you too."

Willy put a bullet into the dresser next to Tony. The

noise made everyone jump, and Jones worried Lauren would pull the trigger accidently. She didn't.

"Holy shit!" Willy came close to losing his balance, and the ladder shimmied back and forth as he tried to find it. "Next one is in your ass."

"Get on the bed," Jones said.

Tony did as he was told.

Jones looked at Lauren. "You wanted to be through with this. You have cash and a car. I'd say this is your shot."

"Speaking of shots," Willy said. "Can we get out of here before someone calls that last one in? I have no desire to go back to prison."

"You should go," Jones said.

Lauren took a step toward the door.

"I am going to find you," Tony said. "I am going to find you and I am going to do things to you. Horrible things."

Lauren froze.

"But I could forgive you, baby girl. I really could. I know these guys got in your ear. I know this isn't you."

Lauren looked at Tony.

"Shoot that old man and give me the gun. That's it. Do that and I will forgive you. I'll forgive everything."

Jones watched Lauren think about it.

"Everything will be like it was. I promise."

It was the promise that thawed her. "I believe you, and that's why I'm leaving."

Lauren moved to the door, keeping a wide berth from Tony.

"Don't you walk away from me, baby girl. Don't you do it."

Lauren didn't look back; even when Tony screamed her name to the night.

"What do we do with him?" Willy said.

"We keep him here until Lauren is gone. Then he can walk."

"We should kill him," Willy said.

"You know I can hear you, right?"

"Then you know I think you should be dead."

"No," Jones said. "No one else needs to die."

Willy screamed, "Behind you," and Jones reacted a few seconds too late.

Marvin brought the blood-stained shower curtain down over Jones' head and pulled it tight. The vinyl fabric formed a tight seal around Jones' head and he felt his breath catch in his throat. The much bigger man tightened his grip on the curtain and used it to swing Jones back and forth like a dog shaking a rat. Jones had no choice but to grab at the huge hands around his neck and hold on. Marvin swung Jones' head into the wall, and he felt the drywall cave as his skull hit it; Jones rebounded and momentum and brute force lifted his body into the air. He came down on the dresser and the furniture collapsed to the ground like a building being demolished. Jones clawed at the hands around his neck, but the pressure didn't relent. He was hauled to his feet and sent airborne again. This time, Jones didn't hit the wall, or the furniture—he hit the window, or at least he would have if there had still been glass in it. Instead, Jones crashed into something that gave almost instantly with a loud scream.

Suddenly, Jones felt himself falling, and he groped for anything to anchor him. Glass bit into his palm and Jones roared as he squeezed his hand tighter around the side of the window frame. He pulled himself upright and ripped the curtain from his face. In front of him was an empty black rectangle. Jones screamed Willy's name and leaned out the window as far as he could. He could make out the Jeep in the gloom below, but not Willy. The Google Earth shot he had looked at on his phone had been taken in the daytime in the middle of summer when the untended grass of the vacant lot next door had been baked dry in the sun. The cooler weather had given the weeds that had been lying dormant in dirt the opportunity to rebound, and they had grown tall enough to swallow the old man whole. As he pulled himself back through the window, his eye caught sight of a flash of silver. The cheap ladder had slid sideways with the intention of falling a few seconds behind Willy, but a ridge on the worn decorative column of brickwork separating the unit from its neighbour had snagged it.

Jones straightened and turned toward the door; he stopped when he saw Marvin on the other side of the room. Jones scanned the space and saw that Tony was gone. The big man was pale and his midsection was stained black with blood. Jones knew from the colour that the wound was serious, and he was surprised Marvin was able to stand let alone throw him around the room. He pointed at the blood. "You need to get to a hospital before you bleed to death."

His words had no effect; Marvin didn't move, but Jones saw him sway a little.

"The girl is gone, so is Tony's ride. That means the only thing that can help you now is an ambulance." Jones looked at the phone on the bedside table. "You need to forget about me and make the call."

"I told you he doesn't talk," Tony said on his way back through the door. "He won't do it, not even to save his own life. My man is committed. So was my girl. At least, she was until you showed up."

"She's gone?" Jones said.

Tony nodded. "She stole my car just like you told her. She took my money just like you told her. All of this after she stabbed me just like you told her. I bet you're real proud of yourself."

Jones looked around the room, lingering on the window. He didn't know if his partner was alive or dead and he had no idea where Lauren was headed. Nothing had gone to plan. "No," he said. "I'm not."

"I'm not going to lie, that makes me feel a bit better. But you know what would make me feel a lot better?"

Jones had an idea what it was.

"If you couldn't feel anything."

He was right.

"Marvin, kill him."

Marvin lurched forward with none of the grace that he possessed when Jones first put eyes on him.

Instead of backing up, Jones ran at Marvin and left the ground to cover the last few feet with his knee leading the way. Despite the blood loss and trauma, Marvin was still fast and he had no trouble shoving Jones aside before he could make contact. Jones hit the ground hard and immediately began to scramble back to his feet. Marvin lunged at Jones while his back was turned and unloaded a vicious overhand right to Jones' kidneys that drove the air out of his lungs but elicited a louder grunt of pain from Marvin. The mute staggered back, clutching the black spot on his shirt and Jones lashed out with a kick that connected with Marvin's torso. The kick to the open wound pitched Marvin forward and gave Jones enough time to grab hold of the other man's belt. He rammed Marvin into the vacant space that had once been a window, but the big man didn't go out. His two long arms were able to splay and grab onto the walls on either side of the window and stop his momentum. Jones let go of Marvin's belt and hooked a fist into his exposed core. Marvin had been concentrating on the window and the sudden blow to the hole in his abdomen surprised him. Jones hit him a second time and Marvin took his hands off the wall to cover up. He realized his mistake when Jones went for his ankles instead of his body. Jones scooped up the tall man's spider legs and tipped him out the window and into the night.

Jones turned, panting hot breath and seeing red. For a second, he was confused because it seemed like Tony could see it too. The pimp glanced up at the ceiling and then looked over his shoulder.

Tony said, "Shit," and then he ran out the door.

Jones saw the red light flicker and understood that the red wasn't coming from him; it was coming from the police car that had just pulled into the lot. Jones crossed the room and pushed the damaged door back into the frame as best he could. He went back to the window and saw that the blackness outside had not been stained red; there was only the one squad car for now. Jones leaned out the window and managed to grab hold of the ladder without falling. He pulled the ladder back into place and reversed onto the rungs.

Jones yelled for Willy before he touched the ground and he heard the old man grunt a reply.

"He's here," Sheena said.

Jones turned his head toward the voice and made out a dark form that turned out to be Sheena. She was kneeling beside Willy who had landed on the ground, a few feet away from the Jeep.

"I think I fucking broke my hip."

Jones rolled the bank robber onto his back and the

old man screamed. He forced his hand over his mouth to silence him.

"We need to call an ambulance," Sheena said.

"We need to go."

"But—"

"He's right," Willy said. "We have to get out of here."

"Can you get up?"

"Not on my own."

"This is going to hurt," Jones said as he wrapped an arm around Willy's back.

"I got news for ya, kid. It already hurts."

"I'm sorry," Jones said as he slid his hands under Willy's knees.

Willy managed not to scream when Jones lifted him. "I'm not complaining," he said. "It could have been worse. Look how things turned out for that guy."

Jones looked over and saw Marvin's leg on the other side of the Jeep. He had been so focused on Willy, that he hadn't thought to look for the other man.

Jones walked around the Jeep with Willy in his arms and saw Marvin with his face in the dirt and his brains on the bumper. There was a lot of blood, and Jones was careful to step around it.

"Get in the car, Sheena. We need to go."

Sheena's knees were rigid and her arms were crossed tightly against her chest. Jones figured it was the first dead body she had ever seen. The dead always made a hell of a first impression.

Jones put Willy into the Jeep and stowed the ladder. He eased the rear door shut and then positioned himself between Sheena and Marvin.

Jones kept his voice level. "What is your job?"

Sheena didn't answer.

Jones asked the question again. "What is your job, Sheena?"

She looked at him. "What?"

"Why are you here?"

She thought about it for a second. "I'm supposed to be the getaway driver."

"That's right. Right now, we need to getaway, Sheena. Things went sideways up there and we have to leave."

Fear widened Sheena's eyes. "Lauren!"

"She got out."

Sheena looked around at what she already knew was there and what she knew wasn't. "Where did she go?"

Jones put a hand on Sheena's arm. "She left. Just like we need to do."

Sheena risked another look at Marvin's body and then nodded. Jones got into the passenger seat, and a second later, Sheena was behind the wheel. She drove slowly across the dark vacant lot, but not slow enough to keep Willy from screaming after each bump. Sheena got back on the road, and as they passed the motel on the way to the highway, Jones saw that a second police car was in the lot. One of the cops was speaking to a man outside the motel office, the other was climbing the stairs. Neither cop looked over at the Jeep as it turned right toward the gas station and the highway on-ramp.

Jones had made Sheena stop at a car wash on the way to the hospital and spent ten dollars on fifteen minutes with a high-pressure hose. Most of the rented time was spent on the rear bumper.

When Jones got back into the car, he saw that Willy was pale but still conscious. "We need to talk about what happened," Jones said.

"You mean get our story straight," Sheena said. She was holding the wheel at ten and two hard enough to make her knuckles white.

"Yeah."

Willy sucked in a breath and spoke through bared teeth. "I'm an old man with a broken hip. The story writes itself. Just drop me off at the door to the emergency room and let me do the talking."

"I meant about the body we left behind," Sheena said.

"What's this *we* shit?" Willy said. "You sat in the car. Nothing that happened in that room had anything to do with you."

"Is that how the cops would see it?"

Willy managed a snort that he regretted. "This one thinks she's Bonnie Parker all of a sudden."

"Who?"

"Bonnie and Clyde," Willy said.

"Like the Jay-Z song? I thought that was based on a movie."

"The movie was about two real people running from the cops," Jones said.

"Did they get caught?"

"Sort of," Jones said.

"What does sort of mean?"

"Died in a hail of gunfire," Willy said.

Sheena stared through the windshield. "Perfect."

Willy pulled himself up so that Sheena could see his face in the rear-view. "That was different. That was about money."

"So?"

"People care about money. No one cares about a pimp trafficking underage girls."

"So we just walk away like nothing happened."

Willy flopped back on the seat and pushed the beads of sweat that had formed on his forehead into his hair. "I'm glad we got that all settled. Now, can you please drop me off at the hospital. I can handle everything except the surgery."

Jones could tell Sheena didn't like it, but she didn't have a better argument, so she pulled out of the bay and accelerated hard toward the street. When the hospital was in sight, Willy said, "Put me down out front and don't look back. I'll tell the cops it was a hit and run and you two were just a couple of Good Samaritans."

"No one is going to believe that. Good Samaritans wouldn't leave you on the pavement," Sheena said.

"Let me worry about that."

THEY DIDN'T DROP WILLY OFF. JONES POINTED AT THE VISITOR'S LOT AND Sheena found a space. Willy propped himself up on an elbow when the Jeep came to a stop and craned his neck to see out the window. "No, no, no, no. This wasn't the plan."

"We're not going to leave you on the ground," Jones said.

Willy flopped back onto the seat. "This is stupid."

"We walked away from what happened at the motel. I'm not walking away from you too."

Willy turned his head toward Sheena. "Kid, you don't owe me anything. You don't even know a thing about me."

"I know you showed up tonight for Lauren, and that means I know everything I need to know about you."

Willy opened his mouth to complain and Sheena shut him down. "If you want to be on the pavement so damn much, get out and crawl your ass over there. Otherwise, shut up."

Willy smiled. "I like you, Sheena. You sound just my daughter."

"I like you too. All that bitching makes you sound like my mother."

Willy laughed and then groaned in pain. "Fine, fine. We'll do it your way."

Jones found a wheelchair and rolled the old bank robber into the emergency room. Jones let Willy charm the intake nurses while he made a call to Irene. Jones pulled out his phone and saw that he had missed five calls.

Jones made the call to Irene first and then checked his voicemail. The first message was from Scopes, so were the next three. The messages were all variations of the same theme. The game was over and he needed to turn himself in. The last message was from Dan Pembleton.

"It's Dan Pembleton. Ruth Verne called me and told me that you would be in need of my services again. She has paid my retainer and told me, in no uncertain terms, that I am to provide you with anything you require whenever you may require it. I will be waiting for your call."

Jones waited until Irene showed up and put in a few more minutes to give her time to get all the yelling out of her system. When the doctors let her in to see her father, Jones went back to the Jeep. Sheena saw him coming and shifted across to the passenger seat. She didn't say a word when he pulled out of the lot and accelerated hard in the opposite direction of her apartment building, and she said nothing when Jones sped through a red light. Jones barely noticed the quiet; his only thoughts were of getting home and what he would find when he got there. He was disappointed. Tony's BMW wasn't in his driveway and Lauren wasn't waiting on his doorstep with his wallet and his license.

Jones profanely broke the silence before he yanked the keys out of the ignition and left Sheena in the Jeep. He opened the door and walked into the kitchen without taking his shoes off. He wrote a short note on the back of a bill lying next to the phone and put it into an envelope. He wrote Lauren's name across the front, taped the envelope to the front door, and got back into the Jeep. Sheena didn't ask about the envelope; she didn't say a word until Jones pulled to the curb in front of a hydrant near her building.

"I'm scared," she said.

"About the cops?"

Sheena shook her head. "No. I should be terrified about getting caught, but it's not that. I was at first, but that went away. I'm scared because I don't feel anything. I should feel something after what we did."

"What did we do?"

"We killed a man."

Jones turned to look at Sheena. The tough woman with all of the tattoos suddenly looked smaller than the birds on her arm. "That happened, but that's not what we did," Jones said.

"What did we do?"

"We saved the girl."

Sheena thought about it while she dragged her finger through the fog that had started to build on the window. "Maybe that's the problem. I'm not even sure we saved her. We don't even know where she is."

"She's alive."

"And that's supposed to be enough?"

"The girl who wrote that message on the door thought there was only one way out of the life she was living. The girl I met tonight wanted something else. She wasn't looking for a way out. She wanted a way through."

"Through to what?"

"Something on the other side of the life she had. Something that put her old life at her back."

"So we just have to hope that she's headed somewhere better?"

"There are worse things than hope."

Sheena took a long time to weigh Jones' words. When she nodded, Jones saw in her eyes that she understood. She opened the door, and Jones felt the tentacles of the night air wrap around him. Sheena put a foot on the pavement and straddled the line between one world and another. She looked back at Jones. "Will I see you again?"

"No."

Sheena's nostril's flared. "Oh. So it's case closed, time to move on."

"I've tried to keep moving this past week, but there's nowhere else to run," Jones said. "At first, I was just running from what was coming, but then I realized that I wasn't running away—I was racing toward something else. Trying to move fast enough to get to the end before I ran out of track." Jones shook his head. "There's no track left for me."

Sheena put her other foot on the pavement and got out of the Jeep. She paused with her hand on the door and met Jones' eyes. "I'm sorry."

Jones thought of Lauren somewhere out there in a stolen car driving away from Tony and he smiled. "Not me. I was fast enough."

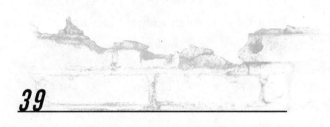

39

SCOPES ARRESTED JONES THE SECOND HE STEPPED INTO THE POLICE station and he had him in front of a judge the next day. Pembleton put up a good fight, but Scopes was ready for it. He and the Crown lawyers presented the judge with all the ways Jones had recently lied to police and the judge was not amused. He denied Jones bail and dismissed every one of Pembleton's objections. After the gavel struck the block, Pembleton provided a short one-word apology that seemed sincere. Jones leaned in close to Pembleton and spoke quietly in his ear. He had known what the outcome would be the second he saw the look on Scopes' face when he turned himself in, so he wasn't surprised, or in need of consolation. He needed only one thing. Pembleton listened and then sat motionless as he considered what Jones had said. The lawyer said, "I'll take care of it," just as the bailiff took Jones by the elbow.

Jones said, "Thank you," and then he let the bailiff lead him away.

A week passed before Jones saw Pembleton again. The lawyer was waiting in a meeting room with his briefcase open and the desk littered with files. The guard walked Jones into the room and told him that he had half an hour. When the door closed, Jones and Pembleton spoke at the same time.

"How are you holding up?"

"Did you find her?"

Pembleton was smart enough to know that Jones wasn't going to answer his question, so he answered the one posed to him. "No, she wasn't there. The key you left in the envelope was still taped to your door when I got there. As you instructed, I took it and left a note with everything she would need to contact me directly. She has not called. Before I arrived, I drove by your house. The letter I left is still there on the door."

Jones slapped the table. "Damn it."

Pembleton tapped his pen on the table. "Does that note that you made me leave on your door have anything to do with your case?"

"Not this one."

"Then you need to forget about it. I've been familiarizing myself with your case, your real case, and you are in some deep, deep shit."

"That a legal term?"

"It's a fact. Don't let my expensive shoes fool you. I spend most of my days wading around in deep shit. I can get you out, but I need you to pick up a fucking shovel because I can't be the only one digging. We have twenty-eight minutes and I can't waste them on things that aren't about my case."

Jones nodded. "What do you need?"

Pembleton opened a file folder and began flipping pages. "Let's start at the beginning."

The guard banged on the door twenty-seven minutes later to let Jones and Pembleton know that they had one minute left.

Pembleton put his pen down. "I think we made some good progress."

"I want to talk to Ruth."

The lawyer frowned. "I'm afraid that isn't possible."

"Tell her I asked to speak with her," Jones said. "Please."

"I will, but I don't think it will change anything."

The guard opened the door, and Jones stood. "Thanks."

Pembleton gave him a small smile. "See you next week."

40

PEMBLETON CAME BACK WEEK AFTER WEEK. EACH WEEK HE GREETED JONES the same way. "No and no." No Lauren had not tried to contact him, and no Ruth did not want to speak with him.

After hearing the same message six times, Jones should have developed a callous, but the news still hurt each time. He was not without other visitors; his brother Tom had come to the prison once. He walked into the interview room determined to contrast the hopelessness that covered almost every square inch of the facility. Tom was upbeat and witty, but Jones could tell exactly how much his brother hated talking to him through the glass by how much he spoke about their father. Over the last ten years, Tom had never once said a thing about their father that wasn't related directly to sustaining his existence. But over the prison phone, Tom spoke on and on about their old man as though he were the kind of dad that people saw on TGIF sitcoms, and not the kind of dad in after school specials. Tom had mined his memories for every funny story and pleasant memory just so they could talk about that and not about the charges and whether or not they were true. When the guard banged on the door to let them know that they had one minute left, Jones saw a flash of relief on Tom's face. Before his brother left, Jones told him that he didn't need to come back anytime soon. He told Tom that he would have his hands full taking care of their father on his own, and he would rather him focus on that. The words weren't untrue and that made them easier for Tom to accept. He said he would visit the next month and Jones knew he would.

The trial had been set for July, and Jones still had three months to go. Pembleton gained confidence in his ability to mount a solid defence with each visit, but Jones did not share his opinion.

"I killed him. The cops have a witness who can put me there."

"You put six bullets in the man. There's no doubt you killed him," Pembleton said. "I'm not arguing that case. The case I'm arguing is should you go to jail for it. Kevin McGregor was clean on paper, but I don't deal strictly in paper. People are better on the stand than any report, and McGregor's ex-wife and child should prove quite interesting. When this is over, you might just get the key to the city."

Pembleton had taken the case for Ruth, but the sudden onrush of publicity had locked him in. The arrest and its connection to Adam's abduction had been major news. Pembleton didn't mention it, but it was impossible to hide—even from a man in jail. The common room played one channel all day, and Jones had seen Pembleton on it more than once.

TWO MONTHS FROM TRIAL, JONES WALKED INTO THE MEETING ROOM TO SEE Pembleton smiling. He pointed at Jones with a finger gun and dropped his thumb twice. "No and no," he said.

"So why are you smiling?"

"Because I got a yes. From McGregor's kid. Dylan is twenty, and he thinks you are a hero."

"What did you ask him?"

"If I could have a forensic team go through his house."

"I thought his mother moved him west after the divorce."

Pembleton smiled. "She did. His father kept the house. His mother never fought him on it. Her only priority was getting her son away from his father. So McGregor lived alone in the house until you killed him in it."

Jones stared at Pembleton. "You're still smiling."

"Most people hate lawyers," he said.

"I get that."

"It's funny. Most people hate us so much that they do their best to avoid us even when they shouldn't. You would be amazed how many people avoid getting a will because of how much they hate lawyers."

Jones saw where Pembleton was going. "Dylan inherited the house."

Pembleton smiled even wider. "Bingo. He isn't going to move back to Toronto. He has a life in Vancouver. I told him that I could assist with some of the legal work involved in selling the house if he would let me have a team spend a few days going over it."

"The police already turned that place inside out. If there was anything to find, they would have found it."

"You're absolutely right. If there was something to find in the house, the cops would have definitely found it." He smiled again. "But what if what they were looking for wasn't in the house?"

"What did you find?"

Pembleton held up two fingers. "Two more bodies."

Jones breath caught in his throat. "Where?"

"McGregor had not planned on killing Adam. At least, he hadn't planned on doing it that day. Putting his body inside the wall was an impulsive decision. It was sloppy, but it worked. I don't know if killing Adam woke something inside him or if it became a high he started chasing.

I'm no psychologist." Pembleton leaned across the table on his elbow and pointed a finger at Jones. "What I do know is that the next time he killed a boy, he had a plan. He used a shed in the backyard instead of the basement and concrete instead of bricks. He built the shed on posts instead of a pad. He must have made it with killing in mind, because the floor was constructed in such a way that he could easily remove it to access the ground underneath. He built a small box for the body, placed it under the shed, and filled it with cement." Pembleton sat back in his chair. "And when it worked, he did it again."

Jones felt sick. "Who were they?"

"No idea yet. Identification is going to have to be done by dental work and that takes time. What I do know is that the Crown is getting nervous. They called my office yesterday to talk about a plea."

"What are they offering?" Jones said.

Pembleton rolled his eyes. "I didn't even let the conversation get that far. If they are calling, it means they know that they are losing."

"Call them back and hear them out," Jones said.

"Their offer doesn't matter because we're not interested."

"I am," Jones said.

"You can't be serious. We are winning here."

"This isn't a game that can be won, Dan. I put a man on his knees and pulled the trigger, and they know it. They aren't going to just let me walk away from that."

Pembleton waived his hand. "Of course the Crown won't walk away. I don't need them to. Their job is the same as mine—to argue a case in front of twelve men and women. It's the jury who has all the power, and they are the only ones I care about. McGregor was a monster. You killed a monster. When I tell the jury about everything that was found in that house, there is not a single person on this earth who would send you to prison."

"I didn't know about those kids," Jones said. "The judge won't let anything about that into evidence."

Pembleton smiled. "I'll get it in. One way or another, I'll get it in."

Jones shook his head. "No."

"What do you mean no?"

"I won't use those kids to save my skin."

"Don't be stupid, Sam—not when things are finally starting to go your way."

"Hear the Crown out, Dan."

Pembleton set his jaw and tapped his pen against the table. The force grew with each tap until the pen flew out of the lawyer's hand, and he slammed an empty palm on the table. The guard heard the noise and opened the door. "Everything alright?"

"No," Pembleton said. "No, it is not."

The guard lifted a hand to his belt and took a step toward Jones.

"No, no," Pembleton said. "Nothing like that. I'm referring to the case. Everything is fine in here."

The guard gave Jones a hard stare.

Pembleton raised his voice. "We need the room."

The guard stared at Jones long enough to let him know who would be paying the tab for Pembleton's mouth and then walked out of the room.

"I will talk to the Crown lawyers and hear their offer, but I want you to know that I think this is a huge mistake."

41

THE NEXT WEEK, JONES GOT A MESSAGE AN HOUR BEFORE HE WAS SUPPOSED to meet with his lawyer that the meeting was off. He had to wait until the next day for a chance to call Pembleton from one of the prison phones. The lawyer's voicemail answered the call and promised with saccharine pleasantries to call him back as soon as possible.

Pembleton blew off their meeting again the following week. Jones called again and again, and each time the voicemail happily swallowed his message. The television coverage was equally unhelpful. Every couple of days there was a small segment from sombre faced reporters standing on location, which contained little more than his name and someone new saying, "No comment."

Pembleton showed up the week after that. Jones was led into the interview room and found his lawyer bent over the table reading a file. He was too engrossed in his work to even look up when he said, "Thank you," to the guard.

When the guard left, Pembleton said, "No and no," without making eye contact with Jones. He gestured at the chair opposite him with the back of his hand and turned a page. Pembleton only stopped what he was doing when he realized that Jones had not sat down.

"We have a lot to talk about, Sam. Please take a seat."

"Where the hell have you been?"

"Getting you your deal," Pembleton said.

"You were supposed to find out what the Crown was offering and get back to me."

"About that," Pembleton said. "I was concerned after our last conversation that you had no idea how the game is played and would therefore play it poorly."

"I told you this is not a game."

Pembleton pointed his pen at Jones. "You are wrong, and that is why you would lose. I, luckily for you, do not lose. I heard their offer and I rejected it."

"That wasn't your call."

Pembleton pointed to the chair. "Sit down."

Jones didn't move.

"Do you want to know what they did next?"

Jones didn't move.

Pembleton smiled. "Ask me what they did next."

"What did they do next?"

"They got angry and threatened all manner of things. You would have been very frightened."

"If you had told me," Jones said.

"Ask me what I did."

"No."

"Sam, play along."

Jones put his hands on the table and leaned across the table. "What did you do?"

Pembleton didn't even blink at Jones' display of aggression. He was too pleased with himself. "I did nothing," he said with a smile. "I waited."

"Waited for what?"

"For the Crown to catch up."

"Catch up to what?"

Pembleton smiled and gestured at the chair. When Jones didn't move, Pembleton crossed his arms. Jones yanked out the chair and sat.

"Catch up to what?"

Pembleton couldn't lose the smile. "Me. It turns out that Kevin McGregor, in addition to the house, had a cottage just outside of Muskoka. It belonged to his father and now it belongs to—"

"Dylan," Jones said.

"Yahtzee."

"There were more bodies," Jones said.

Pembleton pointed a finger gun at Jones and dropped his thumb. "There were more bodies."

"How many?"

"Enough to get me a second offer."

"How many?"

"Five years. You would be out in three."

"No, bodies. How many bodies?"

"Four. All boys." Pembleton leaned back in his chair and grinned. "Don't worry, the third offer will be even better."

Jones thought about four boys, about four sets of grieving parents, and then about using them as bargaining chips. "Take the deal."

"Sam—"

Jones said, "Take the deal," and then stood up and banged on the door.

42

JONES WAS SURPRISED TO FIND THAT HE HAD A VISITOR THE NEXT DAY.
It was just after nine in the morning, and he felt a sudden
irrational panic that it was Tom coming to tell him something about their father. Jones followed the guard down
to one of the video booths and he was surprised to see
someone else on the screen. The young woman sitting
in the visitor's chair was fresh faced with shiny hair set
in a tight bun that contrasted the oversized cardigan she
gripped with two small fists. The hands caught Jones'
eye; her nails had the shine of a new car, but her scarred

knuckles looked used. The young woman on the monitor bore more of a resemblance to the girl in the picture Norah had given him, but there were subtle differences—marks left by a world that only fought dirty.

Lauren pointed to the phone in her hand, and Jones realized that he was still standing. He picked up the matching receiver and sat down at the desk.

"Hi."

"How did you know I was here?"

Lauren smiled. "Are you kidding me? You're famous. You're on the news, or in the paper, at least once a week. Every time Norah reads something about you, she shows it to me."

Jones frowned. "You went back? What about her brother? The one who—"

Lauren shoved the slouched sleeve of her cardigan back over her elbow. "I made him up. Norah doesn't have a brother."

"Why would you make something like that up?"

Lauren shook her head as though she had just heard a child say two plus two was five. "I was scared. Some stranger shows up and tells me that he wants me to leave with him. I didn't know who you were, or what you planned to do with me."

Jones shook his head. He had been so naïve. "I thought you would have jumped at the chance to get away."

Lauren looked at Jones with eyes that were older than

her age. "Leaving with another man would not have been getting away."

Jones rested his elbow on the table. "I made a lot of mistakes. I thought I could save you."

Lauren gave Jones a sad smile. "How could you save me? You didn't even know me."

"I thought I did."

"I'm not the person you think I am, Sam. I've done things. Bad things. I didn't do all of them because Tony forced me to. I made those choices. The girl you were chasing was an idea in your head. A fantasy. You were using me like every other john who answered my ad."

"No," Jones said. "That is not how it was."

Lauren thought about it. "Maybe you're right. Norah says I have a tendency to be cynical. She says that I assume the worst about other people so that they can never disappoint me. You know what she says about you?"

"What?"

"She says you're a hero. She doesn't care why you went looking for me. She's just happy you found me."

"I'm not a hero," Jones said.

"To some people you are."

"What do you think?"

"I think you were trying to find something."

"What does that mean?"

"It means you were lost. Like I was."

"Are you still lost?" Jones asked.

Lauren adjusted her sleeve again. "I think so. I made it through, but I don't really recognize my life on the other side. Does that make sense?"

"I get it. Do you have anyone helping you find your way?"

"Norah knows all kinds of people. After she helped me get clean, she hooked me up with a therapist to talk to. I didn't want to go, but she made me. At first, she'd go with me to every meeting and sit outside the door so I couldn't run away again, but she doesn't need to do that anymore. Talking helps." She stared at Jones, reading something in his expression. "Are you talking to someone?"

"Not the person I want to." Jones realized how it sounded when it came out and quickly made to apologize.

Lauren dismissed the words with a wave and pushed at her drooping sleeve again. "This person that you want to talk to, can they help you?"

"I need to tell her something."

"Something for her, or for you?"

Jones opened his mouth to answer, but closed it when he realized the words were going to be a lie.

"You can't find what you need in other people." Lauren said the words with the practiced cadence of a mantra. "I learned that. Some days, I even believe it."

"I need to tell her I'm sorry. Sorry for failing her. Sorry for failing her again."

"She doesn't know you're sorry?"

Jones thought about it. "She does."

"So who are you really asking to forgive you?"

Jones didn't have an answer for the woman who used to be the girl.

"For what it's worth," Jones said. "I don't think I'm lost anymore. I know where I am. That's because of you."

Lauren looked at Jones and smiled when she decided that he had meant what he said. "That's good."

Lauren shifted in her seat and Jones could tell that the conversation was coming to an end.

"Why did you come here, Lauren?"

She stopped shifting. "I wanted to tell you that I don't feel that way anymore. I don't want to die. I thought you should know that."

Jones smiled.

"And, that I'm glad you looked for me," Lauren said.

"So am I."

Lauren put down her phone and stood up. Jones put down the phone and watched the girl on the screen turn to leave. Before she walked away, she waved goodbye.

Jones waved and then the girl was gone.

MIKE KNOWLES lives in Hamilton with his wife, children, and dog. He has written seven previous novels: *Darwin's Nightmare*, *Grinder*, *In Plain Sight*, *Never Play Another Man's Game*, *The Buffalo Job*, *Rocks Beat Paper*, and *Tin Men*.